# KATIE KINCAID ENSIGN

## Andrew van Aardvark

# Table of Contents

Prologue

| | |
|---|---|
| 1: Katie Steps In It | 1 |
| 2: Katie Settles In | 25 |
| 3: Katie Finds More To Do | 45 |
| 4: Decide Kincaid | 59 |
| 5: Learn Kincaid | 73 |
| 6: Fly Kincaid | 83 |
| 7: Ensign Kincaid's Fine Adventure | 97 |
| 8: Ensign Kincaid Carries On | 111 |
| 9: Ensign Kincaid Digs Deeper | 125 |
| 10: Katie, Bar the Door | 135 |
| 11: Katie, Just Suck It Up | 147 |
| 12: Katie, You've a Lot to Learn | 165 |
| 13: Kincaid on the Spot | 177 |
| 14: Kincaid Shows Initiative | 191 |
| 15: Kincaid Takes a Step | 201 |
| Appendix A: 24th Century Military Ranks | 211 |
| Appendix B: Renown Class Frigate Fact Sheet | 217 |
| Appendix C: Hellas Class Boat Fact Sheet | 221 |
| Appendix D: Typical Ship's Organization | 223 |
| Appendix E: Resolute's Ship's Company | 227 |
| Appendix F: Simplified In-System Navigation | 233 |

Katie Kincaid Ensign

Author: Andrew van Aardvark

Editior: Margaret Ball

Copyright © 2021 NapoleonSims Publishing

www.NapoleonSims.com/publishing

All rights reserved.

Cover image credits:

Female silhoue*e  Photo 149551420 © Sergey Nazarov | Dreamstime.com

Space ship Illustration  139560069 © Mik3812345 | Dreamstime.com

Space ship interior:  127380755 @ SDecoret | www.dreamstime.com

Image of Jupiter © NASA

Starry backgroundImage  © Brandon Siu | Unsplash.com


ISBN: 979-8-50898-094-8

# Prologue

*Hello dear, deeply encrypted diary that no one else is going to get to see before I'm long gone.*
*Today I'm going to write about my experiences as a very junior officer.*
*I did try to be an exemplary junior officer both by my own standards and by those of the wider traditional Space Force too.*
*In many ways, I believe I succeeded.*
*In some there is no doubt I failed.*
*It took some considerable self-confidence for a young Belter girl to try to make herself not just into a successful Space Force officer, but one destined for higher command.*
*And not just higher command, but also herodom.*
*I'll confess that as a young girl herodom had some attraction of its own. Don't most youngsters with any heart yearn for glory, respect, and adoration? All things traditionally associated with heroism. Sure, so are danger, almost certain death, and being sidelined by the powers that be after some ceremony of acknowledgment. However, as anyone who has dealt with them knows, danger, death, and politics don't seem real to people who aren't children anymore, but not quite adults either.*
*A fact that I, and others like me, have routinely used for our own purposes down through the ages, but that's a story for another time.*
*The point here is that I was once a young woman and heroism had that sort of attraction for me.*
*It was never my main motivation.*
*My main motivation was a belief that someone like me, or like whom I could be at least, was needed. Needed if the species was to survive, probably. Certainly needed if humanity was to have any hope of having a say in its own future.*
*It may seem I'm claiming an improbable degree of far-sighted altruism for my younger self.*
*I don't think so.*
*Be that as it may, it also is a question for another time.*
*The current issue is that having gotten into the Academy and graduated from it, I, as a very junior officer on her first deployment, had to be sufficiently impressive to get myself placed on the fast track to command.*
*I had a fine line to walk between being self-confidently ambitious and obnoxiously full of hubris. I occasionally wobbled walking that line. I almost fell off it more than once out of an excess of pride.*
*I have some faint hope my trials and tribulations might be some*

*sort of lesson to some future young person.*
*A very faint hope.*
*Bottom line, I promised myself I'd make a full account of my life to date here. For reasons. Just how clueless and full of myself I was as a young wet behind the ears officer is part of that record.*
*Enjoy.*

## 1: Katie Steps In It

"Ensign Kincaid, do you believe you know how to run a spaceship better than your captain and his senior officers?"

"Yes, sir!" Ensign Katie Kincaid felt compelled to answer. It was the simple truth, and she wasn't going to lie to a senior officer.

The *Resolute*'s Executive Officer, the man she reported to, sighed. "That was not the answer I expected."

"I'm sorry, sir. It'd be wrong to lie, wouldn't it?"

"And pray tell, *Ensign,* why do you think you know more than your seniors? You've been aboard the *Resolute* for a few weeks. It's your first posting. Your seniors have all had months to years more time aboard the *Resolute* alone. Most of us have accumulated years of experience on various postings. All of us have been certified by Space Force boards and our own seniors as having acquired vital knowledge on how to maintain, run, and use Space Force ships to achieve the missions we've been assigned. And you think you know better than us. Why?"

"Because I grew up in space, sir." Katie replied. "I was doing maintenance on ships' life support systems at an age when most of you were first learning the alphabet and how to add. I've done every job a ship has. I did most of it alone, without other people to lean on or to correct me if I made a mistake. I never had to unlearn things I learned growing up on a planet. I've got years more experience in space than the vast majority of other Space Force officers."

"Including, specifically, your superiors on this ship?" the XO asked in a dangerously quiet tone.

"Sir, all of your histories are part of the public record."

"I could bring you up on charges for your attitude. Charges of insubordination and behavior contrary to good order and discipline."

"Sir, I answered a direct question as directly and honestly as I could. I've been careful to never publicly contradict or embarrass anyone even when I was sure I knew best, except when Spacer Jones' safety was in question."

Lieutenant (Senior Grade) Winters, the Executive Officer (XO) of the *Resolute* and Katie's boss, sighed. "Sadly, Kincaid, that was probably the right thing to do. On one hand, I have to commend you for the moral courage to make the right decision despite the problems you had to know it'd cause you."

"Sir?"

"On the other hand, your perception, and the attitude consequent upon it are unacceptable."

"Yes, sir." Katie didn't know what else to say. What did he expect of her?

"Did your previous experience include much time with weapons? Using or maintaining them?"

"No, sir."

"Did you participate in, let alone lead, any boarding actions?"

"No, sir."

"Did you serve with any crews sufficiently large that dedicated food technicians, and victualers were necessary and had to be supervised?"

"No, sir."

"So, perhaps you might be willing to concede that there are aspects of running a Space Force frigate that you aren't an expert on, Ensign Kincaid?"

"Yes, sir."

"How kind of you, Ensign."

"Sir, no offense intended, sir."

"Personally, I don't take any, Kincaid. That is because I'm a remarkably patient man and probably too easy going to be a good executive officer. We all have our flaws. However, others won't be so forgiving. Moreover, your arrogance makes you dangerous. As Executive Officer and your superior, it is my job to teach you some humility."

Katie didn't think that sounded good. But what could she say? Nothing much. "Yes, sir."

"Doubtless you're wondering how?"

"Yes, sir."

"Well, Ensign, it's simple since you already know so much it'd be a shame to waste your time and that of the Space Force, wouldn't it?"

Katie knew there was only one answer she could give. She wished it was otherwise. "Yes, sir."

The XO smiled at her grimly. "Well, at least they taught you something at the Academy."

"Yes, sir."

"So we're not going to take it easy on you like we do most other more challenged new officers."

"Sir?"

"As you already know so much, Ensign, you're obviously not going to need the same time as most newly commissioned officers to master the duties of each possible role you could be assigned. Agreed?"

Katie could recognize sarcasm if it was obvious enough. She knew it'd be best to back down. It'd be a good idea to suggest that it never hurt to have plenty of time to fully master one's responsibilities. Only she didn't have it in her. "Yes, sir."

"Great. That means that, instead of only learning a few roles and specializing, that we have the luxury of rotating you through all the roles a junior officer can be assigned." The XO grinned at her. Katie was sure she was only imagining a certain mean glee in his expression.

"Sounds like a great learning opportunity, sir," Katie replied gamely.

"Indeed," the XO said, "I think you'll find it terribly educational."

"That's good, isn't it, sir?"

"Oh yes, assuming you can handle it. We're going to be gone for a year. I don't think you'll find it too long. It'll mean only a month or two per slot. Hmm, maybe it won't hurt to double up on your tasks. What do you think, Kincaid? Can you manage to put in a little extra effort to learn more?"

"I think so, sir."

"Well, I guess we'll find out, won't we. Normally, we'd only give two or three sets of tasks to a young officer on their first tour; a sub-ordinate bridge watch to learn the routine, a deputy department slot to get used to administrative duties, and, finally last but not least of course, assisting the Officer of the Watch on the bridge. All culminating in your being allowed to stand a bridge watch as Officer of the Watch on your own. If you're not certified to stand watch by the end of your first year, you can pretty much kiss being fast tracked to command goodbye, you know."

And that was the nub and the rub right there. "Yes, sir, I do." Indeed, she did. If all the extra roles and work proved too much, she mightn't get certified to be Officer of the Watch before the year was out. It'd put paid to her dreams of command. She might get jobs counting socks or supervising technicians, but she wouldn't get ship command.

"Good," the XO said briskly. "Usually we'd start by giving you the helm and then a stint as deputy weapons, operations, or supply."

Katie would have loved being given the helm position. For all that it was normally assigned to an enlisted spacer, it was still not just a bridge position but meant direct control of the ship. Supply might be boring, but she knew it was important. Weapons and operations both were bound to be interesting. She didn't say so. The XO didn't seem to be asking a question.

The XO smiled. "However, luckily for you, the individual we intended to take the Baby Engineer's slot won't be available and we can't replace them for a year-long deployment on short notice. So we're going to start you off in the Deputy Engineering Officer's place. Normally a specialist Lieutenant Junior Grade's position. You should be flattered."

Engineering was the alternative track to the command one. Her heart sinking, Katie kept her face blank and managed to reply, "Thank you, sir."

"Just doing my job, Ensign. I'll have a briefing package dispatched to your terminal. I expect you to be fully up to speed when you report to Lieutenant Jeffries in the Engine Room at 0800 tomorrow. Clear?"

"Yes, sir."

"You're dismissed."

\* \* \*

"A long talk with the XO?" Amy Sarkis asked Katie.

Katie had just got back to the cabin she shared with Sub-Lieutenant Sarkis. SLT Amy Sarkis was currently serving as Deputy Supply Officer on the *Resolute*. Katie wasn't sure she wanted to talk about it. On the other hand, she knew Amy was probably trying to be helpful. Amy also knew perfectly well how long Katie had been talking to the Executive Officer. Furthermore, Amy knew that prolonged attention to a junior officer by the XO was not a good thing. What Amy was really asking was what sort of trouble Katie was in and what she could do to help.

"Yep," Katie said, trying to sound casually philosophical about it.

"And?"

"Well, he wasn't really happy with me for showing Lieutenant Shankar up." Katie rubbed the back of her head ruefully. "Then I stuck my foot in it."

"Oh?"

"The XO has given me the Baby Engineer's slot."

Amy whistled. "Wow, right into the deep end."

Katie flinched at the saying. She'd learned to swim at the Academy. She'd even learned to enjoy it during the summers at her grandmother's place. Only for Katie, getting tossed into the deep end literally evoked some of the scariest and most embarrassing experiences of her young life. Spacer born, she'd never seen so much open water in one place before encountering the Academy's pool and she certainly hadn't known how to swim. Unlike her colleagues, who'd been planet born and preparing for the Academy since they were kids. Worse, her fear of the water and lack of preparation had been a perfect metaphor for her entire first year at the Academy. A year she'd barely managed to pass. Katie had been completely out of her element and unprepared for what she'd faced. Not fond memories. And now it was looking like her time on the *Resolute* was shaping up to be a reprise of that uncomfortable time.

Amy broke the silence. "You don't think you can handle it?"

Katie smiled at her cabin mate wanly. Katie didn't know how to begin explaining how she felt. "I think I probably can."

She turned and punched some keys on her work terminal. Their cabin was small. Not much room to stretch. There was a gym for that, but it made it easy to reach everything. "I'll have a better idea when I've read the briefing package the XO has sent me." A few more key strokes and she had the document in question open. Katie scanned it. "Yeah, at first glance it looks doable."

Amy grunted and moved to peer over Katie's shoulder. "You want to be on the command track, not the engineering one, right?"

Katie turned her head to look at Amy. "That's right, but that's not the issue really."

"Okay."

Katie took a breath. She chewed on her lower lip a bit. She wanted to phrase this carefully. "I may have been a little over confident in pointing out that, being space born and having grown up on a ship, that I had an edge in experience over the average junior officer on their first posting."

Amy closed her eyes and groaned. "Only you weren't that diplomatic."

"Yeah, maybe not."

"So how deep into the shit did he decide to dip you?"

"Sort of like Achilles, I don't think my heel got coated."

Amy blinked. "Only you, Katie. You do like your ancient history, don't you?"

Katie huffed and put on a faux serious face. "I don't think people have changed that much. I do think the classics have endured because they reflect that."

Amy gave Katie a thin smile. "Or because they reflected what teachers wanted educated people to think." Amy's cynicism was probably why she'd gone into logistics despite being bright and well connected. "But it's beside the point. You're dodging the issue."

Katie sighed. "I'd rather not think about it too hard." It was a flaw she hated to confess.

"That bad?"

"The XO has signed me up for an accelerated course of learning every possible role a junior officer can have on the ship."

Amy did a spectacular imitation of a baffled owl. "There's not enough time on the entire deployment for that. It's unheard of."

"He's planning on having me work double roles, two jobs at once, when possible."

Amy shook her head. "Katie, there aren't enough hours in a day. Not even if you wanted to give up your mandatory exercise, meals, crapping, washing, and sleeping."

"The XO seemed to think it was possible to make it work."

Katie's roommate gave a humorless chuckle as she shook her head again. "No, he didn't," Amy said. "He knows better. He wants you to understand it too. This is about teaching you a lesson. You're not some sort of super girl. There are limits. You have a lot to learn. He wants you to figure that out and go beg him to let you off the hook."

Katie grimaced. Amy was probably right. Only Katie didn't have it in her to decline a challenge without at least making an effort. "I don't know. You're probably right about what he thinks. Only I wasn't kidding about already knowing a lot of the material. I've been doing ship provisioning, ship repairs, engineering watches, and bridge watches since I was just a kid. Belters and born Spacers get responsibility a lot younger than the planet born."

Amy sat in her allotted chair and gave Katie a hard look. "You really still think the Space Force is composed of a bunch of clueless mud eaters after all those years at the Academy?"

"No, I don't. Only the fact is the space environment training at the Academy was a joke. It wasn't much more than screening out those hopelessly prone to space sickness plus a little familiarization."

It was Amy's turn to sigh. She spoke slowly. "It's true that for me and all the other junior officers I knew, our first real deployment was a tough learning experience. Being in space day and day out and learning the routine and habits, as well as our specific duties, was tough. Overwhelming at times."

"Plus you were feeling physically discombobulated because of the unfamiliar environment. Sure, I understand that. It's a lot to expect even young people to adapt to an entirely new environment and way of life in under a year. Only I was born into that environment and spent years as working crew in it."

Amy looked thoughtful, but worried too. "I see your point," she said. "It makes me wonder why we don't recruit more Belters and Martians if it's valid."

Katie shrugged. "Politics? I've talked to my grandmother about it, but I still don't completely understand it. She sees everything in terms of power. She thinks the people running Earth are determined to control the solar system using the Space Force."

"You're kidding."

Katie waggled a hand by way of saying maybe. "Could be I'm simplifying a bit," she admitted. "Exaggerating too. Her arguments are much more complicated and nuanced. She's got this whole picture in her head about how societies and history work that I don't really understand. Also, she likes to hint at things rather than state them outright. Plays devil's advocate other times."

"That's very interesting. I wish we were going to get to talk more about what the great Admiral Schlossberg thinks." Amy looked apologetic. "Bet you get a lot of that, though. I've been trying not to impose."

Katie nodded. "You've been good. I brought it up. You know I don't get much besides advice from her. She wouldn't be happy with me right now. She'd say a big ego is needed for the job, but you've got to keep it under control."

Amy looked surprised. "I'd say she's right. Sounds like solid common sense to me."

"Et tu, Amy!"

"Hey, Katie, I'm on your side. My advice is you look over the schedule you have and sometime in the next day or two you go to the XO and you apologize profusely and tell him you realize how mistaken you were. Don't quite get down on your knees, but beg him to relent on the too full training schedule."

"Because just knowing about space and how ships work doesn't mean I know how the Space Force does things and can prove it."

"Exactly." Amy held Katie's eyes. "Your grandmother is right. You know it. Don't shoot yourself in the foot out of stubborn pride."

Katie chewed her lips and inspected her toes. "Ouch." She looked up. "I'll sleep on it. You make a lot of sense, but it does go against the grain."

Amy smiled. "If it was easy, we wouldn't get paid the big bucks."

Katie smiled back. One thing about the Space Force, you

weren't going to get rich from your salary. "Thanks, for the advice. I'm going to study in my bunk and get some sleep. I'll make a decision tomorrow."

"I'd be happier if you just bit the bullet, but sure, sleep on it."

Katie folded her bunk down over her desk and climbed in. "Good night," she said before pulling it closed.

"Sweet dreams."

\* \* \*

Lieutenant (Junior Grade) Ravi Shankar slammed the hatch closed behind him. The hatch to the closet laughably called his private cabin.

Ravi knew better. He'd been warned often enough about his habit of treating the ship's fittings roughly. Outright by fellow officers. With glances of reproach by enlisted personnel. He didn't know why. The *Resolute* was a new ship. Her only deployments had been her shakedown cruise and a tour to Mars. She'd then gone right into refit to prepare for her coming year-long deployment out to the Jovian system. She was just out of it.

There wasn't a constant bill of repairs for her hull techs to work on. The lazy bastards could well afford to spend a little time fixing anything that broke. Besides, the *Resolute* was supposed to be a warship. It was supposed to be constructed to take a pounding and keep on working, although the theory had never been tested.

Finally and last, but not least, Ravi was mad, and felt like it. He needed to take out his anger on something and inanimate objects were much safer than animate ones. He had just come from a dressing down by the Executive Officer. One occasioned by his treatment of an enlisted spacer. He did not need another one of those.

Ravi sighed. He had to do a lot more than avoid being dressed down by the XO. He had to impress him and the captain both. LTJG Ravi Shankar's career was not going as planned or as he wished. It was annoying, unfair, and frustrating. It was also frightening. Ravi's family wasn't noted for its patience with those it perceived as failures. Indeed, it tended to show a cruel lack of mercy.

The *Resolute* was still alongside. There were no restrictions on hot water usage. Ravi decided to take advantage. A long hot shower would help him calm down and relax. It'd also help him think. However justified his feelings, he couldn't afford to indulge them. He had to be coldly rational and think his plans through.

His shipsuit stuffed into the laundry hamper and with hot water pouring over him, Ravi contemplated his situation.

His being assigned to the *Resolute* meant his superiors considered him competent. They weren't worried about his messing up on the coming long deployment and having to be replaced. That was nice.

On the other hand, and less fortunately, the assignment also suggested his career was currently going exactly nowhere. A certain amount of time deployed on a working ship was necessary for a successful career. Any ambitious junior officer made sure he got his ticket punched. Any ambitious junior officer also tried to make sure they didn't waste any more time doing so than absolutely necessary. If at all possible, they tried to do so under the eyes of senior officers who could help their careers.

Everyone made sounds to the effect of detesting HQ staff pukes who didn't do any real work. In practice it was senior officers who determined which junior ones got promoted. They tended to promote ones they knew and who'd been of personal use to them. It was only human.

Which meant in the real world it was best not to be too far from and out of the sight of the senior ranks for too long. Year-long deployments to the Jovian system counted as too far and too long.

Also, most career personnel in the Space Force had families they didn't want to spend a year away from. The upshot was that the crews of ships being deployed on the Space Force's longest patrol were carefully selected.

The people picked tended to be junior for their posts and not obvious screw-ups. They also tended to be the dregs of what the officers letting them go thought they could get away with sending.

It was no honor being selected to go on a year-long patrol to Jupiter and her moons.

At least he didn't have to guess why Ensign Kincaid had been assigned to the *Resolute* as her first posting. The girl had Admiral Schlossberg's patronage and was obviously energetic and ambitious. Just as obviously she had the political sense of a houseplant. In addition to being personally brash and impetuous.

Young ensigns were normally assigned to a scout courier as their first posting. At least the ones who weren't complete screw-ups were. The ones that seemed capable of holding down a bridge watch on a spaceship. If they were lucky or well-connected enough, one based in the Earth-Luna system. Not Kincaid.

Ravi wasn't as well plugged into the Space Force gossip network as he would have liked. Sadly, schmoozing wasn't a personal strength of his. But he had heard of how Kincaid had ratted out a scout ship's crew for smuggling. He'd been suspicious of her even before he'd been assigned her as his deputy-cum-trainee for the loading of the *Resolute*'s munitions

It hadn't gone well. They hadn't had enough time to properly complete the task to start with. Then Kincaid had decided to interfere. She'd questioned his authority in front of his enlisted personnel.

He had been willing to give her the benefit of the doubt. Ravi knew all too well what it was like to be misunderstood and unfairly treated. Her behavior had used up all the slack he'd been willing to give her. She'd embarrassed him in front of his people and gotten him a dressing down by the XO.

All because she, a junior officer only weeks into her first posting on a ship, had thought fit to question his interpretation of safety protocols. Spacer Jones had been slow-walking the storage of the ship's heavy missiles and Ravi had found it necessary to light a fire under him.

And then Kincaid, *Ensign* Kincaid, instead of quietly learning from the incident, had had the audacity to directly question his orders. She'd insisted it was necessary to go slow so the missile wouldn't get too much momentum. She'd gone on at length about how being slow and positioning oneself with care was essential to the movement of heavy objects.

He had tried to hint to her that she ought not question him.

She had doubled down with a lecture on how it was especially important to be careful with missiles given how both delicate and dangerous they were. He had been losing his temper with her when the senior Weapons Officer, LTSG

Novak, had turned up. Turned up and sided with Kincaid.

It would have been an unforgivable embarrassment even if it hadn't earned him a trip to the XO's office.

Ravi made a conscious effort to stop grinding his teeth at the memory. They were going to be out of reach of decent dentistry for the next year. Wouldn't do to break a tooth now.

A whole year in close proximity with Ensign Kincaid and in de facto competition with her. A competition in which she appeared to have won the first round. Ravi was going to have to be very good at keeping his temper under control.

At least the shower had helped some. A good night's rest would help more. First, he had to do the inevitable paperwork. An activity that seemed to dominate a Space Force officer's existence. Ravi was actually quite good at carrying out administrative reporting. The sort of thing that still went under the rubric of "paperwork". Not much actual physical paper had been involved for centuries. The careful mechanical application of explicit rules was something that appealed to him. He was good at it. Of course, it was best if the paperwork required had some logical purpose to it and didn't involve contradictions. Two conditions that didn't always apply in the Space Force.

That this was the case was of some theoretical interest to Ravi. Ravi had always taken a particular interest in history. The administrative requirements imposed on junior officers in the Space Force were interesting. Interesting as a fine example of a path-dependent historical process. Each step in the process made some sense. The final result made none. The Space Force promulgated regulations as its main response to anything going wrong. It never canceled them. As a result, there was a thicket of regulations that applied to everything, often contradictory. It was impossible to comply with them all if you ever hoped to get anything done. A fact that young Ensign Kincaid did not seem to have absorbed yet. A successful officer had to exercise judgment.

A successful officer didn't annoy his or her colleagues by nitpicking over precise adherence to rules. It was plain bad form.

The fact that her failure to realize that was bound to cost Kincaid in the not too distant future was already starting to cheer Ravi up before he opened his mail box. What he found there brought him close to a state of happiness.

Amongst all the regular reports and requests for reports was a tentative training schedule for Ensign Kincaid. It was insane. Apparently Kincaid had managed to severely annoy the Executive Officer and was going to be publicly humiliated for it.

"Ensign Kincaid has pointed out she has considerable prior experience in space. She will therefore attempt a more concentrated and complete roster of duties and certifications than usual," one part of the introduction to the document read. Ravi couldn't help chuckling.

The average young officer got three, maybe at most four, training roles assigned to them in the course of their first year on ship. If they were earmarked for ship command, one of those roles would be as the Officer of the Watch on the bridge. The XO had somehow managed to shoehorn every one of more than a dozen possible roles on the ship into Kincaid's training schedule.

Ravi was amazed the Executive Officer had managed to make it appear even theoretically possible. Practically, of course, it was totally unreasonable. It would require an extraordinarily fast pace of learning. It required perfect performance of every duty the first time it was attempted. It left no time for rest and no margin for anything at all going wrong. It made no allowance for extra duties or tasks. The junior officers were always the first ones in line for those.

Ravi didn't believe that the XO expected Kincaid to complete the training course as given. Not for a moment. It was obvious that the XO expected Kincaid to at some point realize the training schedule was impossible to meet. The XO expected Kincaid to back down, eat humble pie, and beg for a more reasonable training schedule.

Having met Ensign Kincaid, Ravi was convinced that was going to take a lot longer than the XO thought it would.

In fact, Ravi was pretty sure Kincaid would drive herself to the point of collapse. She'd likely wreck her career in the process. The girl had no give. No give and no common sense, as far as Ravi could tell.

Ravi knew it didn't make him a good person, but he was going to enjoy watching Kincaid go down in flames.

If he was lucky, he'd get to be the one to add the straw to

her burdens and watch the camel's back break.

Katie Kincaid, the camel with a broken back.

Whimsical, but it had a ring to it.

\* \* \*

Katie was meeting with her grandmother in a suite in Goddard Station's fanciest hotel. Apparently ex-Admirals got generous pensions.

Katie suspected that her grandmother could've had accommodation in the station's Bachelor Officers Quarters for free. As an ex-Admiral. If she'd been willing to ask. Goddard Station was after all the Space Force's main base. Its largest at least, and for the majority of humanity still living on Earth, the one with the most important mission.

A mission no one liked to speak of. No sense scaring the voters. Still, policing near-Earth space was the Space Force's top mission. The goal being to make sure no rogue spacer decided to replicate the event that had made the dinosaurs extinct. Ideally preventing anybody from wiping out a major city too, if possible.

So Goddard Station, orbiting in Earth space, was of paramount importance and its size and funding reflected that. A place for a retired Admiral to sleep would not have been hard to find or have stretched the budget.

And it wouldn't have been particularly Spartan either.

All of which raised the question in Katie's mind of why the Admiral had instead decided to rent an expensive hotel suite on her own dime. Katie had spent the majority of what vacation time she'd had over the last few years visiting her grandmother and had got to know her well.

Katie's grandmother wasn't fond of either waste or extravagance. Whatever her grandmother allowed others to think, Katie didn't believe she was staying in the hotel for the greater luxury it provided.

"A penny for your thoughts," her grandmother said.

"I was wondering why you were renting such fancy rooms."

Her grandmother smiled. It was a mischievous smile. Katie suspected this was a side of Admiral (ret'd) Katrina Schlossberg that very few other people got to see. Katie also very strongly suspected it meant there was no hope she'd get a straight answer to her question. "What? I can't have a last decent meal with my granddaughter in nice surroundings before she goes away for a year?"

Katie's lips twisted as she tried not to smile. It wouldn't do to encourage the old woman. She took too much delight in teasing Katie as it was. "No. We both know neither of us cares much either way about this sort of thing. We could have had a good time together in some hole in the wall Pho shop."

"You weren't much into magic when you were a kid, were you, Katie?"

"Magic is code for things happening for reasons you don't know. Not knowing why things are happening can get you killed."

Her grandmother actually grinned. "Didn't think so."

"I know you're going to tell me it's not possible to know everything, not even everything immediately important to you. Furthermore, I know you're going to suggest, suggest because the heavens know it'd be too easy to simply state it, that given that fact you might as well use it. What I don't know is why you enjoy thinking this so much. Seems a pretty depressing way to look at things to me."

"You're being stubborn."

"I'm not alone. It seems to run in the family."

"An old lady should be allowed to indulge herself some in her golden years."

"You know I don't want to presume, but we have got to know each other over the last few years, haven't we?"

"I like to think so. It's given me great pleasure."

"Okay then. You know, I've never been clear on exactly how retired you are."

Katie's grandmother gave her a small rather sad smile. Katie had the oddest feeling it was an expression her grandmother was allowing herself. The feeling that it was one of those indulgences she'd spoken of. "You don't think that was accidental?" her grandmother finally said.

Katie had learned not to sigh in her last few years at the Academy. It didn't project the calm competence of a good leader. Instead, she allowed herself a moment of solemn contemplation of what her grandmother had said before replying. "I guess, to be honest, I didn't think about it at all. I didn't want to wreck what we had."

"And you wanted to get away from thinking about the Space Force. And thinking about your career in it. Last, but most of all I suspect, you weren't comfortable thinking about what influence I might be having on that career. Am I right?"

Now Katie did allow herself a sigh. "They were genuine vacations."

"I think I have a good idea how hard it was for you. I tried to give you a chance to relax some."

"And you know I think I really liked Kat Schlossberg and wasn't too sure about the ex-Admiral."

"Sensible of you. The Admiral is a rather cold harsh character, all too willing to sacrifice young people to her goals. Not at all a nice person. Not a safe one either."

"Wow." Katie looked around the room they were sitting in. She was getting the feeling the conversation was getting past serious and into things you don't want to be overheard. "You have reasons other than personal."

Her grandmother gave a smile, both cold and proud. "So true in multiple ways. I do like the Socratic method. I have wanted to spare you worry."

"I appreciate that. And?"

Her grandmother gave the room a quick glance of her own. "I've done my best to make sure it's possible to speak freely here."

Katie couldn't help giving the old woman an exasperated look. At times it seemed it wasn't possible to have a conversation with her that wasn't like an onion. Not just that there were layers within layers, but that they were likely to make you cry too. "That's reassuring, but you're not going to spill all the beans, are you?"

"Of course not, dear," her grandmother said. "That would be irresponsible. I know things that are not mine to share. Other things I might be able to share but for which in all conscience I have to do a cost benefit and risk analysis for every time I do. I know other things maybe of not such fraught importance, but which it'd be irresponsible to spread around simply to indulge my personal feelings."

"Or mine."

This time her grandmother pulled a thin smile out of her repertoire. "I'm glad you understand, dear."

Katie sat back and took a deep breath. "So you have secrets and you're not going to share. Not with me and not with the rest of the Space Force."

"That's right."

Katie tried to decide how she felt about that. She bit her lip and looked at the old lady across the small table from her. Said old lady studied her back. Before Katie could figure out what to say, they were interrupted by room service bringing them their supper.

The waiter having left her grandmother spoke. "Eat your meal, dear. Let your thoughts percolate. We can resume our conversation when we're done eating."

The food was good. Katie had learned to quite enjoy prime rib. It came with roasted vegetables and a fine red wine. Life wasn't perfect, but it did have its moments. They ate in silence. Finally, her plate clean and seeing her grandmother had finished her own food, Katie spoke. "This is what got between you and mom, isn't it?"

Her grandmother stared at her bleakly. "A good part of it, I think."

Katie pursed her lips and squinted back at her grandmother. "And you don't regret it? You don't think maybe it's time to do things a little differently?"

"You need to improve your acting, dear," her grandmother replied. "You're not that convincing. I know you know that there are things bigger and more important than either of us, and Allie too. And yes, of course, I have regrets, but that doesn't mean I'd do things differently."

"Nothing?"

"There you go again. Black and white. All monochromatic. I do understand your taste for keeping things simple and binary. I also think we both know you're indulging yourself. Again, I understand your feelings. The situation is less than ideal. Still, it's not helpful. Of course, not *nothing*. Anything significant, that's a different question. One could argue I made a self-indulgent mistake having Allie."

"You think Mom was a mistake? Really?"

"No, not really. It was bound to be problematic. It was as clear as anything ever is that I was likely going to end up short changing any child I had. Despite that, I can't regret that Allie exists or that you do. I could have handled it better. I could have been more direct with Allie and I could have involved myself in your life sooner."

Katie looked at her grandmother and she didn't see

someone making an abject apology. Someone with regrets, sure, but someone standing their ground. That was fair. Katie had become convinced over the last few years that her grandmother tried her best to be fair. Also that she wasn't one to dodge decisions because those decisions might have a cost. Katie figured that her grandmother, aware of those costs, tried to be as strictly rational in apportioning them as possible. Katie figured that was an approach worth trying to emulate.

"Okay, but what you're not saying in so many words is that basically you'd still put the job ahead of your family."

"Job?"

"Okay, not just something you did for money. Not the right word. But you were doing something you didn't tell Mom about that took you away from her, and I'm guessing left you tired and distracted when you were around. Where was granddad in all of this? Is this still going on? Is there still some cause you have that's more important than your family?"

"We've known each other for almost four years now, admittedly off and on, and this is the first time you've asked about your grandfather."

"Your total unwillingness to talk about him is notorious. Promising young astrophysicist drops off the face of the Earth, and nobody is willing to even talk about it. Has spooks and tippy top secret written all over it. I did ask other people. They all immediately changed the subject or said they had no idea what had happened. You weren't just a ship commander, were you?"

"That is a speculation that I can neither confirm nor deny the truth of, dear."

"Yeah. In other words, yes."

Katie's grandmother was beginning to look exasperated. Katie supposed that was fair. They both knew Katie was beating a dead horse out of annoyance at the situation. Situations. Maybe it was time to extend an olive branch and move on. "I guess I'm doing the same. I'm putting my career ahead of my family, too."

Her grandmother first nodded, then extending a hand out flat, palm down, waggled it. She smiled. Katie had the feeling she enjoyed making Katie work for it.

Katie took a deep breath. "Yeah. Okay. It's not just a career to me either. It's not just family. I'm willing to sacrifice my entire personal life, everything, to doing what I want to."

"You want to make a difference, a big historic one, and you're willing to do almost anything to reach a place where you can eventually do that."

"Not very modest, am I? I didn't think I was that obvious. Nobody else seems to have noticed."

"And they'd all think you're crazy if they did. Utterly delusional at best."

Katie colored. "Yes, I think they would. Sometimes late at night when things aren't going well I wonder myself."

Her grandmother nodded. "For what it's worth, I don't think you're an egomaniac. You don't put your own ego ahead of other people or considerations. That's not the young woman I've gotten to know."

Katie let out a breath. "Thanks. It's a relief you think so."

"And if you're crazy, so am I."

"Really?"

"Yes, really. We've talked about this piecemeal and indirectly before. The Star Rats are here. In system, doing the Lord knows what out around Saturn. So aliens are real and so is interstellar travel. Slower than light, at least. Reading between the lines of the little they've been willing to tell us, we can surmise there are species out there with Faster Than Light travel. Genuine FTL. That's all public knowledge."

Katie nodded. "But oddly, there's almost no serious discussion of it."

"What could people say, dear? Anyhow, to continue, it's an open secret that almost every major government is researching FTL. It's more the rule than the exception that promising young physicists tend to disappear."

"Oh?" Katie realized she should have made the connection much sooner.

"You've been busy, dear. Besides, it's something all sensible people pretend not to notice. So given all that, it's pretty clear at some point we're going to develop FTL travel ourselves. And no, I'm not going to speculate on when."

"Okay. But I can, and given the resources being committed and the fact we know it's possible, I think it could be in my lifetime."

"Yes, and at that point we're probably going to be faced with a galaxy containing multiple alien species all more technologically advanced and more powerful than we are."

Katie nodded. "Yeah, it all seems obvious to me."

"Only it's so far out of the mainstream you're afraid of being considered crazy if you admit to thinking that."

"Yeah, I wonder if there's something wrong with me or with everyone else."

"And being the modest young creature you are, you figure there's something wrong with everyone else."

Katie colored again. Katie's grandmother's ability to embarrass her never ceased to amaze Katie. "I don't think I'm wrong."

"Nobody likes to admit it, but when something's too big to handle or to do anything about, sometimes just ignoring it and getting on with life is the best you can do."

"So not stupid or crazy, just willfully blind."

"Everybody has to choose their battles, dear, even if they don't think about it like that. Most people pick smaller battles they have a chance of winning."

"Anyhow, FTL could happen in our lifetimes and we'll be facing powerful aliens and the Space Force will be on the front lines."

"And it is small, and has only a small number of officers, of which only a portion will be anywhere near up to the challenge. And you want to be one of that small number, right?"

It was true and something Katie rarely, if ever, admitted to. Maybe in front of that review board back at the end of Basic Officer Training. Or late at night solving the universe's problems over too many drinks with friends. Neither instances where she'd have expected to be taken seriously and at full face value. Now she was being asked to declare her intent baldly and without equivocation or excuses. She found she was appalled at her own hubris. Didn't change what she believed or what she was trying to do, though. "Yes, ma'am, that's right."

"Good. Given that it's reasonable to sacrifice a lot. Even family and friends."

Katie took a deep breath and started to answer.

Katie's grandmother held up a hand to stop her. "It wasn't a question. It's also not something I want to discuss right now. Our time is limited. Just be careful about how you make those sacrifices, dear. Don't lose track of the human cost."

"No, ma'am, I won't."

"Good. You're only one little ensign right now, though. What about your family? Have you managed to talk to Allie and your dad yet?"

Katie took a deep breath. It seemed like a lifetime since she'd seen her parents in the flesh. In fact, it'd been the four years she'd been at the Academy. A trip out to the Belt took weeks each way and was very expensive. She'd had her grandmother to visit. They'd all thought it likely she'd get a posting out to Ceres as a Scout ship crew member after graduating, or failing that at least enough leave to make a trip home. It hadn't turned out like that. "I've been sending text messages and the odd video at regular intervals. I rented a private booth and sent them a long video this morning. I got one back this afternoon."

"How are they?"

"Good. Disappointed I won't be getting back home for at least another year. Busy. They've hired on non-family crew Mostly members of Calvin's family, the Cromwells. It's been work stepping up operations to take advantage of that and pay for it all. Nothing goes exactly to plan. It takes time and energy, but it seems to be working out."

"They understand you're going to be under a communications blackout?"

"Yep, they don't think it makes sense, but they don't expect the Space Force to make sense."

"With our current technology it's still a big solar system. The *Resolute* is going to be out on patrol by herself for months getting out to Vesta and then Jupiter."

"And any enemy that knew exactly where she was because of poor communications discipline could do a lot of harm."

"Exactly."

"Can you hear Mom being sarcastic about our silly paranoid games?"

Her grandmother sighed. "All too well. Only we're right and Allie's wrong in this. Just because a problem doesn't seem real because it's not something you're familiar with and having to deal with it inconveniences you, doesn't mean it doesn't exist. Allie can keep her head in the sand along with the rest of humanity. We've decided to accept reality, however inconvenient."

"Yeah, us. Somehow that doesn't make me feel as good as it

should."

Her grandmother's smile was warm. It occurred to Katie that the supposedly retired Admiral Katrina Schlossberg had been bearing this burden since before Katie had been born. That her grandmother likely welcomed someone to share it with. That she likely genuinely regretted not being able to do so more fully. "Yes dear, I do understand."

"Sorry, suppose if anyone does it's you," Katie said.

Katie's grandmother looked almost embarrassed at that. She fiddled with her dinner utensils. Katie couldn't remember the last time she'd seen the ex-Admiral like this.

"What is it?" Katie asked.

Her grandmother looked straight at her. "I have a favor to ask."

"Anything," Katie answered.

Her grandmother shook her head ruefully. "Dear child, you shouldn't go handing out blank checks like that. Not that I don't appreciate it."

"I don't. Not to just anybody. To you and maybe my old friend Sam back on Ceres. Not even to Calvin or my Family. I trust their good faith, but not their judgment that much." Katie smiled ruefully herself. "You see, I can be just as cold blooded and calculating as you are."

Katie's grandmother chuckled dryly. "I fear I doubt that, dear."

"Nah, you're just too into being the gray spider manipulating us poor peasants from behind the curtain, that's all," Katie replied trying to lighten the mood.

"About that. What I'm about to share is only because you're already partially read in on it."

"Okay."

"That smuggling ring on Ceres you stumbled into was only part of a larger operation."

"Damn."

"Yes, not good that the Space Force has been compromised and our investigations have led us back to high places on Earth."

Well, Katie had known her grandmother had secrets Katie would be happier not knowing. She just hadn't expected to learn of them so quickly. "That's disturbing."

"Indeed," her grandmother agreed, "but that part's not your

problem. What might be, if you're willing to take the task on, is what's going on out on Vesta and in the Jovian system. On Ganymede base in particular."

"What do want me to do?"

"Mainly, simply keep your eyes open. Maybe talk to a few more locals for a bit longer than you would otherwise and listen carefully. Report back, discreetly, when and if you can. Be ready to tell me all about it when you get back."

Katie nodded. "I can do that."

Her grandmother nodded back, took a breath, and sat back.

Katie braced for whatever was coming.

"Finally," her grandmother said, "about what you can and can't do. I've heard you're being somewhat, shall we say, *ambitious*."

Katie cleared her throat. It was going to be hard framing this so that she didn't end up looking like a complete idiot. "I had a conversation with the XO in which I may have projected a bit too much self-confidence."

"And?"

"As a way of testing me, I guess, he's given me a very, as you say, *ambitious* training schedule."

"In other words, you stepped in it and he's trying to slap you down."

"I suppose that could be one interpretation, ma'am."

"Katie, you've got to learn tact. Once more, you have to pick your battles. The best thing would have been to never have gotten yourself into this situation in the first place."

"Yes, ma'am, but it's too late for that now. What can I do now?"

"Probably the best thing is what he expects. Go to the man, apologize profusely for your impertinence, and ask to be given a more forgiving schedule."

"And look like a braggart with bad judgment?"

A hard look. "Better than demonstrating for a fact that you're a braggart with bad judgment. If you insist on seeing this through, be damned sure you deliver. Pace yourself, be a machine, there is no way it's going to be easy. Back out now or see it through. Do you hear me, Katie? Given what you've told me, it's not just your future or your career at stake, is it? Have you thought this through? Are you willing and able to deliver on what you've promised?"

Katie knew her grandmother was right about the tact thing, and the fact she'd gotten into the situation without thinking first. Katie wasn't proud of either fact. She had thought about it long and hard since. She could do this. It'd be better if she did. "Yes, ma'am," she said.

"Okay, then. About time we turned to things less consequential and more pleasant."

"Yes, ma'am."

## 2: Katie Settles In

Lieutenant (Junior Grade) Iris Gregorian had been busy. The tradition was that ship's boats operations was a world onto itself. Usually they engaged with the various support services directly. It wasn't hard and didn't require a lot of planning and preparation as long as deployments were short. No more than a few weeks out to Mars or days out to Luna. A deployment out to Jupiter via the Belt was a different kettle of fish.

If you needed something and hadn't brought it along, then you were going to have to do without it for everything from months to most of a year. And it was Iris who was having to put most of the effort into seeing that didn't happen. Her assigned role was Deputy Boat Operations Officer. Lieutenant (Senior Grade) Oswald Wong was the Boat Operations Officer proper.

Only Wong, despite his higher rank, was much less experienced than Iris. Iris had had a definite career setback after Katie Kincaid had blown open the existence of a smuggling ring. A smuggling ring Iris had been a minor part of. Also, Wong probably wasn't going to re-up after the *Resolute*'s tour out to Jupiter. He'd have done his mandatory stint in the Space Force at that point. It was apparent that although the man was competent enough, he wasn't outstanding. Iris suspected his heart would be in his family's business in a way it'd never been, and never would be, in his Space Force career.

Wong was running out the clock on his time in the Space Force. He was doing what he needed to, and not much more. Iris was taking up the slack.

So her time to relax a little here in the wardroom with a coffee and a snack was precious to her.

She was looking forward to a little quiet time by herself before spotting Ensign Katie Kincaid sitting by herself poring over her reading tablet with a thin crease between her eyebrows.

Iris took a moment to feel a tiny bit sorry for herself and walked over to Kincaid. "Hi, mind if I sit here?"

Katie looked up. Then she looked surprised. She took a visible split second to process the presence of Iris standing before her. "Oh, hi. Yeah, sure. Please, be glad to have the chance to talk to you."

Iris gave the best reassuring smile she could manage. It wasn't like she'd never dealt with a young, wet behind the ears ensign before. Also for the most part, she and Katie had got on quite well before. Well, before that small, almost career destroying, bump at the end there. Iris sat down with her coffee and cradling it in her hands looked over the top of it at Katie. Katie looked back at her, trying not to appear wary. It was almost amusing. Iris took a moment before letting the girl off the hook. "No hard feelings, Katie. I know we're both busy so I won't beat around the bush. You did the right thing."

Katie blushed. Looked down at her tablet on the table. Iris had only known the girl for a few weeks four years ago, but she knew this sort of embarrassment wasn't normal for a young woman self-confident to the point of being brash. "Thanks," Katie said after getting over her discomfort. "It wasn't easy. I wish it hadn't hurt so many people."

Iris sighed. One thing about being in the dog house and in boats, there wasn't much point in trying to impress people with your command presence. "It hasn't been fun for any of us. John had to resign. Only you know, I think it may have been for the better. We were only going to get in deeper and become more compromised the longer it went on. I don't know where it would have ended."

Katie chewed on her lip, a hard look of concentrated

thought on her face. "It was a lot more than just the *Sand Piper's* crew and even Guy Boucher, wasn't it?"

"I don't know. My role was mostly winking at what Kevin and Sam were up to. I had the feeling it was. Thinking about it since, it only makes sense."

"Lieutenants Wong and Romanov? Is Kevin Wong related to your boss?"

Iris shifted in her seat uncomfortably. Katie's last question was one she'd never felt comfortable putting to the Boat Operations Officer directly. They'd mostly left each other alone. "I think they might be distantly related. Wong is almost as common a name as Smith though."

"The whole thing is a murky mess, isn't it?"

"Yeah, and it was made pretty clear to me that part of the price for not getting cashiered was not stirring up the mud."

Katie made a face. It was as clear as day she didn't like secrets or ambiguity in general. "But it was mainly Wong and Romanov?"

"Boucher, or some associates of his, were running a gambling and girls operation down on the docks."

"They reeled in Wong and Romanov and the rest of you decided to cover for them?"

"Exactly."

"Scout crews are pretty tight, aren't they?"

"They are. You live that close together with people day in and day out, and you either learn to hate them or love them."

"And it started small, and didn't seem a big deal, and it was Captain Anderson's call anyhow?"

Iris winced. It'd been hard won knowledge for her that people tend to believe what they want to. Katie didn't seem to be quite the innocent and naive girl she'd been four years before either. Still young enough, though. "Speaking of starting small, you've stepped in it with Shankar and the XO, haven't you?"

It was Katie's turn to wince. "I'm looking at a rather packed training schedule."

"I don't suppose it's worth telling you that you need to ask the XO to change that?"

Katie sighed. Iris was touched that Katie was willing to be so open about her feelings with her. And a little worried, too. Katie needed to be less trusting. "You're not the first to suggest it. I know it's what makes the most sense. I just can't stomach the idea. I think I can pull it off. It'll be worth it if I can."

"It's your funeral," Iris replied. She didn't like it, but as young as Katie still was, and despite the fact she was only an ensign, she was still a Space Force officer. Katie had to make her own decisions and live with the consequences. "I have a memo telling me I'm to help you qualify on boats. Pilot, co-pilot, flight engineer, and ship's boats division administration. Oh, and you're to demonstrate at least a supervisory level understanding of boat maintenance. The XO also suggested that if you have spare time, a familiarization with the planning and execution of boat operations wouldn't go amiss." Iris couldn't help smiling at the last. It was a cruel joke true, but it was still funny for all that. The XO had obviously been working out a certain degree of frustration with Katie.

Katie looked blank. "I really hadn't thought about how much there was to learn," she said.

Iris gave her a grim smile. "No kidding. I'll try to help as best I can. Any time you have left over from all your other duties, eating, exercise, and sleeping, I can assign you work helping me with ramping up boats for the tour. The heavens know, I can use all the help I can get. Only it means I'm not going to have time to hold your hand. I'm going to have to point you in the right direction and trust you to work things out. Can you handle that?"

Katie smiled. "Are you sure you're not trying to get even?"

"I'm taking a chance on you by trying to help," Iris replied.

"I know. I appreciate it. I'm not up on Space Force routines for everything, but I have a good feel for small spacecraft operations. I'm pretty good at memorizing manuals. I'll need some heads ups when practice deviates from what's in the manuals. I'm confident I can help."

Iris nodded. "Great. I've made up a list of spare parts and consumables to requisition above what we normally carry. I want you to review it to see if I've missed anything. Also to flag things where we might need to light a fire under the yard supply division because they're critical. I'll send it right over to you." Having said that, she took a moment to finger the right incantations into her tablet. She looked up.

Katie nodded in turn and checked her own tablet. "Got it," she said. "Looks good. Oh, I'm due in Engineering in a few minutes. Sorry, got to run."

Iris smiled. "I understand, believe me."

Katie smiled back as she stood. "Thanks, later."

"Later."

\* \* \*

Katie was standing her first watch on the *Resolute*, an engineering watch as it happened. It was their first day out of Goddard Station, and they weren't even completely clear of Earth space yet. Not that that was immediately clear from down in the Engine Room. The Engine Room, more formally the Main Engineering Control Room, was the zero gee part of engineering down in the main spindle. The part with all the machinery and the accessible parts of the propulsion system. The one part of the ship designed to allow crew to move about when the ship was under acceleration and maneuvering.

One of Katie's favorite parts of any ship.

Right now she was sharing it with Lieutenant (Senior Grade) Jeffries, the Engineer, and Senior Petty Officer "Mo" Khoury. Normally under safe peacetime cruising conditions, SPO Khoury would have been holding down the watch on his own and trying to stave off boredom. Out of an abundance of caution, the Space Force insisted on having someone located next to the machinery that was the ship's heart at all times.

In practice, at times other than ones of dire emergency, it was healthier and more convenient for the crew to control that machinery from the comfort of the gravity ring.

At other times repair or routine maintenance might be required, but those weren't things done under acceleration or when it was possible the ship might be maneuvering.

All of which was to say that normally a senior rating was stuck down in the zero gee engineering space with little to do as all the necessary work would be done by the larger watch in the gravity ring's Remote Engineering Control Room. Said senior rating would attempt to keep themselves busy by doing minor maintenance and by manually recording various settings the ship's computers were already monitoring much more effectively.

Only at the current time the *Resolute* was on its first day of a year-long deployment and the short-handed Engineer was attempting to get a head start on training Ensign Kincaid. So "Mo" Khoury had company.

"I wish Lieutenant Roth hadn't decided to break her leg skiing," Allan Jeffries was saying.

"Inconsiderate of her," Katie said.

"Very inconvenient," Jeffries replied. "It's left me with twice the normal workload and constantly on call."

Katie noticed SPO Khoury attentively watching dials and pretending to be deaf and dumb. Smart man. "It's odd that SFHQ wouldn't have replaced her, sir," she said.

"Not really, I'm afraid. It's not like we've a surplus of trained engineering officers or that anyone is jumping up and down to volunteer for a year-long mission to the outer system."

"Still, sir."

"Also, SFHQ seems to be under the odd impression that machinery and propulsion run themselves without the need of maintenance or supervision. Especially practically new machinery that's just been through a refit."

"Isn't that mostly true? Isn't a lot of what we do just watching it all work the way it should?"

"It's true right up to the point something breaks, and then it isn't," Jeffries said, looking at Katie with a serious expression. Seemed he wanted to assure her he wasn't just venting. "Ideally, if we're watching carefully, we catch it before that actually happens. Make sure it doesn't. If we don't and something does break then we've got our work cut out for us. Best case scenario, the ship's ability to do its mission is degraded. SFHQ and the captain worry about a mission failure."

Katie knew where this was going. She'd grown up in a similar fragile bubble of metal surrounding some air and some complicated but vital machinery. "And what do you worry about, sir?"

"I worry about us all dying."

"I see, sir."

"I imagine that unlike most of the young ensigns I could have got you actually do, Kincaid," Jeffries said with a slight smile. "Your unusual background may have been a handicap at the Academy, but I'm damned glad to have you here."

Katie couldn't help smiling back. She wasn't sure Lieutenant Jeffries wasn't being a touch too familiar for a senior officer that was, at least temporarily, her boss, but it was nice to be appreciated. "I'm glad to be here, sir. I love this stuff."

Jeffries nodded. "All very good, young Ensign Kincaid," he replied, "but let's see what you can do."

"Sir?"

"What's our current acceleration, Kincaid?"

"Quarter gee, sir. And subject to variation, though that's not planned."

Jeffries smiled. "Good. It's important to always remember that. If things always went according to plan, there'd be no need of putting jumped up monkeys into tin cans that float in a vacuum. Now on your family ship did you always control things from the gravity ring or did you go down into the spindle at times when she was moving?"

Katie couldn't help thinking that technically ships were always moving. Indeed, to be picky, everything was always moving relative to something else. Only humans were hard wired to perceive things differently. She did have to admit saying "*when accelerating or actually or potentially maneuvering*" was a bit of a mouth full. It wasn't just humans not being designed for space, it was their language too. "The gravity ring, sir. Even in the ring we stayed strapped in when maneuvering. Fact is, a small gee variation is more likely to get you hurt in the ring than in the spindle. You lose your balance and then you fall hard. Our planned accelerations were always small."

Jeffries nodded. "Makes sense on a civilian ship. Especially one I'm guessing was minimally manned."

"Just the three of us, sir. Me and my parents."

The Engineering Officer failed to keep a quick frown from flickering across his face. "New and heavily automated?"

Katie wished she'd not understood. "And under manned for a fact too, sir. My parents were new to space and to technical work too. They were well educated for office work on Earth. They believed everything the ship salesman told them and only skimmed the technical manuals."

Jeffries didn't bother trying to suppress his inner engineer this time. He sucked his teeth. "Ouch."

"Yes, sir." Katie nodded. "Started to worry me as soon as I was old enough to genuinely understand those technical manuals and the safety ones too."

Jeffries had been half watching the control board. He turned to give Katie his full attention and a long, apprising look. "I'm guessing you made it your mission in life to make up the slack."

"Well, sir, people have told me I'm rather over confident and inclined to taking too much on. Maybe to sticking my nose in where it doesn't belong. All I can say is I came by it honestly."

Jeffries smiled. "Well said, Kincaid. I'm guessing you've learned a little modesty the last few years at the Academy?"

"Some, sir, maybe. Anyway regarding my parents and our ship, the *Dawn Threader*, they took on hired crew when I left Family friends, solid people who know what they're doing."

"A big relief."

"It sure was, sir."

"Good, but let's get back to the here and now." Jeffries took a breath and peered off into space for a moment. "Unlike on civilian ships, the Space Force believes it might be necessary for Space Force crew, in particular crew on watch in the spindle, to move around when the ship is accelerating. Senior Petty Officer Khoury here, had to take a special course in it before we'd let him stand watch here."

Khoury looked over and gave a disgusted grin. "Only a few weeks and mostly common sense."

Jeffries assumed an exaggerated mien of official rectitude. "The Space Force does not believe in mere 'common sense', Senior Petty Officer."

"I'd noticed that, sir."

Katie grinned at the good-humored byplay between the men. Looked like his men liked Jeffries. She suspected they respected him too. It's hard to like someone who has your fate in their hands when they're not competent.

"Anyhow, what I'd like to see, Ensign Kincaid," Jeffries said looking at Katie, "Is how you move around this space when it's under acceleration."

"Yes, sir. Now?"

"Yes, you are to go forward to the Damage Control locker by the main entry hatch and check that it's fully stocked and everything in it is properly stored. Understood?"

"Yes, sir. Permission to unstrap, sir?"

Jeffries flicked his channel to the Bridge open. "Requesting permission for personnel to move about in engineering," he said. He nodded at the reply. "Permission granted. On your way, Kincaid."

As it happened, "forward" at this point was straight up against the ship's acceleration in its long, slow burn for Vesta in the Belt. All the same, it was an easy if meaningless task. Any Earther, or anyone else who'd spent most of their life in one gee environments like Katie, could have handled it without a second thought. It was obvious to Katie that that was the whole point. "Yes, sir," she said. "Commencing movement forward to the main hatch."

She freed herself from her safety harness with one hand while keeping her feet hooked in place. She treated it exactly as she would have one of her wall climbing sessions back in the marine fitness complex on Ceres. She was careful to always be holding on in at least three places at a time. She was careful to make sure only one foot or hand was free at a time. In a way it was easier than a wall climb in that she had regularly climbed walls under a full gee or more. A piffling quarter gee was nothing. In a way it was much harder in that she had to establish holds that would remain as solid as possible under changes to forces from more than one direction.

Katie had studied a little about how to do that, and both the ship's "handholds" and the ship boots she was wearing were constructed with it in mind. She hadn't had any real practice. So she took her time and thought about every move. Petty Officer Khoury had almost certainly downplayed what was in that course he'd taken. When she got to the main hatch, she looked back at the two men who'd been watching her, it seemed. She wondered that they weren't getting impatient with how slowly she was moving. She'd gotten into trouble at the Academy constantly at first because of a habit of overthinking things and taking too long to complete simple tasks.
The men were watching with interest, but they didn't seem impatient. That was good.

Having reached the main hatch and the nearby Damage Control locker, Katie worked with one hand to open it and check that everything that was supposed to be there was, and was properly secured.

She was just as careful on her return trip. She secured herself in her position without ever having more than one limb free. It was a bit awkward figuring out how to do that. The description of the method in the manual wasn't the best it turned out.

All that done, she looked up at Jeffries and Khoury.

Khoury, behind the Engineering Officer, winked. Katie kept a straight face. Jeffries nodded. "Well done, Kincaid. You were slow, true, but you made sure you were solidly secured at all times which is what is important."

"Thank you, sir."

"Your marks at the Academy were outstanding, but I wanted to see if you could execute on what you understood intellectually." The Engineer looked serious. "It's important not just to get the job done, but also properly. Safely and reliably."

"Yes, sir."

"I'm not going to beat around the bush, Kincaid," Jeffries said. "Based on what I've seen so far, you've got the makings of an outstanding Engineering Officer. The Space Force needs more engineering officers, even ones who're just adequate. I could use one right now."

Katie wasn't sure what she was hearing. Was he offering her the Baby Engineer's slot? "Sir?"

"Elect for the engineering career track. Have the XO relieve you of training not relevant to that, and I'll put you in the Deputy Engineer's slot. With a year's experience in the slot, you'd be a sure bet for early promotion right past Sub-Lieutenant and to Lieutenant Junior Grade. I'm pretty sure Senior Lieutenant would follow shortly and like as not, you'd be a ship's engineer as soon as you re-upped."

Katie was amazed. It sounded great. Only it wasn't what she'd had in mind. Most of all, engineers didn't tend to get ship command. Still. "Sounds almost too good to be true, sir. Can I have time to think about it?"

"Of course," the Engineer replied. "It's a big decision. But, and I know I'm not supposed to say this, but the ship driver's shop is a closed one. They're not interested in letting disruptive influences in. Especially not young talented ones. They like things fine the way they are. It's not fair, but it's the way things are. No matter how good you are, even if you're never unlucky or make a mistake, it could be a very long time, if ever, before you get ship command. Never is all too likely. Better the bird in hand, Kincaid. Please, think about that. Do what makes sense. You understand, right?"

"Yes, sir."

\* \* \*

It'd been a panicked, hurried rush getting the *Resolute* all stocked up for a year-long deployment away from her normal bases of supply. Amy was looking forward to locking herself in the tiny closet that had been labeled her office and going over the records of what had happened quietly and in detail. She found being alone with records and sorting them out so they made sense relaxing. Applying orderly routines to make sense of the world and ensure things worked the way they were supposed to gave her great satisfaction.

As soon as she came into sight of the door to her office, she realized her hopes were about to be dashed.

Lieutenant-Commander James Hood, the *Resolute*'s captain, was standing outside the door of her refuge. Not arguing, captains don't argue with their crew, but having an animated discussion with a pair of officers half in and half out of her office.

Also senior officers. The XO, Lieutenant Winters, and the Operations Officer, Lieutenant Haralson. Thor Haralson, who Amy had something of a crush on that she was careful to keep to herself. Amy had no idea what they were doing there, but she didn't think it could be good news.

They didn't seem to have noticed her yet. For a second she had thoughts of turning around and getting out of Dodge before they did.

Only the captain chose that moment to see her out of the corner of his eye. "Ah, Sub-Lieutenant Sarkis, the very young lady we wanted to see."

Amy stepped forward, stopped at a conversational distance from the captain, and tried to look the very picture of an eagerly helpful junior officer. "Sir! Are you sure you don't want to speak to Senior Lieutenant Vann, sir?"

Her superiors stopped their bickering to share in giving her a set of small smiles of amusement. "Quite sure, Sub-Lieutenant," the XO said. "We've already spoken to your boss, and he assures us you're the perfect person for the job."

"Job, sir?"

Lieutenant Haralson, the Training Officer in addition to his main role as Ops Officer, grimaced slightly. It was quick. Amy couldn't help thinking many other people would have missed it. "Lieutenant Vann assured us that you had a solid, thorough grasp of all the responsibilities of a Supply Officer. In fact, he said you could step into his shoes today if you had to."

"That's very flattering, sir," Amy replied.

"But not untrue, right?" the XO asked. The captain looked on. Apparently willing to let his officers do the talking for him.

"I like to think so, sir. Lieutenant Vann is very conscientious. I don't think he'd say it was so if he didn't believe it. I do try hard, and I think I've got a knack for the job."

"Great, and I don't imagine you'd have any trouble training someone else for the job?" the XO said.

"Ah, no sir, shouldn't be any problem," Amy said. She wasn't sure where this was going. "One of the best ways to make sure you have a completely solid grasp of a topic is to have to teach it to someone else." So normally she'd welcome the chance to do so, only it now occurred to her that the only person on the ship who could use the training was Katie. Only Katie already had a full plate, didn't she?

"I've found that myself," Lieutenant Haralson said. Rather grudgingly, it seemed to Amy.

"Ensign Kincaid is your cabin mate. You get along well with her, don't you?" the XO asked.

"Yes, sir. She's a good, considerate cabin mate, no bad, or annoying habits. She's bright and energetic. An interesting person," Amy replied in good faith. It was always good to be positive about your fellow officers. Even better when you could be that way honestly and without any reservations, however unspoken.

"Interesting," the XO said, "yes, I think we can all agree on that." He looked over at Lieutenant Haralson. "Well, Thor, you're the Training Officer."

Lieutenant Haralson glanced the XO's way, before biting the bullet and addressing Amy in rather formal tones. "The XO has decided that Ensign Kincaid's unusual background, um," another sidewards glance, "merits a more, um, complete and comprehensive training program than is usual."

"Yes, sir," Amy said. What else could she do?

Lieutenant Haralson took a breath and most definitely did not sigh. He glanced at the captain's encouraging, but implacable, face and continued. "Ensign Kincaid's main current responsibility is to certify as capable of taking an engineering watch. She is also learning all the other responsibilities of an engineering officer. The Engineer, Lieutenant Jeffries, is extremely happy with her progress so far."

"He'd like to get her certified and put her in the Baby Engineer slot," the XO said. "She's good at it, and if she has any sense, she'll jump at the chance."

Amy carefully did not react to this in any way. She noticed the captain also kept his face non-committal. It occurred to her that captains didn't normally get involved in the actual running of their ships. That was the XO's job. Captains used their ships to execute their missions, their Executive Officers ran them. The captain likely wasn't too happy to be involved in all this. So better step carefully.

Lieutenant Haralson rallied and spoke again. "Be that as it may, it behooves us to not preempt a young officer's career path choices too quickly."

The XO grunted.

Lieutenant Haralson's lips tightened, but the XO was, after all, at the end of the day, his boss. "Even a whole year isn't too long to cycle an officer in training through all the possible roles on a ship," Haralson said. "So it's going to be necessary for Kincaid to multi-task and learn multiple roles at a time. She apparently believes she can handle it." He sent a quelling glance the XO's way.

The XO gave him a thin smile back. He was after all getting his way.

"Lieutenant Gregorian has taken Kincaid under her wing and is instructing her in all the ins and outs of boats," Haralson said. "Fortunately, there don't seem to be any hard feelings over that incident that happened prior to the Ensign's arrival at the Academy."

They all shared a moment of grim stillness over the thought of that particular mess.

Katie wasn't just an outsider, she was an outsider with a cloud over her head. Amy wondered if Katie realized what an uphill battle she had to fight.

Haralson plowed on. "It is, in fact, going so well that it is believed." Oh, so no mention of who believed it. Great. "That the Ensign can begin her introduction to a third set of responsibilities."

The XO decided to cut to the chase. "We want you to take Kincaid on in a training role. Make sure she knows the Supply Officer's job in and out. In a couple of months we want her able to pass the standard certification exams for Supply Officer. We want her capable of, in your judgment, actually doing the job. Understood?"

"Yes, sir," Amy replied. "But, sir, that is very ambitious."

"We have faith in both you and Ensign Kincaid," the XO replied.

"Yes, sir."

What else could she say?

\* \* \*

So they were on their way, bound for the Belt and the Outer System. Ravi Shankar was glad for that. He could have wished for more time to have prepared properly for the tour. It'd been beyond hectic there at the end. The kerfuffle with Kincaid hadn't helped. All the same, Kincaid aside, if they'd had a couple more weeks to prepare, he still imagined the yard dogs would have found a way to delay vital deliveries to the last minute. It was almost as if they didn't want the ship's officers to inspect their deliveries too carefully. He snickered to himself. It was exactly like that.

It usually wasn't clear who benefited, or always exactly how they went about it, but little short-cuts, shortchanging, and feather bedding were rife in the Space Force's shipyards. It was political. It went straight to the top. Appointments to positions in the Space Force's supply administration were lucrative. It was an open secret that a combination of political favor and bribes determined who got those appointments. Thereafter, the lucky appointees had to make an extra effort to profit from their positions. Their shifts were often not entirely legitimate.

The common impression was that the improprieties, although unsavory, were limited and did no serious harm. Ravi wasn't so sure. There also wasn't much he could do about it. Still, ship's officers watched yard dogs carefully and double checked everything they did.

Which was exactly what he, along with Lieutenant (Senior Grade) Anne Elizabeth Novak, the Weapons Officer, and his boss, were doing right now. They probably wouldn't be able to fix any deficiencies out of shipboard resources, but they could avoid being surprised by them. Maybe devise workarounds ahead of time.

And so Ravi, as Deputy Weapons Officer, and Lieutenant Novak, as Weapons Officer, were down in the missile bay tearing their newly delivered long-range missiles apart. Or to be more precise, supervising Senior Missile Tech "Dusty" Miller as he did so.

"Stop twitching, Ravi," Novak said. "I know you'd like to get hands-on, but it's below the dignity of superior commissioned beings such as ourselves. Besides, I don't think 'Dusty' would approve of my letting you handle his babies."

"You've that right, ma'am," Miller put in on his own behalf.

"Nice to know who's really running things," Ravi replied.

"New family, aren't you?" Novak asked.

Ravi couldn't help frowning. "Yes, ma'am."

"Nothing to be ashamed of. In fact, to be fair, you can be proud of the fact you doubtless had to work harder to get to where you are. Partly by being willing to do the hard wor yourself, and partly by being determined to see it was done absolutely correctly. Unfortunately, the fact is that you can step on the toes of more relaxed officers from more established families that way. Also, it can make the hands uncomfortable." She glanced Miller's way. That worthy was making a point of being absorbed in his work.

"Guess that's what got me where I am," Ravi replied.

"On a year-long trip out to Jupiter and back?"

"Yes, ma'am."

"Me too," Novak confessed. "At least that's what I suspect."

Ravi looked at his boss in surprise. She was a good solid officer who seemed to take her job seriously. She seemed to be quite competent. Lieutenant Novak had a pleasant personality, and everyone seemed to like her. Including her superiors. Despite the atypical dust-up over Kincaid, Ravi liked her himself. He figured he was lucky to have her as his boss. He should have wondered how she'd managed to get posted to the *Resolute* and its year-long mission. Instead, Ravi had been too absorbed in his own problems. Ravi promised himself he'd pay more attention in the future. "Would it be too forward to ask how so, ma'am?"

"Only fair," Novak replied. "Can't prove anything, but, ironically, like you, I was probably guilty of excessive rectitude."

"You wanted to do the job right and by the book?"

"Yes, I also didn't want to let the bastard into my pants either."

"Ouch." Ravi looked over at Miller. He was ostentatiously absorbed in his work. Ravi figured that in an ideal world they wouldn't be discussing this in front of the man. Still, Miller was no innocent young recruit. He'd know the score. They were all going to have to get along crammed into a small tin can together for the next year. Better air the dirty linen now and get it over with. "No offense, ma'am, but you won't have that problem with me. I like women, but I don't think personal and professional affairs mix well."

"Good, we're agreed on that."

Miller chose that moment to intrude. "Ma'am, sir, I'm done with the sensors and warhead. They're all fine and meet spec. Shall I go right to the second stage engines?"

Ravi looked at Novak.

"Yes, Lieutenant?" she asked.

"Speaking of being slow and picky, we've got the time right now. Let's do it thoroughly and by the book, let's take the shielding off the control leads and inspect them."

"You heard the man, Miller," Novak said. "We should give at least a sample of them a complete inspection."

"Yes, ma'am," Miller replied before turning to start prying shielding off of the side of the missile with the special, very expensive, manufacturer supplied tool for performing that task.

It didn't take long. Pretty soon they were looking at a long section of wire coated with shiny black insulation. Without removing a section of wire and destructively testing it in a lab, it wasn't possible to tell if it was exactly the shiny black insulating material specified. Also, it wasn't possible to see that under that insulation that the wire was anything but normal, being made of braided gold strands. It was not cheap, but it wouldn't corrode in storage, and it wouldn't fail in operation because of vibrations causing a break.

Though it was highly improbable they'd be able to see anything useful, they all gathered around the open side of the large missile and peered intently at its insides. Ravi noticed one tiny section of a long black wire looked a little different than the rest. Almost like a small very flat blister. He reached in and gave it a hard rub with the ball of a thumb. The blister broke, leaving him with a tiny smear of rusty water on his thumb. He stared at it.

There were three facts Ravi felt sure of. That the insulation on the wire wasn't supposed to be so thin or fragile. That gold didn't rust. That his missiles weren't supposed to have moisture in their control circuitry. He looked around at the faces of his companions.

They were grim faced. "Sir, step back, please, so I can have a look at that," Miller said.

Novak nodded.

Ravi stepped back.

Miller stepped in and producing a knife peeled back the control wire's insulation to reveal a single solid, thick strand of rusty, apparently iron wire. Miller swore. "The bastards couldn't be bothered to use stranded copper or even aluminum," he said angrily.

Ravi had to swallow the amusement that bubbled up in him over Miller's apparent belief the cheaters had crossed some sort of line in their cheating. It seemed in Miller's world there were both acceptable expected cheating and indefensible cheating.

Ravi coughed into a hand. "Well, a couple things for sure. We're going to have to look at every one of our birds, and we're going to have to tell the captain."

Novak nodded once more. "Agreed. Telling the captain will be my job."

Ravi looked at her bleakly. "He's not going to be happy. This is big. Going to have to turn the Space Force missile procurement section inside out. Supplier too, I'd think. Heads will roll both places. Can't see it not going public. They'll be angry. Rightly so."

Novak looked for all the world like someone with an attack of bad constipation. Finally, she relaxed and sighed. "We need to keep both our opinions and the facts of the matter to ourselves. You're right, Ravi, they're explosive. I'll brief the captain immediately while you and Miller determine the full scope of the problem. We'll present the captain with the facts and their technical implications and that's all. It's the captain's decision how to act on them. Is that clear?"

Ravi wasn't happy. He looked away and grunted. Then he realized that was disrespectful and likely unfair. Most certainly not enough, let alone correct. "Yes, ma'am."

"I'm sorry, Ravi, but it's like you said regards Kincaid. You have to be realistic."

Ravi took a deep breath and looked his boss in the eye. He managed a weak smile. "It hurts having the shoe on the other foot."

Lieutenant Novak's face was the picture of sympathetic understanding. "I know the feeling. I'm glad you're mature enough to understand the situation and accept it. I worry about Kincaid."

Ravi nodded. "And I'm guessing because of the way me and Kincaid got off on the wrong foot, it's going to be all your problem. It'd be awkward delegating her training to me."

"Too true. Can't say I'm happy about it, but it is what it is."

Ravi resisted the urge to look at his feet and shuffle them. He hadn't felt so guilty and embarrassed by anything for years. Not since he was a boy. "Well can't claim I'm sorry she won't be my problem, but believe me I'm sorry about causing you trouble."

Novak snorted. "I'll take that and cash it at the bank for what it's worth."

"Ma'am, I'll do my best, better than I've managed so far, to help. Some advice maybe?"

"Sure, can't hurt."

"Kincaid is young and an outsider, but she's had a lot more experience getting things done, I think, than most young people her age."

"I've read her record. She's something of a prodigy."

"Unfortunately, most of that experience has consisted of being right when older authority figures have been wrong."

"Something of a problem."

"Could be, ma'am. Unfair as it seems, if you're going to be able to teach her anything worthwhile about being a good officer, you need to correct any false lessons she's learned from that. If she's to learn anything more than technical facts and procedures, you're going to have to show her that sometimes older authority figures actually understand some things better than she does."

"Not happy about that idea. Usually I like to build my

young officers up," Novak replied.

"Most young officers aren't quite so confident."

Novak sighed. "The stars above, that's true."

"With the right attitude, she has the potential to be an outstanding officer."

"But without it, she's a menace. I get it, Lieutenant Shankar. In any case, I have to go break the news to the captain. You get the easy job of watching Senior Petty Officer Miller demonstrate he really doesn't need you supervising him. Then you get to report what he finds. Got that?"

"Yes, ma,am."

"Later, Ravi."

## 3: Katie Finds More To Do

Katie was down in the Port Boat Bay making sketches and annotating them. Engineering diagrams of the *Resolute*'s systems. Pipes, valves, conduits, lights, outlets, control panels, and anything else with some functional purpose. An actual record could have been made much easier using the camera in her Personal Portable Computing Device. "P2CD" being what the Space Force called the special phones it issued its officers. In fact, such records were almost certainly already on file in the ship's database. Only the ship's engineer, LTSG Jeffries, had been adamant that the process of making such records manually aided absorbing and retaining the desired information. So Katie was denied access to those official diagrams and was having to create her own.

Katie recalled that back on Ceres her old friend Sam, among others, had believed the same as Jeffries. She wasn't completely convinced, but she was inclined to trust their superior experience. And in any case, it wasn't like she had any real choice about the task. It was a deliverable required for her to obtain her engineering certification.

Also, she suspected she was being taught how to look around her and figure out what things were and how they worked together. It'd have been almost fun if she wasn't so busy.

Inanimate objects and engineering systems weren't the only things she was finding in her explorations. At the current time, the Port Boat Bay also contained the *Resolute's* squad of marines. They were practicing zero gee entries and exits from Boat Beta, among other combat evolutions. Katie would dearly have liked to have more time to watch.

"Okay, ten-minute break. I want you to think about what went right and what didn't," the head marine yelled. He turned and moved towards the corner Katie had been occupying. As he came up to her, Katie saw he was a sergeant from the chevrons on his shoulders. The name tag on his breast read "Suvorov".

"Good Morning, ma'am," Sergeant Suvorov said. "You find our training interesting?"

"I do, Sergeant," Katie answered, "but I'm really here to trace out the Boat Bay's systems for my Engineering Certification. I just stopped to watch while waiting to have a look in the area you were training in."

The sergeant nodded. "I see, ma'am. We'll be resting for the next ten minutes and it's no problem for me to move the exercise areas around so that you can access any area you'd like."

"I appreciate that, Sergeant Suvorov. The Boat Bays seem to be mirror images. I figure it's best to check, though. Sometimes the builders don't fellow spec. On older ships there might be mods. Still, I expect the Port Bay here will be laid out much the same as the Starboard one was. It should be quick."

"I see, ma'am. Very good. There is one other thing."

"Yes, Sergeant?"

"You're Ensign Kincaid, correct?"

Katie had rank tabs and a name tag too, so she figured this was an opening rather than a serious question. "Correct."

"Had a memo about you, ma'am."

Great. Katie vaguely remembered a long list of training goals that included things like "shore patrol", "boarding operations", and "cargo inspection", among others that might conceivably involve working with the marines. Katie's best friend back on Ceres had been a marine, and she was inclined to like them for all that some of the marines she'd encountered while at the Academy had been rather tough on her. Only she didn't have any time for more training duties. "Yes, Sergeant?"

"I'm in charge of the *Resolute*'s marine detachment under all normal circumstances, ma'am," Sergeant Suvorov said.

"I understand," Katie replied. "I believe I have some training objectives I'm going to need your help in achieving."

"Yes, ma'am, but that's not all."

It was all Katie could do to keep her face straight. Of course, it couldn't be that simple. "There's more?"

"Yes, ma'am. Space Force regulations require that when marines operate in an environment in which there may be contact with civilians that an officer be in charge."

Katie's training instructions had included the phrase "*you shall be fully prepared to take command of such boarding or inspection operations as may be required*". She had thought that meant being adequately trained to do them. Maybe a lot more than that then. Ouch. She stalled for time to think. "I was instructed to be prepared for that eventuality."

"Yes, ma'am, and I hope I'm not being too forward, but I'm thinking you're thinking they'd assign someone with more training and experience to take charge of any actual operation, right?"

Damn right she'd thought that. Maybe she'd been wrong. What could they be thinking? For sure to a large extent the officer in such an operation would be a figurehead and the sergeant would be in actual charge of organizing and running it. The officer's role would be to impress and placate any civilians who mightn't have the sense to respect a marine sergeant. They'd also do a lot of the associated paperwork, and they'd be the scapegoat if anything went wrong. Still, it seemed odd. "I understand that in practice you'd be dealing with most of the details of an operation," Katie said as diplomatically as she could, "but, yes, I'd expect someone more senior than a brand new ensign to be assigned anything serious. Surely there's someone else they'd use?"

The sergeant looked apologetic. "There was, ma'am. Lieutenant Roth was the designated officer. A little engineering knowledge comes in handy, particularily when searching a ship for contraband."

Only Roth, having gimped herself up in a skiing accident, wasn't making the trip. It was becoming an increasing mystery to Katie why nobody had made replacing her a top priority. "I see," Katie said.

The sergeant gave a small tight smile. He might as well shouted aloud that he doubted that. Thing was, small smiles didn't go on the record and had a plausible deniability that bald statements didn't. All the same, Katie found herself flattered he was willing to be so open with her. When the sergeant spoke, it appeared as if he was trying to seem casual. "As it happens, ma'am, we don't usually do much in the way of boardings and inspections when in Earth space. The Customs and Transportation Safety Agency handles most of that at the endpoints."

By endpoints he meant the docks of stations, bases, and the spaceports on Earth itself. Even a long trip in the Earth and Luna area was only going to be a few days, and a spacecraft was going to be under constant surveillance by Traffic Control the whole time. Any contraband would have to be carefully concealed in amongst legitimate cargo. Cargo that would have already been carefully checked at its point of origin and would be checked again at its destination. There was really no point to stopping a transport mid-flight and doing additional inspections there. All of which meant such operations would not be something officers whose experience was all in Earth space would be familiar with. Not something they'd be inclined to think about much either. How to acknowledge she saw what the sergeant was getting at?

Katie took a deep breath. "Even out in the Belt, ship boardings and inspections are pretty uncommon."

The sergeant's smile became fractionally less thin. "That's true, ma'am. But that smuggling operation you exposed? The one everyone has been so quiet about. It likely wasn't confined to Ceres."

Ah, so they were across the Rubicon and the sergeant's cards were on the table. He not only knew who she was, but her history. "I was cautioned that it was need to know and to keep a low profile about it," Katie said. "Have you heard something via the grapevine we should keep in mind, perhaps?"

The sergeant's eyes glinted. "Yes, ma'am, it's entirely within the realm of possibility that local authorities on both Vesta and Ganymede will request the captain's assistance in checking on suspicious individuals and ships."

Katie caught herself pensively chewing on her lip at this news. A bad habit she needed to expunge. "I see, Sergeant. Well, it's clear I'd better bump training for such an eventuality up my priority list. Please prepare and submit a training schedule for me before week's end."

"Yes, ma'am."

The sergeant seemed happy in a subdued marine-like fashion. Both marines, and NCOs in general, seemed to believe allowing themselves to be too happy was a temptation to whatever divine beings they believed in. God, gods, fate, or Murphy as the case might be.

Katie wondered where she was going to find the extra time. Something else would have to give. She'd make it work somehow.

She had to.

\*\*\*

Second week out from Earth and Iris was finding the time for the mandated regular and routine checks of her boat, *Resolute*'s "Boat Beta". It was extraordinarily unlikely she'd find anything wrong, but when your life hangs on something, you make sure it's right. At least Iris did. It was a boring task, and it was almost unheard of for anything to be wrong on a boat. They were purposely designed to be simple and robust. There wasn't much that could go wrong with them. She'd heard some folks signed off on the checks without doing them. If she ever caught someone doing that, they'd end up in front of the captain. On the other hand, you couldn't stop people from being bored, inattentive, and only seeing what they expected to. It was a problem. Iris sighed.

"Yeah, not very exciting, is it?" her co-pilot SLT Robert Maddox commented.

"No, but it's very important, and vital to do it carefully and properly," Iris said. "Boats can be called upon to deploy quickly in an emergency. Easy to miss things when you're in a hurry, so we try to be ready at all times."

Robert, "Bobby" he insisted, grinned at her phrasing. "I do try to be ready at all times, for sure."

"Down boy," Iris replied. "Bobby, sometimes I feel like your mother, not your senior officer."

"Aah, ma'am, you're not that old."

"No, I only feel like it at times."

"Does Ensign Kincaid have anything to do with that?"

"Not as much as you do. You've heard about me and Kincaid?"

"Pretty much everyone has, ma'am. Kincaid just about wrecked your career, right? It'd only be human to resent that."

"It wasn't Katie Kincaid that got me in trouble, Bobby. I did that myself. Kincaid was only the proximate cause of the bill coming due. When I think about it, I think we were lucky that happened before we got dragged in deeper."

Robert made a face. A skeptical one. "So no hard feelings?"

"No, and I'll admit I'm a little surprised myself. Like you said, it'd only be human to resent what happened. I like Kincaid. What's more, I think we could use a lot more officers like her. I want to see her succeed."

"Really?"

"Really. Girl is still young, and she's stubborn, but contrary to what people think, she's very straightforward. With Katie, what you see is what you get. She's not in this out of ego. She doesn't need us to tell her she's a worthwhile person. I suppose she must have her doubts at times, but she's very self-confident. And if you figure she was standing in as the entire crew of a survey ship from a young age, it's no wonder. I spent weeks on a scout with her and believe me, she's a consummate spacer. We don't see that here, I doubt they saw that at the Academy, and in an Earth-born dominated Space Force she's entirely out of her element."

Robert held up his hands in surrender. "Wow. And she managed to adapt to it in the end, didn't she?"

"She did."

"So you're impressed by Kincaid and figure she isn't getting a fair shake from the rest of us."

"I am impressed. As for a fair shake, I don't know. I don't like gossip and sometimes I think the Space Force officer corps is worse than a little old ladies' sewing circle in some small town."

"That's oddly specific."

"I love my family, and I love the place I grew up in, and the people there, but believe me I couldn't wait to leave. Anyhow, I'm not exactly plugged into the gossip and I'm not entirely sure what they're saying about Kincaid, but, yeah, I doubt she's getting a fair hearing."

"Okay," Robert said, "but you have to admit she managed to land herself deep in the doo-doo with the XO."

Iris sighed. Iris wasn't into being the strong, silent commander type, but she did seem to be doing a lot of that lately. "Yeah. Between you, me, and that bulkhead there, I don't think it was right of him to dress her down for doing the right thing. On the other hand, most young ensigns would have known enough to back down and not annoy him further. But not Katie. Katie thinks courage is a virtue at all times and in all places and doesn't have much in the way of give. You would have thought the Academy had taught her better."

Robert nodded. "It taught me to pretend to be humble."

"And you pretend ever so well."

Robert grinned mischievously. Iris was sure he must have stolen cookies as a boy, just for the thrill of it. "She's bought herself some trouble. I'm thinking she's created some problems for us too."

"Yeah, we're officially supposed to get her certified on boats."

"And that means flying time."

"No faking or skimming over that. Wouldn't do it if we could."

Robert nodded. His earlier glee had faded. "The captain isn't going to let us do it in transit away from anyplace we can reach in a boat alone."

"Overcautious if you ask me."

"But he didn't, and it's exactly how every other officer who has ship command would feel."

"Like I said, we need more like Kincaid."

"Doesn't mean the brass wants them. So we'll have a short, uncertain schedule while close to Vesta, and Kincaid has a half dozen other things she's trying to do."

Iris nodded glumly. "Could be awkward."

"It could be the end of her hopes of ever getting ship command. I'm guessing that's what she wants, right?"

"Yeah. And too true."

"So, what do we do?"

"We see what happens and do our best."

"Gee, it's great to have a good plan."

"Sometimes it's a luxury you don't get to enjoy."

"I can see that."

\*\*\*

Entering the third week out from Earth and time was flying. Flying too fast for Katie. So far she was managing to cope with a crammed schedule. Just. She wasn't reading any novels, and she was keeping her meals short. She was reading technical manuals.

Reading technical manuals was allowed even on watch. Good thing or otherwise she didn't know when she'd find time.

"Time to do your regular checks," Senior Petty Officer Pavel "Pie-face" Borzakovsky said. "Part of getting your qualifications. You've got to go through the motions of actually doing the job, not just read about it."

"Understood, and agreed too, PO," Katie replied, stowing her reader in the handy holder provided by her station. They were in the spindle. In the zero gee Main Engineering Control Room to be precise, and it was important that everything have a place it was secured in while not being actually used. The smallest object could become a missile in the event of a sudden, unexpected maneuver.

Borzakovsky watching her nodded approvingly. "At least you're spacer neat."

Katie extracted the engineering log from its storage location and looked his way. "Should be. Grew up out here."

"Keep forgetting that," Borzakovsky said. "Don't even see Martian officers much. Mostly Earth born. Usually takes enormous patience to get them to the point they're not hazards to themselves and everyone around them."

Katie blinked. Surely putting things back where they belonged when you were done with them wasn't such a big deal? Also, the Petty Officer was being very frank. "They don't get much actual time in space at the Academy and like you say they're mostly from Earth."

"Yeah. Guess it's above my pay grade. I forget you're an officer half the time."

Katie gave the PO a smile to show it was all in good humor. "I'll take that as a compliment. It's above my pay grade, too. Though I guess we both know what we think. As for forgetting I'm an officer, that's fine as long as it's just us here."

"But don't forget it other times."

"Just so. I'm not sure I understand how it works myself, but the Academy and even my grandmother were big on the saying that *'it's nice for an officer to be liked, but they must be respected'".*

"Your grandmother the Admiral."

"The same. I didn't pick her, and I'm not apologizing for being born to her daughter."

"Didn't ask you to, ma'am."

"Sorry, Pie-face. People tend not to say anything directly to my face, but it's been a thing. It's a sore spot."

"Apology accepted, ma'am."

"It's good. I shouldn't have snapped. I get too relaxed down here."

"Yes, ma'am, and right now you have readings to take."

Katie turned to the consoles in front of her and started to note values. "Tell me again what the point of this is?"

Borzakovsky gave her an evil smile. Katie figured the truth was that he enjoyed lecturing trainees and putting them through their paces. If they were wet behind the ears, newly commissioned junior officers all the better. "There are several points to it I can mention, ma'am. Likely more that the Space Force Training Command has not chosen to share with me."

Katie gave a dramatic shudder. "Training Command; the true home of sadistic tricksters. I'm familiar with them."

"It's their job, and mine. We have to keep unformed young know-it-alls alert and on their toes," Borzakovsky intoned.

"But do you all have to enjoy it so much?"

"Joy in a job well done is the sign of a superior craftsman, ma'am."

"Well, you do like hammering your metal," Katie said while continuing to record fluid and power flows, temperatures, particle outputs, and the like.

"We also like our charges to pay attention to what they're doing so that they get an instinctive feel for what the systems look like when all is well."

"So we recognize it when something strays out of bounds."

"Just so."

"That makes sense."

"I'll pass your feedback along, ma'am."

"I'm afraid I have trouble believing things simply because someone with authority says so."

"It's been noticed, ma'am."

"Any other observations, Senior Petty Officer?"

"Well, Ensign, it has also been noticed you have a very full training schedule and you're in something of a hurry to get your engineering certs completed."

"Problem?"

"It hasn't been yet, ma'am. It's more an issue of quality control. To be genuinely good at this sort of thing, you need time to get genuinely familiar with the machinery and routines. You need time to let it soak into your bones. That's why the regulations require time on watch doing stuff that seems simple and boring."

"But if it was up to you, they'd require even longer?"

"Yes, ma'am. Regulation qualification times are long enough to allow the average watch keeper to become barely adequate. That's all."

"So I'm not even barely adequate?"

"You don't know it all, ma'am, but you've come in already knowing the basics better than most. Better than anyone else I've ever seen, to tell the blunt truth. You're picking up what you don't already know fast. You're good. You're doing fine. Only you could be outstanding if you wanted to be. If you focused on it."

"Since we're being all open and truthful, I'll tell you straight out I want ship command. They don't give the command of ships to engineers, no matter how good they are. Made the mistake of telling the XO exactly what I thought, and now he's got me jumping through a half dozen hoops before he'll let me try to qualify for a bridge watch. If I don't get qualified for that before this tour's out, no ship command for me. It's an unwritten rule, but a rule for all that."

"Pay grade, ma'am, but if it's power and control you want, you've got it right here. Engineering runs the ship. The rest of them are just passengers. Did you know that we can take direct command of the ship from here? In fact, the entire ship forward of us could be reduced to scrap metal, the command links down, and the thrusters gone or off-line, and we could still maneuver by using the main engines the right way."

Katie looked at him and stretched to record her last number. "Okay, that is impressive. You have to tell me about it. Why isn't it in the standard training manuals?"

"Suspect because it's a single point of failure. A single point of vulnerability. Not the sort of information you want getting out to bad guys, terrorists, or whatever."

"Politics. Always politics, isn't it?"

"Yes, ma'am. Especially if you're an officer, and, seems to me, the more so the higher you go. Seems to me, simple working man that I am, that getting command of a ship is always political. Only so many slots, and it's a lot of power. Engineering is more about being competent at your job."

"I promise I'll think about what you've said. Honestly, I think I might enjoy engineering more personally. Hope I'm not being too trusting in telling you I think it's my duty to seek ship command."

Borzakovsky looked solemn. "Ambitious, ma'am. I'm not going to fault you for it. I'm no gossip either."

"Thanks, PO."

"All the same, ma'am, you've got too much on your plate to do it all justice, even if you've managed to get by so far. Work in haste, repent at leisure."

Katie just nodded.

* * *

Fact was, Katie wasn't expected to be able to do the job of every enlisted hand nominally under her command. They weren't called specialists for nothing, and they'd all had years and several courses in which to learn those specialties. That didn't mean she was allowed to be clueless about what they did.

The month since the *Resolute* had departed Earth had been barely long enough to get some light exposure to routine engineering watch keeping. Katie had also got to follow a few technicians around as they did routine maintenance. Something they had borne with a stoic patience. She had not got to see any of them exercising their repair skills in the ship's work shops. Nothing had broken yet. On a new ship, recently out of refit, that was as it should have been.

Still, Katie was coming to see the wisdom of the points SPO Borzakovsky had made over a week ago in the privacy of the spindle watch keeping station. It'd be a matter of months, not weeks, getting merely familiarized with all of engineering.

Katie wasn't going to get those months. She was close to finishing her minimum mandatory time to qualify for her basic engineering watch certs.

Katie didn't expect the written exams she also had to do to

be any problem. She didn't expect to ace them like she'd like to, but she did expect she'd pass them. After that, she'd be free to go on to the rest of her ever so full training schedule.

"A penny for your thoughts, Ensign," LTSG Jeffries, the Engineer, said. They were sitting in the Remote Engineering Control Room in the gravity ring, along with a number of enlisted watch keepers. Under normal circumstances, it was much easier to monitor and control the ship's machinery and propulsion remotely from there than it was from the spindle. Much healthier and much safer too. Zero gee wasn't safe for those not used to it, and too much of it certainly wasn't healthy.

"I'm getting close to finishing my training with you, aren't I?"

"Yep, don't worry. I've been quite pleased with your performance. All the watch keepers are happy with you. I'll be surprised if you don't do well on the tests."

"Thank you, sir," Katie replied pensively. This was so unlike her. "Thing is sir, is I thought I had a good handle on ship's systems and propulsion beforehand, but now I feel like I've barely scratched the surface of what a good engineering officer should know."

Jeffries smiled. "Which goes to show you've got the makings of a good engineering officer."

"Kind of you, sir."

"No, just honest. To be blunt, if you insist on going, I'll miss you. We all will. We've got good NCOs, but it's not their job to have an overview of the whole department. Even Master Chief McIsaac is more concerned about personnel matters than strictly engineering ones. It's certainly not part of their jobs to deal with the captain or the XO or any other officer. Something I'm always having to remind our colleagues of."

"Yes, sir."

"Sorry, a pet peeve. Anyhow, to cut to the chase, if you do well on your tests I'll offer you the baby engineer's slot for the rest of the tour. As an ensign you'll only be acting, but I'm willing to bet you'll excel. It's like I said before. If you want it, I think you can make both subbie and junior grade in minimum time with senior lieutenant not too far behind."

Katie was intensely flattered. It was a spectacular offer. Most young ensigns would kill for a chance at accelerated promotion like this. And all she had to do was something she enjoyed and was good at. Only there was one huge fly in the ointment. She didn't want to take the engineering track. She wanted ship command, which meant the command track, though that did not assure it by any means. Still, maybe she should be realistic. She was certain she didn't want to turn the Engineer down flat in front of the rest of the watch. "That would mean abandoning the rest of my training schedule, wouldn't it?"

Jeffries looked indulgent. "You wouldn't need most of it as an engineer. I'm sure the XO would be willing to ask Thor to cancel most of it. Don't tell me you've been enjoying learning how to keep inventory and supervise cooks from Lieutenant Sarkis."

"It is more interesting than you'd think," Katie replied, "but no, it's not very exciting."

"See, not like nuclear reactors and anti-matter catalyzed fusion engines."

Katie quirked a grin. "And the ship's waste water systems."

"Absolutely essential those," Jeffries shot back. "Seriously, it's a good deal all around. We need you, and I know you'll do a good job and enjoy it. Ship driver even if you eventually manage to swing it mightn't be as exciting as you imagine. Please, think about it."

"I will, sir," Katie answered. "I have until after my qualification exams, right?"

"You do. It's only a couple of days. Not long for such a big decision."

"No, it's not, sir."

## 4: Decide, Kincaid

A month into the *Resolute's* trip out to the Outer System and it'd flashed by like no time at all for Katie. She was in the little closet graced with a desk and some electronics which was, quite laughably, called the Engineering Administration Office.

Katie had just written the tests for her basic Engineering Certs and unless she missed her guess quite badly, she'd done well on them. Very well, most probably.

And now she had a huge, painful decision to make. One she couldn't put off any longer.

Mentally Katie was between a rock and a hard place.

On one side the fact was the Engineer's offer of the Deputy Engineering Officer's position was objectively a no-brainer. A grab it and run proposition career wise. What's more, it was a course that suited Katie personally. It played to her technical strengths and minimized her occasional issues with being properly diplomatic. Nobody expected diplomacy from engineers. Katie knew she'd be happy doing the job. From a purely personal point of view, it was a no-brainer too.

On the other side, Katie had assigned herself a mission some years ago, a couple of years before going to the Academy. It was a mission that had required getting into and then graduating from the Academy. It'd been a hard slog. A heart-breakingly painful one at times. Katie had almost forgotten what it was like to be in her comfort zone. But she'd done it. Now she was a commissioned officer, albeit the lowest rank possible, and she was on board ship with real responsibilities again.

That mission the younger version of Katie had assigned her required ship command, which meant taking the command track, not the engineering one. It was cut and dried that if she was to cleave to that mission, she had to refuse the Engineer's offer. No matter how tempting it might be.

Was it possible that younger Katie's mission was a quixotic quest dreamed up by a naïve young girl with an imagination that was altogether too active, and who had been arrogantly ignorant of the impossibility of what she proposed to do? Was it time for a more mature Katie to set more realistic goals?

Katie didn't know.

Usually she'd put her feelings to one side and objectively ascertain the knowable facts. Then she'd apply rigorous logic. Usually that was enough.

Not now. Katie was finding it impossible to be fully objective about herself. She couldn't ask anyone else. The blunt facts of the matter would make her look entirely delusional. Logic didn't help. It was obvious the best option for her was to take the Engineer's offer. It was equally obvious that doing so would mean abandoning the goal of command she'd assigned herself.

Sadly, it looked like pursuing that goal had a high chance of failure at great cost to her.

A light rap on the hatch to the office came. "Are you done, Kincaid?"

"Yes, sir."

"Great," Jeffries said, opening the hatch and squeezing himself in. He closed it behind him. For some personnel issues, privacy was desirable. "You've been thinking about taking the Deputy Engineer's slot?"

"Yes, sir. I have. It's a great opportunity. I'm really flattered you've offered it to me."

Jeffries gave Katie a wary look. "You don't sound that thrilled."

"Command was my dream, sir."

"Was?" Jeffries smiled warmly at Katie. "Does that mean

you've come to a more realistic assessment of who's really got the more important and interesting role in our wonderful Space Force?"

It was a joke, so Katie tried to smile at it. "I've given it a lot of thought. I decided I wanted to command ships in the Space Force back on Ceres before going to the Academy. That was the whole reason I did. I was a young girl back on Ceres, though I didn't think of myself that way. I knew there were things I didn't know. I knew it in a theoretical way, though. I had no real idea how much I didn't know."

Jeffries nodded sympathetically. He seemed content to give her time to talk. "We were all young once."

"You'd think," Katie agreed. "Still thinking about it, I'm amazed at how young I was. I can't believe how ignorant I was of so much. And so lacking in awareness of it. Kind of painful to contemplate, to tell you the truth, sir."

"I think most people have youthful dreams that don't work out well," Jeffries said. "I wanted to be a farmer, because I thought farm animals were cute. Nobody told me that they shit and you have to clean it up, that it's hard to ever take a vacation, and that it's an enormous investment with uncertain returns."

"And instead you ended up an engineer in the Space Force."

"It's a funny old world, Katie."

"Amen, sir."

"So?"

"The safe and sensible choice would be to elect for the engineering track, sir. Not only that, but I know it'd be a good fit for me. I'd be happy being an engineer."

Jeffries stopped short of frowning. "Is that a yes or a no?"

Katie took a deep breath. It would be taking a big chance trying to take the command track. Only it was what she believed she ought to do. She had to have the courage of her convictions. If it all went down as she expected, there'd be more than the odd time she'd not only be risking her future, but maybe her life. And not just her life, but those of other people too. She had to be brave. This was no time to take counsel of her fears. "It's a no, sir. I believe I ought to try to take the command track, not the engineering one."

Jeffries slumped against a wall of the little office. He

sighed. "Well, that's clear anyway. Not the answer I hoped for or expected. It seems misguided and quixotic to me, but I don't doubt you have your reasons. I won't press you further on the matter."

"Thank you, sir."

"I think the Fleet is losing a potentially outstanding engineering officer. I just hope it gets a good ship driver out of it."

"Me too, sir."

\* \* \*

Katie was alone in the cabin she shared with SLT Amy Sarkis. As a supply type Amy didn't have formal watch-keeping duties, only tonight she was "working late." Amy's boss, Lieutenar Vann, was as gray and clerkish as you could wish for in a Supply Officer, but he was also very conscientious. He made it an informal policy that either he or Amy be awake and around for every part of the *Resolute*'s twenty-four-hour, seven days a week operating schedule. And so Amy was away, hanging over the shoulders of her reports, and Katie was alone.

Katie had been trying to review her jammed-packed training schedule with the aim of prioritizing what she needed to study. A task you'd have thought she'd be a whiz at given her time at the Academy. If the Academy taught you nothing else, it taught you how to cram ten pounds of work into a five-pound bag.

Only Katie was too overcome with fear and dread. She couldn't concentrate.

Katie sighed. She couldn't let herself be paralyzed by emotion like this forever. Obvious. Also obvious, she was going to have to take a bit of time to work it through.

Fact was, she was deathly afraid refusing the Engineer's generous offer of the Baby Engineer's slot had been a ghastly error. So much so that she was questioning both her own long-term goals and how she saw the world. Gee, she wasn't doing things by halves, was she?

If she believed in her goals and she believed in the analysis of the world that led to them, she'd done the right thing.

Only she wasn't sure in her own mind anymore.

She'd been in a this is my objective, this what I need to do to get there, and don't let anything distract me from that mode for years now. She hadn't allowed herself many, if any, moments of retrospection like this to reflect on the question of whether those goals were still valid.

Maybe she should have.

Katie had been very young and, now she could see, not exactly sheltered, but still very ignorant of much of the wider world when she'd set those goals. Set them based on a set of old histories and biographies her parents had bought her to read because they were cheap. Might be a narrow basis on which to plan a life with the aim of changing the world. Ya think? Katie took a moment to be amused at herself. She really was over the top and full of it. She could understand why it bugged some people so much.

She mulled that over for a bit.

Truth was, a lot of people likely saw her as an egomaniac. Many likely thought she was at least a little delusional. She could see why. She was trying to do things differently than everyone else. She didn't hide her hopes for ship command. Implicit was a hope for higher command beyond that. All that without any family pushing her to it or any obvious reason to believe she was that exceptional.

Katie had her reasons for sure, but they were ones based on a young girl's reading of history. History and the men, they'd all been men, who'd been able to change it. She hadn't realized at the time how out of fashion history and heroism had become. She'd learned quickly when trying to discuss it with first her teachers and then her parents. Even her friend Sam the ex-marine had thought it an odd hobby and not worth taking too seriously.

"The map is not the territory," he'd said. As if history books had nothing useful to say about the real world. Where people weren't completely dismissive, that seemed to be the general attitude.

So the idea that humanity would be facing a crisis soon, and would need heroes, and that she was well suited to be one of those heroes, was something she'd learned to keep to herself.

The closest she'd come to opening up was with her grandmother, the intimidating retired Admiral who maybe wasn't so retired. Only her grandmother spoke in riddles and suggestions. Katie was never quite sure if she was only being humored, or if she was being taken seriously. She was pretty sure her grandmother did think some sort of major crisis was possible, even overdue. She also had the impression her grandmother approved of efforts to address that fact.

Somehow, she wasn't sure exactly how, it was only a feeling, she didn't think her grandmother believed in heroes. If she did, Katie suspected the ex-Admiral didn't think heroes were that important. To the ex-Admiral heroes were just "chrome". Unnecessary decoration added to models that ought to be kept as simple as possible. They didn't really change that much.

Katie's grandmother seemed to think history was something that happened to people, not something they made.

Sad fact was that although her grandmother apparently approved of Katie's efforts, she didn't really seem to think they'd make any decisive difference in the end.

Katie figured her grandmother was taking an entirely too high-level and fatalistic point of view.

Not that she was going to bother telling her that. No need, really.

And what did all this mean?

Well, basically that she had a view of the world and goals that wouldn't seem reasonable to the people around her. If she shared her thinking, they'd think she was dangerously misguided. If she didn't, they'd think she was an egomaniac with an overblown sense of her importance in the scheme of things.

And she couldn't blame them.

Only she knew in her own heart it wasn't so. Katie was convinced that she could have been happy quietly doing some technical job and being underappreciated for the fact she helped keep things running.

Katie figured the Engineer's offer validated her own feeling that she'd have had no problem finding such a place in the world. Heck, she could have stayed back on her family's ship, the *Dawn Threader,* doing asteroid surveys and been content. She'd likely have always wondered if she could have done more with herself, but she'd have been happy enough. It would have been the easy thing to do.

No, one thing Katie was sure of, she wasn't doing this for her own happiness.

Good. That was progress. It was tiring to be thought of that way, but she could handle it.

So that was how she felt about the big picture. She wasn't completely crazy. She wasn't an egomaniac. Whatever anyone else thought, she was someone trying to do the right thing as best as they could. For rational reasons.

What about the immediate situation? Sun Tzu had written a couple of millennia ago that good strategy and bad tactics made for a slow and costly victory. She'd rather not do this the hard way, and it wasn't like she had a whole army at her command that she could expend. She only had her little old self.

Had she mis-stepped with the XO and the Engineer?

To some extent it was clear she had. The easiest and most expedient thing to have done would have been to have ignored Lieutenant Shankar's harassing Spacer Jones for trying to work safely. Odds were they would have lucked out and nothing bad would have happened. Only Katie wouldn't be in the pickle she was now.

Still Katie had resolved she'd work hard on always having the courage to do what she thought was the right thing. It was an attribute all the heroes of the past seemed to have had. Given that she'd had to challenge Shankar, maybe she could have been less blatant and more tactful. Katie wasn't sure. She suspected, given the Deputy Weapons Officer's obvious hurry and stressed-out state of mind, and his apparent unfamiliarity with what the work actually required, that a confrontation of some sort hadn't been avoidable. But she could have tried harder.

Being bluntly honest once she'd ended up in front of the XO had been a mistake. The honest part, no, although omission of annoying facts that hadn't been asked for would have been a good idea. She should have been a lot less blunt. If nothing else she could have made it clear to the XO, that she understood the gravity of the situation and was very, very sorry to have found herself in it. She could have at least conceded she might have acted in error. Such a thing was always possible, even if she didn't really think so. It was unclear. Again, she should have tried harder.

Strangely, the last decision she'd made, refusing the offer of the Deputy Engineer's slot, was the least problematic. Personally, she might regret it intensely. Logically, it'd been the right thing to do.

Finally, as painful as it might be, she had to admit the XO had been right about her not knowing as much about running a Space Force frigate as she might have thought she did from her previous time in space.

Katie did have a big leg up regarding living in space when compared to the average young Space Force officer. She didn't know as much about running a warship as she'd thought she had. Looking at her training schedule, that was obvious.

Strangely enough, so far she was managing to hit all her targets. The training schedule was an improbability, not an impossibility. So far, her luck had held. By dint of hard work and talent, she'd hit all her goals. Getting the Engineering Certs all out of the way was a major step forward. As regards pure technical difficulty, she'd already overcome some of her major hurdles. The supply routines and procedures Amy was schooling her in had proved more elaborate and important than she'd realized, but she was close to having adequately mastered those. Amy should be able to sign off on her Deputy Supply Officer Certs, and in good conscience, soon.

Boats was problematic, because it wasn't all cramming in book knowledge and memorizing protocols, actual operational flight time was going to be required. It'd be a few weeks before they reached the vicinity of Vesta, and Katie could get some of that. Worse, the schedule whatever it turned out to be wasn't going to be arranged for her convenience. Well, she'd cross that bridge when she came to it.

Ironically, the point was that Katie had come to realize that she ought to go to the XO and ask for her training schedule to be relaxed. Only things were going well enough that she really had no excuse for doing so.

Katie sighed. Again. It wasn't an ideal situation. She was alone.

She was tired of rambling around the problem space now. Time for decisions. What were her action points?

One, she wasn't going back to the Engineer to repent of her previous decision. She was taking the command, not the engineering, track. Good.

Two, she needed to double down on the training schedule while she could and try to buy herself as much slack as possible.

Three, when problems arose, as they inevitably would, praise Murphy, she wouldn't hesitate to go to first the Training Officer, Lieutenant Haralson, and then the XO and ask to have her schedule relaxed. To ask that getting certified on a bridge watch be bumped in priority.

There it was, a plan.

She did feel better now.

Time to get back to studying how the nutritional requirements of spacers on a long tour varied and how to effectively ensure they were met.

Maybe Amy found this stuff interesting.

Katie was just glad there were people like Amy to handle it.

\* \* \*

Ravi had just ducked out to the wardroom for a cup of coffee. Ravi hadn't planned on eavesdropping on the conversation between Lieutenant Jeffries, the Engineer, and Lieutenant Haralson, the Training Officer. He hadn't lingered to hear the whole conversation either.

What he had overheard had been enough. Kincaid was being awkward again.

Back in the Weapons office, looking at SPO Miller's preliminary report on the state of their missile stores, it was helping lift his mood some. With respect to Kincaid, at least some small corner of the Universe was unfolding as it ought to. Somewhat at least. Too bad the same wasn't true regarding their missiles.

Miller's report was damning. It was even more depressing. It'd turned out that every one of the missiles he'd checked had been defective. They might work. Their electrical specs when tested were still mostly close to what they should be. Only those readings might not hold. Iron rusts in a way gold does not.

Miller was recommending every one of them be fully checked. He was also recommending a liberal application of water displacement product. He'd found a lot of moisture in the missiles and had concluded they hadn't always been properly stored. A lot of WD might help. Short of re-manufacturing the things it was the best they could do.

Miller's report also suggested their supplies of short-range missiles, anti-missile missiles, and torpedoes hadn't been always stored in the mandated manner. They also appeared to meet operational spec and Miller hadn't found any sign of scrimping in their actual manufacture yet. Yet. He hadn't stated it outright, but the man had strongly hinted a complete teardown of a sample of the things might be a good idea.

It all gave Ravi a headache.

Ravi knew Novak had passed the fact there was a problem on to the captain. He wasn't sure if she'd made the gravity of the situation perfectly clear. It wasn't certain that the ship's longest ranged and most important weapon system would actually perform under operational conditions. It wasn't certain it wouldn't either. They just couldn't know for sure. Ravi knew he'd have been tempted to shade the situation to the brighter side of things if he'd been reporting it to the captain.

The situation with Ensign Kincaid was a reminder of how being too forward and negative with one's superiors could have a negative career impact.

It was one that both pissed Ravi off and elated him. One thing about Kincaid, she made life interesting. Ravi, though, preferred his entertainment pre-packaged, fictional, and delivered via his vid terminal.

Kincaid had stepped in it big time challenging Ravi while an ensign trainee, while Ravi was trying to do a difficult and stressful job. Going on to anger the XO sufficiently that the XO had felt he had to punish her and not just issue a harsh reprimand.

Kincaid should have been in the XO's office begging to be let off the hook and to be given her chance of having a successful career back.

Instead, she'd stumbled into a chance at advanced promotion and career success Ravi would have killed to have been given as a young officer. And refused it.

It was infuriating and amusing all at once.

Ravi had to admit he wasn't that ambitious himself. He wanted to do something useful and be appreciated for it. Ravi's family had higher expectations. They'd invested heavily in him to get him into the Academy and launched on a Space Force career. His family expected him to succeed sufficiently that it'd reflect well on them. They had money, they even had a lot of influence and power, they didn't have the social prestige older more established families did. It was Ravi's role to provide some of that. Ravi had worked hard at all the tasks he'd been given to that end.

Ravi was falling short.

Becoming a ship's engineer would have sufficed. Engineers were capped career wise, but they were definitely part of the Fleet's core command group. Ship's captains and SFHQ expected ships to be able to perform the tasks requested of them. It looked very bad if they couldn't. The Engineers were critical in seeing they could. That got them respect. That got their opinions paid attention.

Kincaid was throwing away a chance Ravi would have been happy to have had.

It seemed to Ravi that, despite her supposed outsider status because of having been raised in the Belt, she really was Admiral Schlossberg's granddaughter when push came to shove. Simply by birth she was part of the established aristocracy everyone pretended didn't exist. Ravi wasn't impressed by that.

Ravi had to get back to work, figuring out how to handle Miller's bad news. But at some point in the future, even if Lieutenant Novak took over the bulk of her training, his path was going to cross Kincaid's again.

When it did, she'd get what she genuinely earned from him. No more.

\* \* \*

Amy was having an uncharacteristic bout of self-doubt.

Katie Kincaid's fault, of course. Amy liked Katie. She also respected her. Everybody, including Katie herself, seemed to forget she was just a young girl getting a start in the world. It seemed to Amy that they all, again including Katie herself, tended to measure her against a set of unreasonable expectations. They found her actual performance wanting measured against those. They failed to see how impressive it was that she managed to do as well as she did.

It exasperated and disturbed Amy in equal measure. Exasperated her because she wished Katie and her colleagues would be more reasonable. Disturbed her because Amy herself had taken just such a more reasonable approach to her career and life. She'd done so deliberately and after careful consideration. And now Katie had her wondering if she'd not played it too safe.

"Isn't there a rule against this or something?" Katie asked. Katie was shadowing Amy in her duties.

Amy shook her head. They were sampling the midnight "scran", snacks verging on a full meal, in the enlisted hands' mess. "Nope, no written rule anyhow. It's understood informally that officers don't intrude on the enlisted people's space, and it's socially verboten to be too familiar with them, but there's no formal rule written down against it."

Katie looked around. Clearly trying not to be too obvious about it and failing dismally. "Still?"

"Still, it's the job of supply officers to make sure everybody is well and properly fed," Amy said. "Some officers are hands off and delegate everything to their NCOs without ever checking themselves, but that's not Lieutenant Vann's way of doing things. I think he's got the right of it."

"So we're not horning in on the enlisted hands' snacks, we're sampling them to make sure they're up to snuff?" Katie asked.

Amy noticed an enlisted hand, a weapons tech if she wasn't mistaken, smirking behind Katie. This wasn't a private conversation. Still, there were proprieties to be observed. She pretended not to notice. "Exactly," she said.

The mess wasn't crowded, the evening watch was still on duty and the middle watch was grabbing something to eat and getting on with their duties. They were due on watch soon, and many of them had rounds to do first. Nobody was lingering. It was the quiet time for everybody not going on or off of watch. So the mess wasn't crowded, and it wasn't hard for Amy to find them an empty corner with no one sitting nearby once they'd collected their "samples".

Amy could only imagine Katie was getting similar surprises about how things were done versus how they were described in the manuals in most of the rest of the roles she was being trained in. Never hurt to ask, though. "So, you did the mandatory courses on programming languages as part of qualifying for the engineering track, right?"

Katie looked at her quizzically, but answered her literally. "Sure, I think everybody who could hack it did. Yet another delightful informal test on the part of our beloved alma mater. Imagine you did too."

"I did. Unlike a lot of our classmates who didn't intend to

go that way in the end, I rather enjoyed them."

"Yeah, I'd have guessed being rigorously logical wasn't a big challenge for you. You're not at all what I imagined a supply officer would be like."

Amy gave Katie a thin smile. She knew the stereotypes. They only irked her a little. She figured other people's narrow-mindedness was mostly their problem, not hers. "Yeah, we're not all mediocre rejects from the more exciting career tracks. Most of us chose to do this because it's useful work we're good at and enjoy. Not because we couldn't have chosen a different path."

Katie grimaced. "Sorry, sometimes I don't think things through before speaking."

"Not a big problem with me," Amy answered. "Anyhow, making sure all the techs have the parts they need and everyone is clothed and fed properly is pretty important even if everybody takes it for granted until something goes wrong."

Katie nodded. "I can see that. Engineering is a bit like that too."

Amy smiled. "So yes, us supply officers take considerable satisfaction in our work, even if we feel a little underappreciated at times. Anyhow, back to you and your problems."

Katie's lips twisted in a crooked expression that was half smile and half grimace. "A source of fascination to all. You have some helpful advice?"

"Not really. It's more I'm trying to vicariously enjoy your adventures. I was wondering if you weren't finding all the things you're having to try out a bit like many programming languages where when you first read the manual they seem to be completely specified right down to the last detail."

Katie nodded. "But when you go to apply them, you find there're all sorts of things that are 'unspecified' and 'implementation dependent'. Yeah, just like this here. I don't think there's a manual in existence that addresses how proactive a supervisor should be in checking up on the work of their people."

It was Amy's turn to nod. "Yeah, you have to learn it on the job. I was pretty happy in my little world doing my thing before you came along. Now I'm wondering if I shouldn't have been more ambitious. I wonder about what I might be missing."

"Well, you might be missing some interesting experiences, but believe me, Amy, you're missing a lot of heartache, worry, and angst too," Katie replied.

"Maybe you can share some of that with me?" Amy asked.

Katie flashed a grin. "Be glad to."

"Thanks."

## 5: Learn, Kincaid

Formally speaking it was none of Iris' business what training schedule the Training Officer and XO decided to give Katie Kincaid. Not beyond the part of that schedule that she was assigned.

In practice, Iris, like every other officer and not a few of the enlisted ranks, was watching the unfolding drama intently.

Iris was more than a little disgusted by the whole thing, but resigned to just taking it day by day, and hoping it all worked out. She didn't think either the XO or Kincaid were dim-witted fools, or too stubborn to recognize when they'd made mistakes. Surely one or both of them would eventually back down and they'd reach some sort of compromise.

She felt more than a little sympathy for Lieutenant Thor Haralson, who was the designated Training Officer and caught in the middle of the conflict. Haralson was a superior officer who in a just world would be headed for early promotion. His responsibility as Training Officer would normally involve some minimal paperwork signing off on plans decided on at a much lower level, and a little light supervision that amounted to a check that the paperwork and reality weren't completely out of sync.

Of course, normal was something rarely found when

Ensign Katie Kincaid was involved.

Right now, Iris was sitting in Boat Beta's co-pilot seat as Kincaid ran through simulation after simulation. The boat could be configured to act as its own simulator when not in operational use. Until they got to Vesta space and the captain released them from their in transit restrictions, simulation mode was the only mode they were allowed.

Iris was finding it intensely frustrating. Katie had not only swallowed all the relevant manuals and could regurgitate them both backwards and forwards, she had all the piloting skills down pat too. Her time on her family ship and Ceres mightn't translate directly, but it gave her a major head start over most trainees. She was as good in simulations as could be hoped for.

She must be frustrated too. Only she wasn't showing it too obviously. Her performance was perhaps excessively precise and quick, but that was it. Iris was starting to throw increasingly complex and unlikely scenarios at the girl just to keep her from being bored.

Right now they were theoretically dodging a whole salvo of missiles that had just been fired at them.

"Wouldn't we be blacking out from the gee forces if this was real?" Katie asked as a fictional missile just missed them.

Iris sighed. "I'm sure we'd be feeling them, but you're doing fine keeping us within the official parameters. Not like we can simulate this accurately sitting in the boat bay."

"I understand it's important to train in muscle memory until it's all automatic," Katie said, "but I'm not sure it's not counterproductive doing so much simulation time when it can't be fully accurate."

"There's an ongoing argument about it. Some evidence that too much time in simulations that are close to, but not exactly, real can produce confusion in real-life situations. But it's what we have."

"And it counts towards training time."

"It does."

"At half value, but you're skeptical."

"Aren't you? Look I admire your guts and your desire to do things right, but having turned down the Engineer's out, and having decided to try to get through the XO's, um, shall we say *ambitious*, training schedule you don't have the option of trying to optimize and do everything perfectly."

"So I've got to settle for being second rate?"

"You've got to settle for adequate enough to scrape by on paper for most of it, Katie."

"Ouch."

"Yeah, sucks to be you."

"But I made my own bed."

"You did. Not even saying you did the wrong thing. Just it's not going to be easy. Or perfect."

"Any good news?"

"Couple of weeks out of Vesta, we'll be able to get you some real flight time. I'll have you signed off on boats and pushed off down the gauntlet in no time."

"Great."

"As good as it gets."

\* \* \*

The *Resolute* was a bit more than a week out of Vesta. In transit restrictions on boat operations had been relaxed. Katie was finally getting the real flight time on boats she needed.

Katie was going through the paces that her trainer on boats, Lieutenant Iris Gregorian, had set her. Iris sat in the co-pilot's seat, saying very little beyond the occasional grunt.

Katie found it somewhat unnerving. "It's not the same as the simulator. Not with any acceleration," she said, trying to crack the ice.

Iris grunted, then relented. "You're doing fine for a trainee. Great for the number of hours you've done. Bit sloppy and not at all as sure on the controls as I'd like, but that takes time and practice. No way around it."

It was Katie's turn to make noises of dissatisfaction. "Be learning quicker if I wasn't so tired."

"Go ahead, vent," Iris replied. "Nobody else here and I'm not going anywhere."

"Spent all morning doing exercises with Sergeant Suvorov and the marines."

"Thought you enjoyed that sort of thing."

"I do, and I'm learning a lot too."

"Only it cuts into your sleep and your allowed zero gee time both."

"Yeah, and Amy had us up at midnight, and then again in the wee hours of the morning, helping the stewards with preparing first midnight scran, and then breakfast, for both the captain and the wardroom. Is it really necessary to do everything several times over, for the hands, and NCOs, and then the officers, and then again for the captain, too? Seems inefficient."

Iris heaved a sigh. "Still a Belter at heart, eh Katie?"

"My grandmother has tried to explain this business of classes to me. People getting treated different because of the parents they chose. Seems like nonsense to me."

"Still real. Something real you have to accept and work with. Maybe if the Space Force was all Belters it'd be different, but it's not. People from Earth have certain expectations, and if you get too far away from those, you're going to confuse them."

"Hope we're not losing too much catering to Earth born quirks," Katie grumped as she yanked their boat around in a hard maneuver.

"Not the world that's out of step, Katie," Iris answered with exaggerated patience. "Besides, it even makes operational sense to give the captain special treatment."

"Because he's in command and is more important?"

"Because he's in command, and the ship is essentially in operations an extension of his will, and it's important he be at his best when making decisions, and able to concentrate on them to the exclusion of any mere mundane issues."

Katie subsided for a few minutes to chew on that and concentrate on her own flying. "Okay, I can see that. Guess it's an important point."

"Thank you, ever so much, for that gracious admission."

"Sorry. Don't suppose being tired is any excuse?"

"No. There'll be a lot of times you're tired and you'll still be expected to perform up to spec."

"I'm beginning to wonder if I'm up to it. Maybe I did bite too much off."

"Not much doubt of that," Iris said with grim amusement. "You wouldn't be the Katie we all know and love otherwise. But buck up, so far you're actually managing to keep your head above water."

"Really?"

"Yes, really. Getting your Engineering Certs signed off in only a month was pretty impressive. You're just about done with the Supply Certs with Amy, right?"

"Yep."

"You're finally getting real time on boats here and you've got the written parts of it all done."

"You figure I'll be able to get my flight hours in during the next couple of weeks? You haven't given me a schedule. I assume there's a reason for that."

"There is. Strangely enough, Ensign Kincaid does not get first call on the ship's boats. We can use them to train you when we're not using them for other business."

"I'm guessing we're not going to be docking at Vesta?"

"Nope, we'll be mooring off of her. Big wide sort of orbit. Not many dedicated docking structures for a ship as big and oddly shaped as the *Resolute*. There's back on Goddard Station, Callisto and Mars stations and that's it. So, yeah, the boats are the only way we're going to be able to get people and things back and forth from Vesta."

"Ouch, so no flight time for me while we're off Vesta."

"Not with the captain or other people. Maybe we'll let you transport marines or other cargo with me in the co-pilot's seat depending on how it goes."

"But not if I'm tired from other duties."

"Your biometrics are logged and there are regulations."

"Yeah, I know. I just memorized them."

"I saw your exam results, but getting answers right on an exam and applying the knowledge in the real world aren't the same thing. Not for most people."

"Not for me either, though I do try. It's hard work."

Iris nodded. "It is. Sometimes there just aren't any shortcuts."

"I'm not sure I won't be called away to lead up a marine away party either."

"You sure you're supposed to be sharing that with me?"

"Probably not," Katie admitted. "Only we've spent a lot of time together the last few weeks. I've had the odd epiphany myself. I think I can recognize when someone else has. After Ceres, I think you decided to never be caught offside like that again. You're probably one of the most trustworthy people on the ship."

Iris didn't answer for a few moments. Finally, she drew a deep breath. "Means a lot, you see that. I'd been thinking virtue was going to have to be its own reward."

"Yeah, I'm a girl what likes visible results myself," Katie replied, "but one thing I learned from my time with Jeffries in Engineering and Amy in Supply is that often doing things right means being underappreciated. When everything is going well, nobody notices the effort that goes into it."

Iris nodded. "Something to keep in mind when you're tempted to feel sorry for yourself."

"Yeah, I get that. Anyhow, long and short of it is, there's a chance I'll be called away to lead a marine away party while we're at Vesta. Not sure. Sergeant Suvorov has been playing it close to his vest, and I don't think it's up to him anyways, but there's a chance."

"And they'll need the boats for that, too."

"Yeah, I hope not. No chance I'll get my hours if that happens. It'll mean no chance at all of qualifying and getting on to the rest of the stuff the XO and Haralson have lined up for me. Not before we're departing Vesta, and maybe not before we get into Ganymede space. That'd be a disaster."

Iris tsked. Katie could tell she was frustrated. "That's the real world, kid. You never have the time to fully analyze anything and then never the time or the resources to do the job you'd like to."

"I thought the Academy was tough."

"The Academy was just simulator time for real life in the Space Force."

"Great."

\* \* \*

Katie couldn't help thinking Amy kept odd hours. It was particularly odd when she was one of the few people on the ship that wasn't required to stand a watch. Or maybe not. Maybe Amy believed it was up to her to informally make up for what wasn't formally required of her.

In any case, it was mid-morning, and they had the wardroom to themselves. Everybody else was either on watch, "turned-to", or resting. Being "turned-to" during one's "non-quiet time", was what everyone else besides the Space Force called a normal working day. The folks that had had the middle watch were excused the first part of that. Having missed most of their night's sleep they were now getting some rest in compensation. So, Amy and Katie had the wardroom to themselves.

They weren't just goofing off.

A couple of days out of Vesta and Amy was making up a list of supplies she hoped to try to procure on the asteroid.

Katie had already been signed off on her Supply Certs, but she figured she owed Amy, and was trying to help. Mostly by being a sounding board for Amy's thoughts.

Most of the list consisted of small odds and ends that had been completely overlooked in the original orders or which had been consumed at a higher rate than expected.

One request from Weapons was different. Amy had been adamant in insisting Katie not discuss the matter with anyone else. Weapons wanted gold braided control leads in quantity. Failing that, it wanted fine gold wire or simply gold bullion. It was a desperate request that hinted at a serious problem. It almost certainly meant some considerable quantity of the weapons the ship was carrying weren't up to spec. No surprise Amy wanted it kept secret.

Only Katie couldn't help thinking that was a lost cause. "If it's anything like Ceres, there'll be small amounts of control lead available and plenty of gold in bar or powdered form, but not precisely what you need in the quantities you want from any one source. As soon as you put out a request for this, everyone on that rock is going to know about our problems."

"Damn, I'll have to get back to Lieutenant Vann with that thought and I bet it goes all the way to the captain."

"Please don't mention my name if you can help it," Katie asked. She was already associated with far too much bad news.

Amy snickered. "For all the trouble you get into, you seem to manage."

"Really?"

"Engineering signed off. The engineer wanting you as his deputy. Supply done, and, Katie, you could use more experience, but you could do my job adequately right now. From what you've told me, and from what I've heard, you just need flight time to be signed off on boats. And you're getting marine away ops training too. It's pretty impressive. People are noticing."

"Wow. It's nice to hear that, but my training schedule is still nuts."

"Tell me about it."

"Don't say you didn't ask."

Amy smirked. "If you could handle a month's worth of doing inventory, I can handle a few minutes listening to you go on about all your training tasks."

Katie figured Amy was being too modest. "If there's anything I've learned in the last few weeks, it's that supply isn't just keeping inventory. You guys have to know how everything on the ship works and how it's going in real time, so that you can anticipate what people are going to need. Plus you convinced me: keeping people well fed is crucial to morale."

"Yeah, the way to a spacer's heart is their belly."

Katie smiled. "A simple lot, really. Anyways, I've got to get the boats and marine stuff done so I can start standing watches in various bridge positions, Helm, Navigation, Sensors, Weapons, and Comms. Also have got to do at least a few damage control watches and pass some exams on the protocols for that. Plus Weapons is more than just watches. Some technical stuff to get hands-on with there, and some serious exams."

Amy gave a quick frown at that last. "And Ravi Shankar not being inclined to be too helpful, I'd guess, and one suspects Novak is up to her neck in alligators."

"It gets worse," Katie said. "Theoretically I've got a year to qualify for bridge watches, but some of the tasks I'll need to do aren't going to come up on a long transit. I'll need to get my qualifying time in while still in Jovian space. I need to get everything else signed off on before getting there. At the very least, very soon after reaching Ganymede."

Amy nodded. "I can see why you're worried. Nothing to be done about it right now. Maybe helping with me with my problems will help take your mind off of it. I've got one sanitation station down in enlisted space using almost as much bum wipe as the rest of the ship put together and no idea how to even start looking into it."

"That's disturbing. You can't just order more and ignore it?"

"Tempting, but it suggests something is not right. Use too much of that stuff and you can end up gumming up the works."

"Hull techs will be unhappy about that. Being plumbers is not their favorite role."

"Still, environmental control is as much about taking away

the bad stuff as it is about supplying the good stuff."

"I could make some discreet inquiries," Katie allowed.

"Appreciate that. Some things it's best not to ignore. Hoping they'll just go away isn't a viable strategy."

Katie couldn't help thinking that was applicable in multiple ways. "Too true."

\* \* \*

It's a funny old world, Amy had to think. She was adding a selection of hobby materials to her Vesta shopping list. Craft materials really. Things like paper, glue, scissors, colored pencils, etc., were all going on the list. She was thinking of adding games and puzzles too. She wasn't sure what the Safety Officer, LTJG Cara Campbell, would think of that. Cara's main duty was being Deputy Ops, second string to Lieutenant Haralson. But she took being Safety Officer very seriously. Puzzles and games both tended to have a lot of small parts. Pieces that could become a hazard under the wrong conditions.

Amy could see Cara requiring that someone be appointed the holder of the games and puzzles. Making them responsible for the tracking of each individual piece. Cara Campbell wasn't a bad person, but she was something of an overcautious control freak. It was indeed a funny world.

Even Lieutenant Campbell's probable overreaction to the prospective dangers of board games wasn't as funny as what Katie had found out. She'd tracked down the reason for their overuse of restroom supplies. A certain Able Spacer Milligan had been misappropriating them for craft projects. He'd been making little colored statuettes, really cute ones. He'd been misappropriating certain shop supplies too. Who'd have guessed?

Whole thing did have a couple of serious sides.

Seemed not every member of the crew was overworked. Some of them had been growing rather bored on the long trip out to Vesta and Jupiter. Hard to be sure how many. It wasn't like anyone was going to complain about not having enough work.

It shed a certain light on the fact that the Space Force's larger units did not generally do long deployments. Amy had been aware of that fact from her miscellaneous small supply woes, but she hadn't thought about what it might mean for crew morale. Maybe somebody should bring that up with somebody who had real power to do something about it. She had a feeling a junior Deputy Supply Officer wasn't one of those somebodies.

Katie might have some thoughts on the matter. She was even more junior than Amy, but she didn't seem to realize it, and she did have an admiral for a grandmother. Plus, she'd grown up out here in the Belt.

Only Katie was pretty busy already and getting busier it seemed. Now that Katie was signed off as capable of doing a Supply Officer's duties, Amy wasn't getting to see that much of her.

She wasn't even spending much time hunched over her tiny Pull-out desk in their shared cabin. She seemed to be spending all of her "spare" time either flying boats or practicing zero gee tactics in them with the marines. That was in addition to damage control watches.

Amy wondered if that'd change when they finally reached Vesta in a few days from now. Asteroid bases aren't big tourist destinations. Only Amy had never been away from the Earth-Luna system before. She was looking forward to seeing what Vesta was like. Maybe Katie would be able to find some time to show her the sights. As far as Amy knew, Katie had never been to Vesta before either, but how different from Ceres could it be?

The *Resolute*'s visit to Vesta was supposed to be a show-the-flag exercise. Also a chance for the crew to get a break from their operations tempo while under way. Amy was beginning to have doubts.

Katie hadn't said anything explicitly, but she'd been awfully busy. Amy had the feeling both the boat crews and the marines were preparing for the possibility of something. Something that'd keep them quite busy during their Vesta stopover.

Suggested that their Vesta stopover might not go as advertised.

Amy hoped for her own peace of mind, and for the sake of Katie's already strained schedule, that it didn't come to much.

Some surprises are harmless and amusing.

Some aren't.

## 6: Fly, Kincaid

Iris was rather impressed with the statistics package incorporated into Boat Beta's training software. She hadn't had much chance to use it before being assigned Katie Kincaid as a student.

She frowned. Starting tomorrow, she wouldn't be getting to use it much either. They'd be mooring off of Vesta tomorrow. Both her and Kincaid were being put on around the clock standby. Iris was to be ready to launch her boat at short notice. Boat Alpha was going to handle the bulk of the regular traffic. They were putting out a story that Boat Beta was sidelined for maintenance. Which wasn't true. It, along with Iris and her regular co-pilot SLT Maddox, were on standby to taxi the marines led by Katie wherever they had to go. Out to another ship or to some place on Vesta. Iris didn't know.

Somebody was taking Ops Sec, Operational Security, very seriously.

It bugged Iris. It bugged her because it worried her.

Also, it meant Kincaid was getting the short end of the stick. Katie was in the pilot's seat beside Iris, running a virtual obstacle course provided by the computer. She was performing adequately. Iris' fancy statistics package showed her that. It also showed her that Katie wasn't as sharp as usual. Katie was tired.

Iris decided some helpful advice might be in order. "Katie, looking at my stats, your reflexes are okay, but not what they usually are."

"Yes, ma'am."

"Katie, when we're done here, and while you're waiting for the XO and Haralson to tell you what they want you to do with the marines, you should get some sleep."

Katie frowned as she guided the boat around an obstacle that only existed in its software. "Because I'm on standby around the clock with the marines, they've postponed giving me any bridge watches."

"Right, and you want to try to squeeze in extra study time to speed things up once you get started on those. I understand."

"So, I'm not comfortable with the idea of lying in my rack trying to sleep. Not when I have other things to do."

"Be that as it may, you're only human, Ensign Kincaid. If I could order you to get rack time, I would. If or when you're called out with the marines you want to be as sharp as possible."

Katie jerked Boat Beta around a bit harder than she really needed to. Iris let it pass. Katie sighed. "Okay, that makes sense. Not going to make it easy. I haven't been so worried or stressed out since my first year at the Academy. That was a nightmare. I'm still not sure how I made it through."

"Yeah, something of an adjustment for all of us. I can't imagine what it was like for you. For what it's worth, you're doing fine here so far."

"Nothing really gone wrong so far. Only now I'm responsible for what happens if the captain decides to use the marines on Vesta. Don't know what's happening, but I'm worried. Sergeant Suvorov is super competent, and he thinks I'm doing well, but I'm only a green ensign. I don't know what's going on. I'm not sure anyone else does."

"Well, there's a good chance it'll all work out and your stepping up is bound to look good."

"Still, it's a week's chunk taken out of a tight training schedule and I'll be missing chances to be on the bridge during approach and departure from a busy area of space."

"Maybe this'll give the XO an excuse to let Haralson relax

your schedule without looking like he's backing down."

"Maybe."

"Bottom line, Katie, you can't always be sure what's going to happen, or how people are going to step up. You have to have trust in the people around you. You have to trust that your superiors have some idea what they're doing, that your peers will be more help than hindrance, and that the people working for you know their jobs and will do them."

Katie nodded. "I think I understand. I thought I knew what running a space ship was like. Only I'm not used to working as part of a large team. It's been a learning experience."

Iris had an insane urge to pat Katie on the head and tell her it was all going to be okay. She'd never thought of herself as the motherly sort, but maybe she wasn't entirely lacking in those instincts. Not appropriate in the circumstances, though. "Get some sleep. Deal with whatever happens. Don't sweat what you can't change."

"Hope is a plan after all?"

"Your career is going to be full of surprises. Just hope the ones we get here are to the upside."

"Not the downside."

"Precisely."

\* \* \*

Ravi was tired and he was exasperated.

Currently he was watching Senior Petty Officer Miller finishing up tests on one of their long-distance missiles that they'd discovered problems with. It wasn't hard work "supervising" the PO. Practically speaking Miller didn't need Lieutenant Ravi Shankar present. Miller knew his job. The tiny Weapons Workshop would have also been a lot less crowded without Ravi's presence. Only the odds were a board of inquiry was going to end up being called to investigate what had happened. So Lieutenant (Senior Grade) Novak, the Weapons Officer and Ravi's boss, had decided that "commissioned eyes" needed to be present throughout the whole process.

Lieutenant (Senior Grade) Novak had decided that Lieutenant (Junior Grade) Ravi Shankar, the Deputy Weapons Officer, was going to be that set of eyes. They really didn't want to share the bad news about the missiles around, so it had to be one or the other of them. The job also had to be completed before they moored at Vesta in less than twenty-four hours. A formal report to the captain about the problem and a training program for Ensign Kincaid both needed to be done before then too. Novak had to do the first, and after Ravi's run in with Kincaid earlier, it was better if she did the training program too.

And so by default, supervising the missile inspection had fallen to Ravi.

Ravi had been up for most of the previous twenty-four hours and hadn't got that much sleep in the days before either. Miller, on the other hand, had been relieved by the other two Petty Officer weapons techs, Korona and Pong, at regular intervals. They were Miller's subordinates, but just as technically competent as far as Ravi could tell. They were the ones that were hands-on and couldn't afford mistakes, so that was fair. All the same Ravi was dead tired, right to the bone, and as grumpy as he could be given his total lack of energy.

"Still hanging in there, sir?" Miller asked out of the blue.

Had Ravi been visibly fading off? "Still here, PO, but I'll be glad when we're done with this tonight. I might just sleep for our entire stay at Vesta."

Miller nodded in a distracted way. He was staring intently at the blown up image of some missile control circuitry. Ravi peered over his shoulder. As far as he could tell, there was nothing wrong. "It's fine, sir. I was just wondering why Lieutenant Novak didn't borrow an officer from another Department. Perhaps brought Ensign Kincaid on board a little earlier than planned."

Ravi frowned. It was a good question. He wasn't certain Miller ought to be asking it, but Ravi wasn't exactly thinking straight right now either. Given his mood, best to cut the man some slack and give him as straight an answer as possible. "I'm not entirely sure myself," Ravi admitted. "None of the other officers have a weapons background, but we could have just given them an hour or two of instruction on the procedures you're doing and that would have been enough, I think. So I imagine it's a couple of other things. One, this mess is a political hot potato and Novak probably thinks the captain wants to keep it as quiet as possible. Kincaid's grandmother in particular probably has the clearances to be briefed on it, but it could be awkward if she asked questions in the wrong corners."

"Glad we've got you officers to handle the politics."

Ravi snorted. "Don't tell me NCOs aren't political. I'm not quite that wet behind the ears."

"No, sir, but this isn't like working out something like a job or a problem child over a few brews in the mess."

Ravi sighed. He couldn't argue with that. "Anyhow, all the other officers besides Kincaid have their own duties. Turns out deployment for weeks on end isn't the same as a few day trips out of Goddard Station. Kincaid has been signed off on engineering and supply, and you might think she'd be available, but between flight time on boats and a lot of time training with the marines, she's apparently too busy."

Miller was still peering at his work, not looking right at Ravi, but his jaw tightened. "Odd how much the marines are training. This isn't my first long tour. Usually they train half the time and help the rest of us with housekeeping and scutwork the rest of the time. Not this trip."

Ravi blinked. It wasn't something he'd been paying attention to. Also, it was his first long tour. Only, as foggy as his brain was, it seemed to Ravi that Miller was on to something. "I'm not sure myself, PO," he said. "I think you're right, though. It is odd. Kincaid's training schedule was already full. Chucking in extra time training with the marines on top of that seems excessive."

Miller grunted.

Ravi smiled. He was grimly amused despite himself. Miller knew very well Kincaid was on Ravi's bad side and hadn't impressed the XO overly much either. Miller didn't want to come anywhere near a grudge match between officers. "Could be the XO figures Kincaid needs to learn a little humility. On the other hand, it might be a good face-saving excuse to loosen up Kincaid's training schedule. Unforeseen circumstances and all that. Despite how very junior she is, she is a Belter and familiar with the local environment. Heaven knows she's not one to shrink from a fight. Above my pay grade anyhow."

"Amen, sir."

"Also could be the XO and Lieutenant Novak are too busy right now to spend all their time worrying about Ensign Kincaid."

"Kincaid is supposed to start training with us sometime in the next couple of weeks, isn't she?"

"Well, Lieutenant Novak is working on a training plan for her. Still, we do have more serious concerns. The Lieutenant didn't bring that training forward so she could help us with this. That suggests to me that the Lieutenant thinks Kincaid is not going to be a big help. More an extra task on top of everything else."

"Not thrilled with that, sir?"

"Tired right now, PO. Not thrilled with much of anything. I'll do my job. The lieutenant is probably going to be busy keeping the captain happy so I'll have to take up the slack. I'll do that. I'll be conscientious and thorough about seeing the ensign gets trained properly. I'll expect her to be equally conscientious and thorough in her learning. I won't cut her any slack."

"I see, sir." Miller's tone suggested the conversation was over as far as he was concerned.

Ravi was fine with that. He suspected he really shouldn't have been as open as he had been. Ravi wasn't sure. He was too tired. He was sure that Kincaid was in a place where she needed all the help she could get. Ravi would give all the help he had to in order to preserve appearances.

No more.

\* \* \*

Amy was fuming. Currently, she was waiting in the Port Boat Bay for the marines to finish their latest exercise so she could talk to Sergeant Suvorov. That wasn't what was upsetting her.

LTSG Oswald Wong had managed that. Quite an achievement. Amy didn't think she was flattering herself by thinking that she was hard to upset. If anything, her usual sin was being too laid back. Amy was a bit of a fatalistic hedonist if the truth was to be known. She wasn't proud of it, but she believed that there wasn't much you could do about a lot of things, and that there was no point being unhappy about what you couldn't change.

But she'd come down here to the Boat Bays on the spindle and in zero gee in order to go the extra mile and be helpful.

Both Wong and Suvorov had put in orders for extra consumables above the standard baseline issue. Amy took her job seriously. Both the manual and her own experience told her that such orders meant activity out of the normal. Alternatively, they meant the baseline issue was for some reason inadequate even for normal operations. But not usually, usually they meant something unexpected and not normal was happening. When that happened, people tended to realize they needed more supplies. They also tended to miss some items.

Amy had come down to find out what was happening and determine what they'd be needing, but had forgotten to order. They wouldn't be getting anything they'd missed on the trip between Vesta and the Jovian system. Probably wouldn't find it at Callisto or Ganymede either. Callisto and Ganymede were at the back end of nowhere, which was to say the end of a very long supply chain.

Wong had stopped just short of blowing her off. Nothing that would look bad on paper or that was actionable. He'd made the right sounds. Thank you for checking on us. No, can't think of anything more we need. Sorry, we can't tell you what's going on. Operational security, you know. All the time projecting an attitude of exaggerated patience and the sense he thought she was wasting his time.

Lieutenant Wong had also given Amy the feeling of being worried and distracted by something. All very disturbing. Amy would have liked to have had a short conversation with his deputy, Lieutenant Iris Gregorian, but Iris was out giving Katie some last-minute flight training. The ship would be mooring off of Vesta tomorrow and this was the last chance for a while.

It didn't take the marines long to finish their current evolution. Suvorov spotted her and giving his men a break came right over to her. Moving in zero gee didn't seem very dignified to Amy, but somehow Sergeant Suvorov managed to project an air of professional, but welcoming, competence as he approached. Perhaps it was simply his calm focus. It was respectful in a way Wong had completely failed to be.

"Good day, ma'am. What can I do for you?" he asked, having arrived in front of her.

"I noticed you ordered some extra consumables, ammo, suit propellant, lubricants, replaceable seals and filters, and the like."

"Yes, ma'am. I hope there's no problem. We do need them. I can get verification from the Ops Officer, or even the XO, if need be."

"No, that's not necessary. There's no problem. It's just that usually when we get orders above baseline like this there are even more extra items the customer has forgotten about that are needed."

The sergeant smiled. "Customer?"

Amy returned his smile. "Yes, unlike some other groups, some civilians in the dockyard sometimes maybe, we don't feel like we're paying for your supplies out of our own pockets. Us shipboard supply officers try to keep our shipmates happy."

"Well glad to hear that, ma'am. I can go over it with you to see what I might have missed, but I can tell you right off it wouldn't go amiss if you doubled everything I asked for."

"Double?"

The sergeant nodded. "Yes, I'm afraid it's very hard to predict what our usage will be. For instance, I very much hope we don't have to use any ammo. We're not planning to if we can avoid it, but if we use any at all, the boys aren't going to skimp on it if it's their lives on the line."

"Okay, I'll double everything you've already ordered. No problem."

The sergeant almost grinned at her. He seemed very happy. "Great ma'am, I would've ordered more in the first place, but I thought it'd seem like too much and might be questioned. I'm very happy to find that's not the case. We could also use some items like ready to eat meals. They're more nice to have than necessary, but it'll help morale."

"That's doable," Amy replied. Compared to the cost of running a spaceship, a few more expensive than usual meals were almost literally a rounding error. The fact that some bean counter in a headquarters office might not understand that didn't change the fact. "You can't tell me more about what you're doing, can you? It'd help with figuring out what else you might need."

"Op Sec's an issue, ma'am." He looked around. "In fact, ma'am, if you could keep it under your hat that we're looking at operations beyond the normal at all, that'd be best."

"I understand, Sergeant. You know you've been keeping Ensign Kincaid pretty busy. I'm her cabin mate, but it's possible others have noticed too."

The sergeant grimaced. "Not much to be done for it, ma'am. The Ensign has talent, but she's as green as grass, and needs the training. Too bad we can't order a fully trained Away Ops Officer from you."

"Unfortunately, the Space Force hasn't yet figured out how to freeze-dry and store trained officers, Sergeant. I'll let you know when we do."

Sergeant Suvorov smiled. "I'd appreciate that, ma'am. In the meantime, I imagine you have a list of all our stock keeping units. We can go through the SKUs together and see if we spot anything we've missed. Sound good?"

"Sounds fine."

It took a while and there were only a few minor items to add to Amy's list, but she felt good about the exercise. The marines shouldn't fall short of anything they needed. She'd done her job. "Anything else, Sergeant?"

"You're Ensign Kincaid's cabin mate, ma'am? She listens to you?"

"I am. As for listening to me, sometimes she even takes my advice."

The sergeant shook his head ruefully. "That's good, ma'am. If you could get her to make sure she gets all the rest she needs, that could make a difference. I know she's got a lot on her plate, but if we need her, we're going to need her rested up."

"I'll do my best," Amy replied. "Is that all?"

"Yes, ma'am. Think the boys have had enough lollygagging about. Good day, and thanks, ma'am."

Amy watched the sergeant swim away towards where his marines were resting. It bothered her that the sergeant had noticed Katie's tendency to burning the candle at both ends and was worried enough by it to bring it up with an officer, even one as friendly and innocuous as herself.

Amy was also bothered by the fact that neither Lieutenant Haralson nor the XO had seen fit to relax Katie's training schedule in light of her potential duties with the marines. Seemed like asking for trouble.

If Amy had been Katie she'd have gone to them, directly to the XO most likely, and told them bluntly they couldn't give her both sets of tasks and expect her to do both well.

Amy figured maybe she ought to tell Katie as much.

Amy had doubts it'd help.

Katie tended to be a can-do sort of girl.

To a fault.

*\*\*\**

Katie was standing in the closet-like space that passed for the Ops Admin Office. Standing, because the tiny office only had two chairs and they were already occupied by the XO and Lieutenant Haralson. Lieutenant Haralson had requested her presence, ostensibly to discuss her training schedule. Finding the XO present had been an unpleasant surprise.

The timing was also odd. They'd just moored off of Vesta, and most of the crew was securing the ship prior to being allowed shore leave. You would have thought both Haralson, and the XO had other things to think about. Things that weren't Katie's training schedule.

Also odd was that they were waiting on the arrival of "another party".

Some of Katie's frustration must have shown. She really had to work on her poker face. Lieutenant Haralson spoke up. "Your training schedule was just an excuse," he said. The XO scowled.

"Sir?" Katie asked.

"To settle your mind, you're not here because of anything you've done," Lieutenant Haralson replied.

"I'm not in trouble?"

The XO gave her a thin, grim smile. "Not for anything you've done. We have a task for you. A potentially dangerous task we'd prefer not to burden any junior officer with, but one that needs to be done, and you're who we have."

Oh, that didn't sound good. "Details, sir?"

"When the captain gets here," the XO said. "You'll have to be patient until then."

It wasn't long before the captain arrived, quietly slipping into the office and closing the hatch to it behind him. It was definitely a cozy fit. "I'll stand, gentlemen. Not planning to be long. Brief us, Lieutenant Haralson. Assume the XO and I don't know anything, we want Ensign Kincaid to be fully briefed."

"Yes, sir," Lieutenant Haralson replied. "Almost two weeks ago we received a high security privately encrypted message from the governor of Vesta. Governor Porter reported that he believed his administration and both the police force and the Space Force detachment on Vesta had been infiltrated by local criminal elements."

The lieutenant paused and looked at Katie. "We believe

those criminal elements might be associated with the smuggling ring you revealed on Ceres several years ago."

"A system-wide conspiracy, sir?"

The XO sighed.

The captain gave him a quelling glance. "It was pure wishful thinking to hope the problem was confined to Ceres. Continue, Lieutenant."

"It appears likely," Lieutenant Haralson said. "However, SFHQ hasn't seen fit to share any intelligence it might have regarding that."

"Just good security. Need to know," the XO interjected.

"Yes, sir," Lieutenant Haralson agreed. "In any case, our task is much more limited in scope. The Governor identified the local criminal leader and when and where they'd be vulnerable. Our task is act on that intelligence, and to apprehend, and then interrogate that individual."

"Us, sir? Not the local police, not even the local Space Force detachment?" Katie asked.

All the senior officers frowned. They were not happy. For a second Katie was afraid she'd stuck her foot in her mouth again.

Once again it was the XO who was the most forthcoming. "As the lieutenant indicated, Governor Porter suspects they've all been infiltrated. Some combination of bribes and extortion, no doubt. He's not certain how deep the rot has gone, but he doesn't think he can act without the crime boss getting tipped off."

"One of the main things we're hoping to learn from our target is exactly how compromised the local institutions on Vesta are," Lieutenant Haralson said.

Katie looked around at her senior officers. Yeah, they were very unhappy. A slight gleam of light was that unhappiness didn't seem aimed at Katie in particular. "I see, sir."

"Maybe you do, given Ceres," the lieutenant conceded.

The XO snorted.

Katie noticed the captain was keeping a carefully blank face. It occurred to her that captains weren't allowed to sigh or to look exasperated. Also, that they had to avoid undermining their XOs.

The captain made a small noise in his throat to get everyone's attention. "I want you all to understand." He looked directly at Katie. "This is an extraordinarily sensitive matter. Operationally, of course, but also public-relations wise and politically. It won't help anyone for the public's faith in the administration and the Space Force to be undermined. Our senior leadership will be extremely displeased if any of this comes out before the problem has been put to rest. You are not to discuss the facts of this matter with anyone, let alone indulge in speculation. You will not bring the matter up yourselves. If you are asked about it, you can say that you don't know anything you can discuss. And that is all. Is that clear?"

"Clear, sir." Katie said.

"Yes, sir," Lieutenant Haralson replied.

The XO nodded. "Clear, sir."

"Good. Lieutenant."

"The *Resolute* has therefore been tasked with carrying out a no-warning, no-local-support extraction mission," Lieutenant Haralson said with careful enunciation. "Ensign Kincaid will be in command."

"A very irregular and high-risk operation, Ensign, but we have our orders," the captain added.

"It's not as bad as it might sound," Lieutenant Haralson said. "The Governor has provided excellent local intelligence. Seems the bad guy has operated with impunity for too long and become arrogant and sloppy. We have a location and time when we can be sure he'll be present and as icing on the cake it's during the rest of the settlement's down time."

The XO nodded. "Sergeant Suvorov already has a good plan in place and has briefed his marines on it. He'll brief you. You have final say, but the sergeant is very experienced. All you have to do is follow his plan and keep your head down and it should all work out fine."

Katie understood the logic, but she was more than a little miffed. She was technically responsible for the outcome of the operation, but it didn't appear her bosses intended to give her much say in how it was organized or run. Bucking the captain, the XO, and the Ops officer wasn't in the cards though. Katie kept her feelings to herself.

Her superiors watched her work it through.

Lieutenant Haralson looked resigned.

The captain actually gave her a slight smile.

The XO didn't let the moment stretch to the point where it

was uncomfortable. His smile was very slight, and much grimmer. "So listen to the sergeant's advice. Avoid exercising any of your trademark energetic, but sometimes ill-calculated, initiative and it should all work out. Understood?"

"Yes, sir."

## 7: Ensign Kincaid's Fine Adventure

So far, so good. Katie hated to even think it. Katie hated to tempt Murphy. All the same, they'd managed to reach and disembark at an unused mining rig's private dock using permissions the Governor had given them without being challenged or even noticed as far as Katie could tell.

They were on Vesta and on their way to their target's location. So far they hadn't seen so much as a single living soul. It was creepy, but it made sense. Vesta was a settlement, not a ship, it ran on a twenty-four-hour cycle that matched that of a normal town on Earth itself.

It was the wee hours of that cycle. There would be a few watch keepers in Traffic Control and minding vital machinery, but the majority of the asteroid's population would be in bed. Some would be tending to the needs of spacers in the entertainment district, many of those spacers being on shore leave from the *Resolute,* but that was far away from here. They'd be getting close to the district. Their target was close to it. But they were approaching from the direction of the largely deserted docks.

So far, so good.

Katie was leading the marines. Taking point. She was in light armor, but was much less a visibly armed intruder than any of the heavily armed and armored marines. From a distance in the dim downtime lighting, odds were good she'd spot any chance encounter before they saw her, let alone got a good look. All the more so if they were tired, distracted, in a hurry, or drunk, or, as was likely, all four at this time of night. She'd warn the marine squad behind her if that happened, then slip out of sight herself.

It was a slight modification to the basic plan Sergeant Suvorov had presented her. He'd relied wholly on speed and its being downtime. A couple of the marines carried non-lethal weapons in the event a chance encounter proved unavoidable. Both the Governor and SFHQ had signed off on using them without warning on any unsuspecting innocents they came across. A scary thing in Katie's mind. This was some serious stuff to be dumping on one green ensign and a marine sergeant.

Katie wasn't happy with how their plan depended on a run of good luck either. It was a series of die rolls and they had to roll twos or threes or above for each one in a sense. Katie had never actually played games that used dice like that. She hadn't had the time. Katie didn't like relying on luck either. Well, didn't look like she was getting much choice today. She didn't blame the sergeant for the plan. He'd had his orders and done the best he could given them. She had her orders, and she'd do her best too.

Their next die roll, or required sub-task in the mission according to your taste, was to approach and neutralize their target. Hiding under that neutral imprecise language, that meant they were to sneak up on the office where the bad guy and some of his thugs regularly spent this part of the night, get access to their air supply, and gas the beejeesus out of them. Katie only hoped none of them had medical conditions. A random unintended fatality wasn't in the plan. It'd be a bad thing.

So far they'd been skulking through natural gravity access tunnels in the backside of the docking area. People didn't spend much time down there, even during the active part of the day.

As even bad guys need higher gravity than Vesta's 2.5% of a gee to stay healthy, they were going to have to make a surreptitious entry into the gravity ring housing the bad guy's office. Katie wondered briefly what the guy's name actually was. Nobody had felt she needed to know that.

In any event, they'd assured her the ring would be deserted except for their target and his henchmen, and that the security cameras monitoring their entrance point would be showing images from some other night.

All the same they weren't going to use the main entrance, they were going to use the maintenance access at the top of the ring. And so once they got within a hundred meters of the target gravity ring, Katie got to literally crawl up the walls and into the "roof". Katie looked behind her and saw the marines following like a long line of black humanoid flies. The sergeant was in the lead. Katie flashed him an okay sign. He responded in kind.

Not being able to communicate either by voice or radio was one of the creepiest things about this whole exercise. Not only didn't they want to be detected, they wanted to leave as little record behind as possible. So they weren't putting out any EMF, and they weren't creating any sound waves either. The marines all knew the plan and had drilled on it extensively. Katie hadn't had that luxury, but as long as nothing went wrong and they retained visual contact with each other, it should be fine. Visual contact and hand signals should suffice.

Not that she could afford to sit around and agonize over it. They had a generous window, as much as an hour, to carry this off, but best stick as close to the schedule as possible. Currently they were a few minutes ahead of it. That was good, but Katie made herself move up into the last stretch of the maintenance tunnels before the ring top and crawl swim along to their target.

Reaching it minutes later, she looked back to see the marines close behind her. No making excuses and ducking back around a corner at this point. Katie checked with the sergeant with a hand signal. The sergeant flashed an okay sign back. Katie reached down and entered the security code the Governor had provided. A little indicator light flashed green, and she reached down and levered the maintenance access hatch to the center of the ring below them open. From the ring's core, they'd have direct access to its life support systems.

Katie reached down further, grabbed a handhold, and pulled herself down and into the ring. She kept going. She halted at the ring's midpoint and looking behind her counted her marines. All accounted for.

So far, so good.

The next phase went well too.

They introduced gas into the air supply without any issues. When they stormed into a room really too big to be called a normal office, throwing yet more gas and smoke grenades ahead of them, they met with absolutely no opposition. Everybody there had already been knocked out.

And then Katie got her first unwelcome surprise.

The room held a number of large rough-looking men, passed out and dressed in bad taste. The target's thugs, no doubt. It also held one merely normal sized, rather handsome and better dressed middle aged man who Katie rather thought was probably their target.

Katie waved at the marine with the biometrics scanner to check, regardless. You know about assumptions and what they make of you and me. It'd be damned embarrassing if she just assumed the well-dressed guy was who they wanted and it turned out to be one of the other guys. A very career limiting assumption that'd be.

Still, that was all as planned.

What they hadn't expected was to have broken in upon an interrogation. There was a rather bloody and beat-up looking individual tied to a chair in the middle of the room. The bad guys were arrayed in heaps around him where the gas had got them.

The sergeant gestured to a marine who walked over and examined the prisoner. The marine made an okay sign. Presumably that meant the prisoner was alive, because it was obvious they were anything but okay. In fact, even if they hadn't been unconscious from the gas, Katie didn't think they were in any shape to have walked out of the place.

Worse, when the marine lifted the prisoner's head, Katie recognized them. It was Lieutenant Oswald Wong, the Boats Officer, Iris' boss. Damn. Katie didn't know what it meant, but she certainly wasn't leaving him here. They were going to have to carry out two bodies, not just one.

The sergeant looked at her. She just nodded.

One marine hoisted the target over his shoulder. Another couple policed up the scene as best as possible and they were on their way again.

So far, despite the surprise of finding Lieutenant Wong, their luck was holding. Please Murphy, not today.

But their luck didn't hold. They'd got clear of the ring the way they'd come and were half way back to the mining dock where Iris and SLT Maddox were waiting for them with Boat Beta, when it ran out.

They came around a corner to find three men in police uniforms waiting for them.

"Halt and identify yourselves," one of them with lieutenant's rank markings on his uniform yelled.

Katie felt rather than saw the marines behind her sort themselves out into an impromptu skirmish line. She kept her eyes on the police lieutenant.

Katie moved forward slowly with her empty hands spread out and open. "Space Force marines on a special mission."

"*Resolute*? You've got no jurisdiction here."

Well, that was interesting. The police lieutenant knew they weren't from the local detachment and apparently their uniforms were identification enough for him. It was almost as if he'd been expecting them. "You know better than that, Lieutenant. Space Force Federal jurisdiction overrides all local authority except in specific instances on Earth itself."

"So looks like we've got ourselves a baby space lawyer here," the police lieutenant replied. One of his companions snickered at this. Nervously. Looked like he'd noticed that Katie, the sergeant and the half dozen marines following them outnumbered the policemen as well as being more heavily armed. "I'm no lawyer myself so I'll tell you what; you're going to wait until the rest of my people join us and then we talk it over with the governor and the police chief in a nice warm well lit office."

Katie didn't think so. Katie thought the police lieutenant was bluffing. She wasn't authorized to talk to the local police, let alone threaten them. Her bosses wouldn't be happy if she did. Only Katie thought the police lieutenant was playing for time, waiting for reinforcements to arrive. Katie's bosses would be even less happy if she got herself and the marines surrounded and taken prisoner, thereby failing her mission. "No. What is going to happen, is that you're going to stand down and let us pass by. Now."

"Says who? You're not in charge here."

"Says a half dozen heavily armed marines that I command, two railgun armed boats, and the even more heavily armed warship that's hanging just off of this rock. Says all the trained and willing to fight spacers she carries many of who are already on this benighted piece of crap floating in space under the guise of being on shore leave. That's who says, *Police Lieutenant*."

The police lieutenant's companions went white. The police lieutenant himself was made of sterner stuff, but looked grim. He wasn't quite ready to give it up. The police lieutenant seemed to sense Katie was bluffing. Katie wished that was true. "Who's the beat up one?" the police lieutenant asked. Still stalling for time.

"Propulsion Engineer Wong," Katie answered. "Seems to have fallen into bad company. We're giving him a lift home."

"Wong?" the talkative one of the police lieutenant's subordinates muttered. "There's more than one?"

That angered and distracted the police lieutenant. "Shut up," he said, turning to the offending policeman.

Katie stepped up close to him, putting her hand on her side arm, unclipping it as she did. "Enough stalling. Make way. Now," she said quietly, but very firmly.

Uncertain, the police lieutenant stepped to one side. The other policemen followed suit.

Katie pushed past him and carried on.

It wasn't until the policemen were well out of sight that she looked back at Sergeant Suvorov, who just nodded.

They got back to Boat Beta and then the *Resolute* without further problems.

As she exited into the port boat bay, it was all Katie could do not to stop and prop herself up against a wall. She felt like all her strings had been cut.

That could have gone much worse.

It could have gone a lot better, too.

\* \* \*

Katie was in the Med Bay with Iris Gregorian looking at the still sleeping and beat up Lieutenant Wong. He wasn't looking very good, though much better than when Katie and the marines had found him on Vesta.

The other body, still sedated, but also still living, that they'd retrieved from the asteroid, presumably that of the individual who'd had Wong beaten, was being kept in a spare part of the Marine barracks. Alive and intact, despite Iris' feelings when she'd seen Wong. Kept locked in there pending his interrogation, Katie assumed.

Katie didn't know. Nobody felt she needed to. She was just the poor sap that had led the team to capture him. It annoyed Katie to no end.

The spooky house-of-mirrors quality of the whole exercise was deeply disturbing.

Katie was torn between anger and depression. She wanted to rip someone, anyone almost, a new one. Only she had no clear target, and the closest ones were her immediate superiors. Indulging her anger with them would not only be career ending, it likely wouldn't achieve anything besides that. The captain, XO, and ops officer hadn't come out and said it directly, but it was pretty clear they'd been acting under direct orders too, had not had much choice about it, and had not been very happy about it either.

So she was left with a lot of frustrated anger and nothing to do with it. That was depressing.

Katie looked over at Iris. Iris looked back. "Keep a lid on it, Katie. It's not great, but you got Wong out, and nobody got hurt."

Katie just nodded.

Katie thought about what would happen if she demanded to be told what was going on, or if she asked to have her training schedule relaxed as a reward for the operation's success.

Nothing good.

They probably wouldn't have told her anything, even if her grandmother hadn't been Admiral Schlossberg. Katie's reputation for discretion wasn't sterling. Also, although she thought the extraction operation had been a success, and she'd done as well as could be expected, her superiors might not agree. Katie had a feeling they'd be getting a complaint about how she'd treated that police lieutenant.

The threats she'd implied when she'd bluffed her way past him might just be considered a little overboard. She'd vastly exceeded her authority. She'd put the captain and SFHQ in an awkward position. If they backed her actions up, they'd be owning up to having threatened a civilian settlement and its police. On the other hand, if they didn't their already tenuous authority in the Belt would practically evaporate. They weren't likely to be happy with Katie for putting them in that dilemma.

So probably the best thing to do was to go along with keeping the whole thing under wraps. Be a good little soldier.

Hope she didn't end up a sacrificed pawn.

\* \* \*

Amy was worried. She'd just put Katie to bed.

Katie had been grim.

And taciturn.

It wasn't that Amy hadn't seen Katie unhappy, frustrated, or worried before. The stars in the heavens knew she had. Katie was nothing if not an emotional roller coaster ride. Only even at her lowest points, Katie had always kept a basic underlying optimistic energy about her. You always had the feeling that whatever was bothering her currently she'd buck up, tackle it, and sometimes against all reason prevail.

Katie had tried not to wake up Amy when she returned from whatever her mission had been. It'd been in the early hours of the Zulu time cycle both the *Resolute* and Vesta maintained. Only Amy had been waiting for her, lightly dozing, but waiting.

Amy hadn't been sure about that. It wasn't like she wa Katie's Mom or anything, only she'd felt Katie might need some emotional support, and that she ought to try to provide it.

She hadn't been wrong, as it turned out.

As Katie had come through the hatch into their shared cabin, Amy had turned over. "What's up?" she'd asked.

Katie had grimaced. She'd looked not just tired, but depressed and beaten. Like someone who was managing to keep going out of sheer determination. "Oswald Wong got beat up on Vesta." She looked pensive. "I guess it's okay to tell you that. He's in Med Bay. Whole ship's going to know soon anyways. Shore leave is canceled. Iris is going crazy having to make sure everyone gets back safe. Offered to help, but she told me to get some sleep."

Amy could understand that. Katie was young and before had always looked fresh-faced. Right now she didn't just look tired, she had something resembling black lines under her eyes. It gave Amy an unaccountable twinge of sadness. "No offense, but looking at you, I think she's right. What happened?"

Katie'd pulled an even blanker face. "Can't say. I was told to say there's nothing I know that I can discuss."

Oh, damn woo-woo spook stuff. "Okay. Well, whatever it was, I'm sure you did your best. It'll all look better after you get some proper rest. To bed with you."

Katie had smiled a little at that. She'd done as she was told, pausing only to quickly pulse their "shower" for a quick cleaning and to change into a new ship suit. They'd all been trained not to sleep in dirty clothing. To Amy's relief, Katie's fatigue seemed to overwhelm her distressed mood and she almost immediately fell asleep.

Something Amy looked forward to doing herself. She'd requested the forenoon off from her boss Lieutenant Vann in anticipation of not getting any solid sleep during the night. First, she needed to process what'd happened.

Katie didn't seem to realize it, but Amy had known as soon as they started imposing on Katie's already short time with all that marine training that something unusual was up.

It'd also been clear that it went high up. Through the training officer and the XO and all the way up to the captain at least. Clear too, that they were trying to keep it all under wraps. Hadn't been much Amy could say or do about it, so she'd kept her peace.

Wong beat up. Shore leave canceled. Katie looking like a ghost escaped from a war zone. Something was up. She'd been right about that, unfortunately. Something big, and very messy.

Something that was being handled in a way that involved Katie very directly, and in a manner that seemed entirely unfair to Katie in Amy's mind.

Probably the sensible thing was to keep her nose out of it. To be as emotionally supportive as she could be of her young cabin mate, but not go meddling in affairs she didn't understand. Possibly causing more trouble for Katie rather than helping her.

Only Amy wasn't sure her conscience was going to let her off the hook. No, she wasn't at all sure it was the right thing to do, but she was going to look into this and make sure that

Katie's superiors understood they could ask only so much of the young ensign before breaking her. Make sure they understood they held a young officer's career in their hands.

Amy would try to be discreet.

She'd start by quietly sounding out Lieutenant Haralson. Amy had a feeling he wasn't thrilled with what was happening either.

Amy would make it clear Katie hadn't asked for help and was managing to bear the burden so far, only that it was Amy herself wasn't pleased.

She'd be nice about it.

Maybe it'd work. Maybe it wouldn't. That worried her.

But she had to try.

\* \* \*

Ravi was annoyed. Only one short step from being angry and annoyed.

Inconvenient, as he was now back in his cabin and trying to get some long delayed and badly needed sleep. It was early morning, coming up to the middle of the morning watch. Even if he slept in and didn't report for the forenoon, he didn't have long to get the rest he needed.

Ravi hadn't planned to be sleeping on board the *Resolute* at all tonight. He'd had shore leave and had managed to find and rent a small room in that small part of Vesta dedicated to the needs of better-off tourists. Vesta wasn't a great tourist destination. It was mainly an industrial and mining outpost, but there were always a few intrepid souls who wanted to visit out of the way places. There was some profit in providing for them. Ravi had looked forward to taking advantage of that.

It hadn't worked out. Everybody's shore leave had been canceled.

As much as Ravi ached for rest he needed to process what had happened.

The evening had started out well enough. Ravi had gone ashore along with Cara Campbell, the Deputy Ops Officer, and Oswald Wong and Myleen Zhang, who'd piloted the away boat over. They'd all had over a month to get familiar with each other in their professional capacities, but it'd been interesting starting to get to know each other as simply people trying to relax and forget work for a while.

They'd had no problem agreeing to start their leave by

having a meal in one of Vesta's best restaurants. Outrageously expensive, but it wasn't like they'd had much of anywhere to spend their salaries the last while. It'd been a faux Italian place and the pasta, cheese, and meat, though doubtless all vat grown had been quite superb. The wine was from Earth itself.

The first inkling of something going wrong had been when Oswald had got a call half way through their meal. He'd sighed and said he needed to meet a friend of his brother's quickly but should be back soon.

Next Myleen had got a call from the enlisted hand standing watch at the boat. The local authorities had some questions only an officer could answer. She too had expressed the hope she'd be back soon.

It'd left Ravi alone with Cara Campbell. A not entirely unpleasant experience, as it turned out. They were both junior lieutenants, and she was only a year or two older than him, and, critically, not in his chain of command. She was an attractive woman and turned out to be rather fun with an ironic sense of humor where duty wasn't involved. They found that they shared a basic discomfort with the slapdash way the *Resolute* and Space Force generally were run. They were both careful not to denigrate their senior officers, but it was obvious they shared a certain outlook.

Ravi had really been warming to Cara before their evening was rudely interrupted by a broadcast notice that shore leave had been canceled and all personnel were to immediately report to the boat and return to the *Resolute*. Ravi knew it was petty and not reasonable, but he'd been severely annoyed.

Still, they'd hastily paid for everyone and were some of the first people back to the boat. They found Myleen there worrying about where Oswald was. To Ravi's surprise, it wasn't long before Cara had everybody accounted for except Oswald. Some of the enlisted hands were so drunk they could barely stand up, but their mates had dragged them back.

With everybody back but Oswald, Cara had had Myleen request direction from the *Resolute*. They'd been ordered to return without him. Myleen took the pilot's seat, Cara the co-pilot's, and Ravi was left in the passenger-configured cargo compartment glowering at the roughly forty percent of the *Resolute*'s enlisted complement that'd been granted shore leave.

Mostly they seemed too drunk and too happy to care much.

They'd also been very curious about what could have happened. The rumors were wild, but in general the hands seemed excited by something happening rather than apprehensive and concerned.

Ravi had rather envied them.

Disembarkation on the *Resolute* had been hectic. They'd all been chivvied out of the boat bay and up into the gravity ring and through Med Bay, where they were checked for injury. The drunks got sober up shots. Ravi didn't envy them. The shots worked. They sobered you up quick, but it was rather like concentrating the hang over into a half hour. Not fun.

The med techs fed each of their victims some pablum, gave them the shot, and stuck them in the attached heads to quickly puke their guts out before being dispatched to their quarters.

Ravi had been careful to seem fully sober. He'd also kept his eyes and ears open.

To his relief, he heard Oswald was back on board. Ravi had even caught a quick glimpse of him. Oswald looked beat up, but alive. So there were some solid facts. Shore leave had been canceled. Oswald had been beaten up. Thank heavens they'd retrieved him and he was alive and rumor said wouldn't suffer permanent damage.

Rumor filled in the gaps.

Once again speculation, but Katie Kincaid and the marines with the other boat figured prominently in all of it.

Some rumors had Kincaid and Oswald getting into a fight over her having ratted his brother out. Ravi wondered if it was true Oswald was related to the Wong Kincaid had reported. Some of them had her beating Oswald up. Others had her ordering the marines to beat him up.

Ravi thought both sets of rumor to be ridiculous. Oswald was a slight man, but Kincaid was only a medium sized young woman. Both of them would know better than to get into a fight. It was even less credible that marines would follow an order to beat up an officer.

Slightly more credible was the rumor that Kincaid had led a team to rescue an Oswald that had been captured and beat up by unfriendly locals, some said over a gambling dispute, some said maybe over a woman.

That also seemed unlikely to Ravi. Ravi figured most likely

Kincaid had been assigned to the marines as a necessary figurehead to satisfy regulations and that she'd tagged along when they'd been sent to retrieve Oswald.

Ravi did wonder how Oswald had got into trouble. Ravi also wondered how they'd managed to react so quickly.

Ravi would have liked to have hung around the Med Bay and listened to more of the rumors, but the med techs had eventually got around to checking him and shooing him back to his quarters. They'd explicitly told him to get some rest. Medical professionals had prerogatives that trumped mere rank, it seemed.

And so Ravi was back in his cabin, trying to sleep.

Ravi guessed the first thing was to accept there was only so much he could do. Whatever had happened that had led to their shore leave being canceled and Oswald being in the Med Bay was water under the bridge.

Only useful question was what impact it was likely to have on him.

Well, clearly Katie Kincaid was in the middle of whatever was happening. Also, he knew the Weapons Department was going to get her as an officer trainee in the near future. Between the missile mess and whatever had just happened, he was guessing that Novak was going to be busier than she'd planned and more of that training was going to fall to Ravi than either of them would have liked.

Figurehead or not, Kincaid's involvement in Away Ops had to be a drain on her already limited time.

Ravi figured there'd be pressure to take it easy on her. Not unreasonably either, he had to admit, she was carrying an unusual workload even for a new junior officer. Usually their seniors liked to see just how much a junior officer could handle, but there were limits.

Ravi wanted to be reasonable. He also didn't plan to sign off on anyone handling weapons duties who wasn't up to snuff.

Ravi would work hard and go the extra mile to make sure Kincaid got properly trained. He'd give her every assistance he could.

But when it came down to it, he wasn't going to relax his standards for her.

Not one whit.

## 8: Ensign Kincaid Carries On

Iris was tired and busy. She'd finally managed to get all the non-essential personnel clear of the boat bays and up the spokes into the gravity ring. Chivvied them through Med Bay and would have liked to have gone to bed herself.

Only she couldn't. She had to make sure the boats were ready for whatever came next. To that end she was depriving the marines and SLT "Bobby" Maddox of their badly needed rest too. Lieutenant Myleen Zhang, she'd ordered to bed. "Get yourself a quick bite and then some solid sleep. I'm going to need you to be rested and ready to take charge of boats by noon. Got it?" she'd told her.

Zhang had nodded. "Yes, ma'am," she'd replied and turned and gone on her way.

Iris and Bobby had led the marines back to the boat bays and were now re-configuring the cargo bay of Boat Alpha from passenger carrying to cargo/combat. Boat Beta, thankfully, was already configured to carry marines. Iris had done a quick check of the weapons and sensors on both boats before chipping in to help the marines with the re-configuration work.

It wasn't by the Space Force officer manual to do so. Not maintaining proper separation of roles or some such thing, but Iris hardly cared. She had a job to get done.

Neither had the weapons check been by the book. More of a worry that. She'd do proper checks when the reconfiguration was done. She'd get Suvorov squared off - he wasn't in he chain of command technically, but there was no one else around taking charge - and then assign poor Bobby to standby duty before going off to get rested up for whatever the rest of the day brought. She figured she had only a few hours before the captain and XO figured out what was happening and decided to act on it. She had little doubt it'd involve her and her boats. From what she'd seen of Wong's condition, he wasn't in any shape to handle the job.

They'd just finished the Boat Alpha reconfiguration when Lieutenant Cara Campbell, the Deputy Ops Officer, appeared. She came right up to Iris and without preliminaries declared, "You're Boats. Right from the XO and captain, Wong's out of it for days at least." She half winced, half sighed. "Maybe the rest of the tour. Bad shape. Up to his neck in something fishy too."

Iris looked at her blankly. "Okay."

Campbell gave her a tired twitch of a half smile. Iris usually found Cara a bit too stiff for her taste. She liked her better tired. "Not by the book, is it?" Cara said. "Probably shouldn't have said that, you know."

Iris nodded slowly. "Think we're going to have to improvise some the next couple of days. I don't know what the captain plans or what's happening on Vesta, but I think we'd better be prepared to act quickly on short notice. Give me a few minutes to get my people squared away?"

"Sure."

Campbell, as Deputy Ops, was in theory Iris' superior, so Iris was glad she was being so reasonable. Vaguely surprised, but glad too. "Bobby, Suvorov, come here," she bellowed.

Waiting for Maddox and the sergeant Iris noticed that her whole body ached. Head was foggy too. It didn't take long for them to report, thank heavens. "Okay, reconfig is good, right?"

"Yes, ma'am," they both replied.

"Weapons, gear, all secured?"

Another chorus in the affirmative.

"That all?"

Bobby Maddox spoke up. "Flight engineers report boats both good and all fueled up and ready to go."

Ouch. Iris had forgotten about the engineers, and worse

about making sure the boats were ready. "Great, thanks for taking care of that, Bobby. Could you go tell them they're off for now, but they're on call and better get all the sleep they can while they can? You're standby until noon. I want you in the ready room fully suited up, but nap as much as you can. Clear?"

"Yes, ma'am," Bobby answered, snapping off a salute. Not entirely joking, it seemed to Iris' vague surprise. He kicked off to go and do as ordered without further ado.

"Suvorov, a few words," Iris said to the marine sergeant. "For the time being, let's short circuit the formal chain of command. Okay?"

They both looked at Campbell to check her reaction. She was in that chain of command. Technically the sergeant reported directly to Thor Haralson, who was the Ops Officer. He'd normally be acting pretty directly under the command of the captain in using the marines for anything out of the usual. Only Iris had a feeling they were all pretty busy with other things. A simple nod from Campbell confirmed that appreciation.

"We'll confirm everything through Ops, of course," Iris said.

Campbell smiled.

"Yes, ma'am," Suvorov replied.

"Well, Sergeant, thanks for your work today. Unfortunately, it may not be the last thing we need you for. I suggest you do the quickest debrief you can and see your men get some rest. Be ready for another deployment at short notice."

"Yes, ma'am. That all, ma'am?"

"Yes. You're dismissed."

The sergeant saluted too before departing, snapping orders at his men as he did so. In a seconds, Cara Campbell, and Iris were alone.

"We're short Wong and sleep both," Iris stated.

Cara looked unhappy. "Try to get your people as much sleep as possible, but the captain has said he'll waive safety regulations if he has to. Operational necessity. He's giving you Kincaid almost full time too."

"Almost?"

"She's been training with the marines. Seems to be good with them too." Cara looked a little uncertain. "She might be too aggressive, but somebody who fumbled or froze would be worse."

Iris figured that paraphrased something someone senior had said. "Awful lot to ask of one poor junior ensign. You want her to be a pilot and Away Ops Officer both?"

Lieutenant Campbell stiffened.    Then she relaxed and sighed. "Nobody likes it. Not much choice, though. If we need to do ops on Vesta, an officer has to go along and she's the best we've got for that. Regarding pilots it's the same. Technically, me or even Ravi or Amy could do it. We're all junior enough that we've recently been flight qualified, but honestly from what I've heard she's better than any of us ever were. Also, and not unimportantly, turns out we're all busy too. The boats are going to be needed, but so is the *Resolute*. They're even talking bout putting Amy on a bridge watch. Me and Thor are deep into ops planning, we might need the weapons, and Novak and Ravi are neck deep into that. We don't have time to get anyone up to speed on new tasks. So we're down to everybody being overloaded, including our trainee ensign. Sucks, but that's the way it is."

Iris sucked her teeth. "Geez."

"Yeah, not the most professional evaluation, but that sums it up. Any more questions? I think we both need to finish up and get what sleep we can."

"What about Kincaid's training schedule?" Iris asked. "It's not fair to dump two major roles on her and not waive the unnecessary parts of her training."

Cara looked exasperated. "True, but right now, Thor, the XO, and the captain have a lot of other more important things than an ensign's training plan to worry about. I'm not going to ask them about it, and I suggest you don't either."

Iris grimaced. "Still not fair."

"Doesn't matter. It's good to try to be fair, but it's not always possible. It's why we have rules and chains of command so that when we have to make unfair demands of our people, they understand it's not arbitrary or personal. Sure it's unfair, but we both know being fair to Katie Kincaid or anyone else is not the primary mission of either the *Resolute* or the Space Force. She needs to understand that. So do you."

"Right," Iris said grudgingly. "Is that all?"

"I think so. Look, maybe it'll look better with some sleep."

"Maybe."

Cara nodded ruefully. "Anyhow. Later. Get some sleep as soon as you can. No solid plans yet, but we're looking to move quickly."

"Right. Will do," Iris replied.

"Later," Cara said. With that, she kicked off back forward to the spokes to the gravity rings. She'd be back in her cabin before Iris. Iris would do a few checks and follow posthaste. Maybe it would look better with some sleep.

Maybe.

\* \* \*

Technically, it wasn't the next day. Technically, it was just before noon on the same day that Katie had led the extraction op. The same day they'd found Wong beat up by the bad guy they now had in custody. Technically, it was the same day the *Resolute* had canceled shore leave too.

For Katie down in the Port Boat Bay again, with too many zero gee hours on her log, and with too little sleep, all that seemed to have happened a long time ago. Days or weeks ago in a prior age, not mere hours before. Funny how time seemed to go wonky when the ka-ka hit the fan.

"Sorry, about rousting you out of your rack without enough sleep," Iris was apologizing. "Damned sure I'd have liked more sleep myself, but there's an emergency in progress. It's time sensitive and we're shorthanded."

"Right, got that. No problem," Katie answered. Not exactly true on either point, but Iris seemed to need reassuring.

"I'm acting Boats now. Wong's in the Med Bay, for we don't know how long, but days at least. We're down a pilot. Bad timing. Ops says they're going to need us to stand by both to ferry the marines to Vesta, and to help prevent suspects from fleeing. We could use another boat or two and several more pilots."

"Ouch," Katie replied. "Have you told them that?"

"No need. They're aware of the problem, but needs must. The captain has waived both zero gee hour caps and requirements for down time sleeping. He says he wants us to do our best with regards to both, but that operational needs have to take priority."

"So what do you want me to do?"

"I want you to take over as Boat Beta's co-pilot under Bobby, Sub-Lieutenant Maddox, as pilot. Me and Zhang will take Boat Alpha. We'll take watches in the Ready Room in the ring so we can react quickly if need be. For the time being, I suspect they're going to station a boat off the far side of Vesta to prevent escapes but I haven't seen formal orders yet. So, yeah, it's a stretch, but there's a bright side. A bit of good news."

"Good news?"

"Yes, you're going to have all your qualifying time on boats done before the week's out. In fact, we're treating you like you're qualified already. That's in the bag."

Katie steadied herself against a bulkhead and looking at Iris smiled grimly. Katie knew Iris well enough by now to hear what wasn't spoken. "And what's the bad news?"

"Everything you were studying or working on besides Away Ops and Boat Ops, you've got to drop for the time being. Any time you're not working for me or with the marines you have to be sleeping or eating under gravity."

Katie felt a glimmer of satisfaction that qualifying for boats was basically done. It'd been tremendously educational, and she'd rather enjoyed it. That she'd not messed up so badly with the marines that they were relieving her of Away Ops was also a good boost to the ego. She was sure her superiors weren't entirely overjoyed with her actions last night, and would have ideally liked to have given someone else the responsibility. Still with over a dozen officers on the *Resolute* when push had come to shove, they'd decided to stick with her. Katie could feel proud of that. Not happy, though. It was a tremendous responsibility and being on call for both Away Ops and as a pilot was burning the candle at both ends big time. With no end in sight either. "I understand. How long is this for? Is the XO going to adjust my training schedule to compensate?"

Iris sighed. "I'm glad you understand. I'm pretty sure I don't. This is a classic Charlie Foxtrot. To answer your questions; I have no idea, and no. Looks like the captain, the XO, and Lieutenant Haralson all have other priorities than your training schedule right now. The administration on Vesta falling apart is a bit more important than an ensign's training program."

"I see," Katie said. "Okay, I can suck it up and take one for the team. But it's not fair, and when it's all done, I hope they'll be reasonable. It's more than just me, though. I think they're pushing their luck with this. Accidents tend to happen when tired, stressed-out people are cutting corners."

Iris grinned without humor. "Above my pay grade and yours too. Ours but to do, and sigh."

"Out of the hearing of our superiors."

"Just so."

"But I'm a bit of an expert on pushing one's luck," Katie said.

"And?"

"It doesn't always end well."

\* \* \*

Katie was in the Ready Room, just after lunch, and she was supposed to be sleeping. Oughtn't be too hard. The Ready Room was dark. It was quiet too. The marvels of modern sound proofing. Certainly Sub-Lieutenant Robert "Bobby" Maddox wasn't having any problems sleeping. She could hear his soft snoring.

Only Katie was too frustrated and angry to sleep.

It wasn't fair to keep piling duties on her. She didn't know if she could handle them all. Unfortunately, it was pretty clear the XO wasn't going to cut her any slack. Realistically her best bet was to keep her head down, do her best, and hope her superiors gave her a break once the crisis was over.

Katie couldn't help thinking that'd be dodging her responsibility to provide her superiors accurate feedback. They were asking dangerously too much of any one officer. Katie thought she was basically pretty competent, but there was no denying she was both young and green too. Being both head of marine Away Ops and a pilot needed for effective Boat Ops was a dangerous stretch that assumed they'd never need her both as a pilot and to lead the marines at the same time. A rather big assumption. And that was without taking into account the heavy training schedule they'd given her and not rescinded when they dumped those additional responsibilities upon her. Surely that'd been an oversight. They couldn't want someone who'd be making critical decisions to be both tired and overly stressed out. Wasn't it her duty to point that out?

In an ideal world, maybe. But it wasn't an ideal world, was it? In the real world the XO already saw her as a troublemaker and a whiner, Lieutenant Haralson was overwhelmed with planning to fix the mess on Vesta, and the captain too was focused on that, and not inclined to get involved in the internal running of the ship, anyway.

In the real world Katie was going to have to do like her friend Sam, the ex-marine back on Ceres, liked to recommend: "Suck it up, buttercup."

She could start by getting some sleep.

\* \* \*

Amy hadn't planned to have to scoff her lunch down and rush to an all officers meeting in the *Resolute*'s briefing room. Only here she was, having done just that. She was tired too. And confused. She'd barely managed to get an hour's sleep after Katie's return before being woken by Lieutenant Vann, her boss. He'd been apologetic, but needs must. Apparently the XO had off-loaded most of his housekeeping work to Vann. There was urgent work that ought to have a supply officer supervising it. And that meant Amy.

The canceling of shore leave had thrown a wrench into the works of the ship's smooth functioning. Lieutenant Vann was anticipating yet further disruption. The well-being of their people who'd been on Vesta needed checking. Good meals for more people than planned at unexpected times had to be provided. Med Bay had been busy, and there was the disconcerting prospect it'd be even busier in the future. It wasn't just the supply department that was scrambling, Operations and Weapons were both kicked over hives of activity and Vann was alert to the possibility they'd be making unexpected, urgent demands on supply.

Also, whatever was happening on Vesta looked like it might be affecting more than just the crew's leave there. The various largely routine resupply orders they'd put in with various entities on the asteroid were now looking much less routine.

Their various NCOs were all competent and experienced. They could handle anything routine without needing direction from Vann or Amy. In fact, they could probably handle most non-routine events just as well too. Only that wasn't their job, and it wasn't fair to ask them to do that. Either Lieutenant Vann or Amy had to be available to give general direction and to sign off on the solutions their people proposed.

It hadn't taken Amy long to sort everything out and make sure everyone was happy and knew what they had to do. It'd only been a little more than an hour. Only by the time she'd grabbed a quick breakfast and got back to bed, it'd only left a couple more hours to sleep before getting up again for lunch.

Turns out two or three bouts of a couple of hours of sleep isn't the same as getting a solid night's worth. Amy was tired.

At least maybe this briefing would help with her confusion. All the officers except Sub-Lieutenant Maddox and Katie were here. Amy knew from Katie that she and Maddox had been ordered to standby in the Ready Room. Not just allowed to be, but expected to be, resting. But dressed, and ready to spring up and take the dedicated lift down to the Boat Bays at a moment's notice.

The rest of the *Resolute's* officers were settling in and looking quizzically at each other. There was a low buzz of discreet speculation mixed with gossip going on. Sergeant Suvorov was also present. Standing in one corner stoically imitating a piece of furniture, he was not participating in the general conversation. Because of social discomfort or because he knew too much he couldn't share, Amy could only guess.

In any event, it wasn't long before the captain walked in. "Attention!" declaimed the XO. The chatter came to an immediate end as the room came to attention.

The captain made his way to the podium at the front of the room. "At ease," he said once there. He gave everyone a few minutes to settle in.

Everyone having sat themselves down, the captain looked around to make sure he had their attention. "On our approach to Vesta we received an urgent secret communication from its governor," he said.

You could have heard a pin drop. Most of them had been wondering what had happened. Even those in the know wanted to know what the captain had planned for the ship. "Governor Porter had ceased to have full trust in all of his subordinates. He suspected at least some of them had been subverted by local criminal elements."

The room grew grimmer. Amy didn't wonder why. This was worse than she could have imagined.

The captain, having let the gravity of the situation sink in continued. "The governor identified an individual he believed was the leader of the local criminal element. The governor requested that the *Resolute* apprehend and interrogate that individual."

Once again the captain paused to let his words sink in. "Early this morning our marines, under the leadership of Ensign Kincaid and Sergeant Suvorov, extracted the individual in question from Vesta and brought him back to the *Resolute* for questioning. In the process, they found Lieutenant Wong, who'd been taken captive and beaten. They rescued the lieutenant and brought him back to the *Resolute* where he is being treated for his injuries."

The captain looked around. "This occasioned our cancellation of shore leave. Clearly Vesta is not currently a safe place."

He looked down at his podium. "Governor Porter's concerns were justified. I have ordered that he be extracted from Vesta, along with his family and senior staff. Lieutenant Winters, Lieutenant Haralson, and Sergeant Suvorov are currently in the process of planning that operation."

He looked up at the individuals named. "They will be co-ordinating with Lieutenant Gregorian, who is replacing Lieutenant Wong in command of Boats. Lieutenant Wong is on indefinite medical leave. Lieutenant Gregorian becomes the pilot of Boat Alpha as a result. Lieutenant Gregorian's position as pilot of Boat Beta will be taken by Sub-Lieutenant Maddox. Ensign Kincaid will be Boat Beta's co-pilot. Ensign Kincaid will do double duty as operational commander of marine Away Operations."

There was some restless rustling with this last announcement.

The captain gave the room a hard stare. "We're short-handed ladies and gentlemen. Ensign Kincaid has trained for the role and did well this morning. Although despite any rumors to the contrary, the *Resolute* will never use its weapons in a way that would endanger innocent civilians."

Amy was definitely going to have to ask Katie what the captain had meant by that.

"That said, we're not letting the bad guys off the hook either. Our securing of the governor will doubtless put them on notice. They will try to escape or hide. Our first priority will be preventing escape."

Once more the captain paused and looked around the room to emphasize his point. "The *Resolute* will be instituting a blockade of Vesta. To that end, she will immediately go to a modified form of Battle Stations. As we have no reason to expect our opponents to have any weaponry capable of damaging a frigate, there is no need to go to a full Zulu state and lock down the gravity ring. We'll be running at Yankee with some modifications, we'll be at full weapons readiness and may have to maneuver at short notice. On the other hand, as we may be at the higher readiness state for some days, we will relax restrictions on moving about, and regular meals will be served."

Amy couldn't help thinking a heads up would have been nice on that point, as she was the one who'd have to be organizing that.

The captain smiled. "I'm sure some of you have questions about the details. We'll be passing out hardcopy with them at the end of the briefing. You'll also find more detailed documents in your in-boxes. We'll answer any questions about the new readiness state that you submit as time permits."

He looked around again. Everybody had got the message. The captain and his senior officers were busy. Any questions anyone asked better be important and to the point.

Nobody spoke.

The captain continued. "Which brings us to the next point. Given the weight of the decisions they may have to make, we've decided that it's critical that the officers on watch be our most senior."

And so not Amy, which to her mild shame she realized was a relief. Rather belatedly, she also realized that there was some serious tension between the captain's aims of not hurting innocent civilians and not allowing any bad guys to escape. What if the bad guys took hostages? Would the *Resolute* be willing to fire on an escaping ship that also had innocent civilians on board?

"To that end," the captain was saying, "we have decided that Lieutenants Haralson, Campbell, and Novak will be responsible for all bridge watches. They are being excused most of their normal responsibilities. Our executive officer, Lieutenant Winters, is taking over Operations, especially planning. His regular duties will be assumed by Lieutenant Vann. In his absence, the Supply department will be run by Sub-Lieutenant Sarkis."

Well, Amy thought, nice to be told ahead of time. Not that she didn't think she could do the job or that being acting

Supply Officer wouldn't look good on her record.

The captain finished off his outlining of the re-organization. Presumably temporary. "Lieutenant Shankar will be acting Weapons. Note that all routine maintenance and housekeeping beyond that necessary to sustain operations is to be deferred. We want our people as rested and alert as possible for the next few days."

Another pause for emphasis. "Finally, our blockade of Vesta is going to require stationing one of the boats on her far side. That will be in addition to ferrying the marines and others to Vesta when needed. I want you all to render Boats and the marines as much help and support as possible. Understood?"

The captain looked around. "Yes, sir," Amy said quietly, as did the other officers around her.

"Good," the captain said. "That should be all, but are there any questions?"

Another of those Catch-22, damned if you do, damned if you don't, predicaments the military so loved. Anyone who failed at a task because they'd failed to ask a necessary question was in trouble. On the other hand, the captain had already been clear he wasn't open to questions he felt were unnecessary. Amy decided to emulate Katie for once and have the courage of her convictions.

"Sir, I have a couple of questions," Amy said, raising her hand.

"This isn't grade school, Sub-Lieutenant Sarkis," the captain replied. "You don't need to raise your hand. Spit it out."

"We were planning to do a degree of resupply from Vesta, sir," Amy said. "Do you know if those supply sources are still viable?"

"No, I don't know. It hasn't been our most immediate priority, but I suspect once the situation has been restored to some semblance of normal that your usual sources should be accessible. Does that answer your question?"

"Yes, sir. Also, sir, given our higher state of readiness, does that mean regular training schedules are being waived?"

The captain gave Amy a thin smile. Before he could reply, Lieutenant Winters, the XO, jumped in. "Your thinking of your cabin mate is commendable, Sub-Lieutenant, but really the captain and all the rest of us have more pressing matters to worry about right now. We'll sort routine administrative matters out once the crisis is over. Clear?"

"Yes, sir." Amy knew a lost cause when she saw one.

The XO looked at the captain who nodded.

"This briefing is over. Dismissed," the XO stated loudly.

## 9: Ensign Kincaid Digs Deeper

Katie was pretending to be a civilian. A local native of Vesta, or at least someone off of one of the local mining rigs. She had to get to the governor, and it wasn't possible to do so without transiting some fairly densely populated parts of the asteroid colony.

Katie was doing so alone and dressed in a Belter shipsuit. Katie's heavily armed marine squad in battle dress would have stood out. Even if they hadn't been outnumbered by criminal thugs operating on their home turf, that would have been problematic. The crooks didn't need to worry about harm to the local civilians. Katie and the marines as representatives of the Space Force did.

Katie's job was to get to the governor and lead him out to where the marines were hiding in a lesser traveled part of the colony. One of the side maintenance tunnels running between gravity rings out towards the mining rig docks. Boat Beta and Sub-Lieutenant "Bobby" Maddox were waiting in one of those docks. That was their ride home.

It was a big task, but Katie wished she could do more.

The civilians around her in the concourse of the Admin ring's shopping district were obviously worried and distressed. They didn't know what was happening. Not completely. Not for sure. Evidently what they did know worried them. Katie hadn't heard or seen any official reports of what was happening. She was overhearing a lot of rumors. Words and phrases like "coup", "kidnapping", "pirates", and "military operations" kept popping up in the snatches of conversation she was catching. She dared not linger to listen to what people were saying. Katie was on a mission.

If Katie had been in command of a battalion of troops, maybe she could have taken control of Vesta and put all the concerns of the civilians on the asteroid to rest. But she wasn't. Katie didn't have a battalion of troops. Katie had the *Resolute*'s squad of marines. They weren't in touch with the small number of marines actually stationed on Vesta. Also, although most of the local marines likely remained honest and loyal, the *Resolute*'s command staff had learned for a fact that the local marines had been infiltrated. The same was true of the Space Force personnel based on Vesta and the local civilian administration.

With the police, the situation was worse. They might not all be rotten, but it was a fact much of their command structure was compromised.

And so all Katie and the *Resolute*'s command could depend on was their own troops. Their single squad of marines. Until the governor was safe, they didn't dare openly do anything to challenge the locally entrenched bad guys.

A lot of the civilians around Katie didn't seem to be there in the shopping concourse with any clear purpose. A lot of them seemed to be just out and about, so they didn't have to sit at home alone and fret. People also seemed to be trying to gather news. Hence all the rumors and speculation.

Katie was moving through a food court now. She was trying not to linger, but not to too obviously seem in a hurry either. She hit a knot of people, mostly younger women with kids, in front of a "frozen dessert" kiosk.

For some reason - maybe the central payments system was down - the kiosk was only taking currency tokens.

"Mommy, I want an ice cream," one very young girl barely past being a toddler was complaining.

"I'm sorry, dear," her young mother explained, "I forgot to bring tokens."

Katie had a pocket full of tokens that *Resolute* crew

members who'd returned from shore leave had donated. "I'll buy her an ice cream," she volunteered.

At first Katie didn't think the young mother was going to accept Katie's offer. Annoyance and suspicion were the first emotions that flashed across the woman's face. It pained Katie to see it. The child's mother seemed so young. Katie knew she had to be at least Katie's age or a little older even, but she seemed so young. Then she looked at her young girl and Katie and relented. "You will?" she said. "That's very generous."

"Well, not really," Katie said. "I've a pocket full of tokens and I'm not planning to hang around on Vesta long. I'm just here to get some people and take them back to my ship."

The young mother glanced around quickly. "You have a ship?" she asked quietly. "Can you take a couple more people? It's not safe here. My husband is out on a mining trip. I can pay. Eventually anyway."

Katie was surprised. Shouldn't have been, really. It was a split second's decision. Katie couldn't save all the civilians on Vesta, but she could help these two. "Sure, no need to pay, but it'll be spartan and crowded. You'll have to come right away and play along with me. Can't take everyone who might want a ride."

The young mother swallowed. "I'm Mary," she said. "This is Susan. Whatever you say."

Katie put on what she hoped was a reassuring smile. "I'm Katie," she said, bending over to talk to Susan. "Here are some tokens to buy an ice cream. Let's all pretend we're going to a birthday party."

It slowed Katie down to have Mary and Susan along, but it also made her stick out a lot less. Spotting some hard-faced men lounging here and there, Katie was glad for that. She'd not be coming back this way.

The private residence the governor was holed up in wasn't that much further. The governor and his small entourage, just his wife and a couple of staff, were even less trouble than Mary. They weren't guessing things were bad, they knew. They were happy to take direction from Katie. The governor even volunteered to carry Susan.

Mary proved to be a font of local knowledge. With her help, they had no problem getting back to the marines and then to Boat Beta.

Seeing the largely empty cargo bay of the boat, Katie felt a quick twinge of guilt. She squashed it. Katie had done what she reasonably could. Katie went forward and slipped into the co-pilot's seat.

"Bobby" Maddox looked over at her in greeting. "How'd it go?"

"No problems, but this place is a mess. Nobody's in charge, but the thugs aren't on the run yet."

"Damn, I was hoping this was just an abundance of caution."

"Afraid not," Katie answered. "Vesta is unstable. I can see the bad guys using the civilians here as hostages."

"Damn," Bobby answered as he started his pre-flight checks.

Katie didn't really relax until they docked with the *Resolute*.

Even then, she couldn't shake a sense of foreboding.

\* \* \*

There was no way Ravi could be certain the *Resolute*'s weapons were all ready to be used. Several weeks of weapons tests on a proper range would have been necessary to achieve some degree of certainty. And even the best range couldn't fully simulate operational conditions.

Hardly mattered, as they had neither a proper range nor several weeks in any case.

So Ravi was doing the best he could. Along with Senior Petty Officer Miller and the rest of his senior missile and gun maintenance techs, he'd inspected the *Resolute*'s weapons systems to within an inch of their lives.

Currently, both he and Miller were deep into the access space around the forward part of the ship's inline railgun. Capable of launching a variety of 60mm projectiles at velocities of several kilometers a second depending on operational requirements and how much wear on the barrel was acceptable, the railgun was the *Resolute*'s main armament.

Given the expense of projectiles, the danger they posed if not backstopped, and the cost of barrel wear, the railgun was rarely fired. "We can't just whack an uninhabited part of Vesta by the way of a test, sir?" Miller asked whimsically.

Ravi sighed. He'd long since abandoned decorum with Miller. "Don't even think about it, Miller. And for heaven's sake, please, don't say anything like that around the captain or the XO. Not even in jest. It could be our careers."

Miller gave Ravi an aggrieved look, like a hound dog that'd been scolded. "Please, sir, give me some credit. I know better than that. Still, you'd think with all their education and all and with their careers riding on it they'd know enough to test their weapons regularly."

"You know the practical problems as well as I do, PO. The bean counters have a fit every time."

"Aye, sir, I do, but a man can dream, can't he?"

"Quietly and with decorum. Far away from senior officers he can. Anyhow, I didn't hear any disappointed grunts. Does that mean the thing looks good?"

"As far as I can tell by just looking at it and running diagnostics, it's fine, sir."

"That's good."

"Better than our long-range missiles."

Ravi winced. "Well, at least we likely won't have to find out how well they work in reality."

"How so?"

"Missiles hit their targets where they want to and they tend to make a mess of them with their big warheads."

"True, sir."

"So, even if the bad guys are kind enough to flee without taking hostages, we want them alive enough to question."

"Makes the railgun the better option."

"Just so. Also tell me, PO, given a choice of fleeing past a frigate or a ship's boat, what would your choice be?"

"The boat."

"Exactly. So as unfair as it might be, the problem will likely fall into the hands of Boat Ops."

Miller frowned. "Well, I helped check their guns and those dinky little missile packs they have and they look good."

"But, yes, it's not fair to Lieutenants Gregorian and Maddox, let alone Ensign Kincaid, who they've got double timing as the marine leader as well as a co-pilot. I get it, Miller. Only best not bring this up with anyone else. Again, not career enhancing."

"We're supposed to get Kincaid for training sometime soon."

"And I'm not cutting her the least slack when we do."

"Sir?"

"If the XO wants to cut her training schedule back to something easier to handle, shall we say, that's fine."

"But?"

"But, if I'm going to sign off on someone being able to act as a Weapons Officer, then they're going to be able to do the job. Do it well at that."

"Guess that makes sense, sir."

\* \* \*

Iris was spooked. It was inconvenient that she was having to stretch two boats to do the work of at least three. For a genuinely sustainable blockade, a half dozen boats would have been better. What had her spooked was that Vesta had a detachment of Space Force scout-couriers that ought to be doing most of the work. Only they weren't.

The XO, when he'd handed down his operations plan, had presented it as a win that Governor Porter had managed to cajole the local commander into standing them down.

Nobody had said it explicitly, but it was clear they didn't trust the local Space Force detachment to do its job. That was scary.

"A penny for your thoughts," Lieutenant Myleen Zhang asked her from the co-pilot's seat.

"To use technical language," Iris replied, speaking slowly and deliberately and in as a calm and conversational tone as she could fake. "We're way beyond the usual state of SNAFU and more than normally FUBAR'ed."

Myleen snickered dryly. "It's bad of me, I know, but I'm glad I'm not the only one freaked out."

"You're not young and naïve enough not to be."

"That why you put Bobby and Kincaid together?"

"Partly. Seriously considered giving you the pilot's seat on Beta, Myleen."

"Only I'm still pretty inexperienced and more comfortable following procedures in predictable situations than improvising. I'm just not assertive enough either. It was the way I was brought up. It feels impolite to be too pushy. I understand, ma'am."

"Glad of that. Not sure myself it was the right call and believe me it wasn't all about you. Bobby is too laid back. He would have drifted along waiting for you to take the lead.

Kincaid's just the opposite. She's strong wine. I admire the girl and appreciate her get up and go, but she gives me headaches after too long and we're all going to be paired up and on duty for far too long, I suspect. Bobby handles her just fine and I think she'll keep him on his toes."

Myleen frowned thoughtfully. They were essentially on guard duty off of the far side of Vesta. Things might be tense overall. Action could break out suddenly at any time, but right now they were just killing time waiting for that. Plenty of time to think. Not daydream, they had to stay alert, but they had plenty of time to think. "Personally, from a purely selfish point of view, I'm kind of glad this happened. It's proving to be very educational. Balancing personalities to get the best possible teams is pretty important."

"Damned important," Iris agreed.

Myleen nodded. "You know it's odd, but thinking about it now, it seems like Oswald was just killing time. Stuck in a rut and going through the motions. Heck, he had you doing most of his work, didn't he?"

Iris felt her face tighten. Subordinates openly criticizing their superiors to each other was verboten. Her instinct and duty were both to immediately slap Myleen, Lieutenant (Junior Grade) Zhang, down. Only Myleen wasn't wrong. What's more, Iris was going to be spending a lot of time in close quarters with her. Potentially they'd have to co-operate in a very stressful and time critical crisis. Iris didn't want to create hard feelings or to even intimidate the young woman. Not personally and not as the person responsible for Boat Alpha and Boat Ops overall. "Well, young Lieutenant Junior Grade Zhang," Iris finally said in an exaggerated drawl, "it's fine that you're paying close attention to your superiors, but it's not your job or mine to second-guess them."

Myleen blushed. "Sorry, ma'am."

Iris smiled to show all was forgiven. No hard feelings, right? "On the other hand, it's perfectly reasonable to note that Lieutenant Wong's command style tended to be hands-off and rather conventional in nature."

Myleen gave Iris a cautious look. "Yes, ma'am."

Iris looked out at the space surrounding them before smiling thinly. "We all know he wasn't planning to re-up. He was on his last tour before mustering out."

"I guess he just wanted to run out the clock without having anything go wrong. Guess that didn't work out for him. Kind of sad and unfair, I guess. I mean, he wasn't a bad guy, and he was pretty competent when it came down to it. What did he do to deserve ending up in sick bay?"

Iris checked on the location of their flight engineer, Petty Officer Alice Morgan. She was back in what passed for "engineering" on the boat. Her vital signs were suspiciously low and regular. Iris decided not to notice. In any event, she wouldn't be overhearing Iris and Myleen, which suited Iris. "Between you, me, that bulkhead, and the empty vacuum beyond it, I kind of wonder if the bad guys didn't have a hook into him and he balked at what they asked him to do. Maybe it was his brother." Iris had learned Oswald Wong was indeed related to the Kevin Wong Iris had shipped with on the *Sand Piper*. "Maybe they had more on Kevin than came out after the *Sand Piper* incident."

Myleen fidgeted. "That's a depressing thought, ma'am. Almost makes you feel sorry for the guy."

Iris sighed. "Yeah. Whatever the exact details, I'm pretty sure they didn't beat him up because he was being co-operative."

"No, ma'am."

"Anyhow, this is just our first watch, but we're going to be doing regular watches two-in-one out here. We've got problems of our own. If you were to relax and doze off, I don't think I'd notice."

"Yes, ma'am. I think I'll rest my eyes a little now. Maybe you can do the same next watch?"

"Maybe," Iris replied. She wondered if she dared to subtly suggest to Bobby that he and Kincaid do the same. Ideally, she'd have liked to put a single pilot on each watch. Only Space Force regulations required a co-pilot except in a dire emergency. Also, somebody was needed to handle the weapons if it came to that. So once again she had to fudge regulations in order to do her job properly. And take responsibility if it didn't work out. Who said life was fair?

She had a feeling when the crap hit the fan, it'd be Bobby and Kincaid out here. The bad guys would need some time to get their acts together. Once they did, they'd likely have the sense to wait until they knew the boat crews were tired and not fully alert.

If they had hostages or they used more than one ship, at least some of them were almost certain to get away.

The boats were scarecrows.

Push come to shove, they were going to have a hard time of it.

It didn't make Iris feel good to think it, but Bobby and Kincaid were junior enough it shouldn't hurt their careers too badly if they were left holding the bag.

She hadn't deliberately put them in that situation. This mess wasn't her fault.

Not that that helped any of them.

\* \* \*

Katie quite liked Sub-Lieutenant "Bobby" Maddox. Only he didn't seem to take anything seriously. And Katie was pretty sure the current situation was a damned serious one.

Maybe she simply hadn't had enough sleep. She'd had a couple of hours before the operation to extract the governor, and she'd had a couple hours afterwards. That was all, and now she and Bobby were supposed to be taking a watch or blockade duty.

"You manage to get enough sleep?" she asked her formal superior.

"Nope," Bobby replied cheerfully. "But I didn't spend last night leading one marine operation, and this afternoon another one either. Sucks to be you, doesn't it?"

"It's been a busy day," Katie admitted, "but I'll manage."

"I'm taking the controls for the trip out to our station." They were making their way back to the Port Boat Bay. They were due to relieve Boat Alpha with Iris and Zhang in just over twenty minutes. "Once we're there, you're going to doze off. That's an order."

One that violated standing Space Force regulations, Katie couldn't help thinking.

Bobby stopped short of the Boat Bay and looked at her. He grinned mischievously. "You like doing things by the book," he said. "By the book you reply '*yes, sir*' to acknowledge an order. But you know sometimes it doesn't work to do things by the book. You used to run short on your home ship, didn't you? Relied on the alarms to wake up the non-watch keepers if something went wrong, right?"

"Yes," Katie said, "but we really shouldn't have."
"Only you didn't have much choice about that did you?"
"No, sir."
"Just like neither of us does now, right?"
"Yes, sir."
"So let's carry on and do the best we can. Okay?"
"Yes, sir."
"Cheerfully."
"Yes, sir."
"Gotta love that fresh out of the Academy training."
"If you say so, sir."

## 10: Katie, Bar the Door

Being on guard duty is boring right up to the point it isn't anymore.

Katie was feeling frustrated as well as bored because it meant she had to remain alert and focused on what was going on around the boat in anticipation of that swift change. She couldn't afford to be heads-down studying.

Heavens knew she had enough study to do. Both Weapons and Operations involved a lot of physics as well as doctrine and design choices. All embedded into protocols and routines the Space Force insisted its responsible members have down pat.

That was as true of the various bridge positions, helm, sensors, fire control, and, of course, last but not least, of Officer of the Watch (OOW), as it was of command or maintenance roles. More so, really. The bridge crews were supposed to work together like precise and well-oiled cogs. The machinery of ship command made no allowances for imperfections or grit.

And so here Katie was sitting in the co-pilot's seat of Boat Beta as it hung off the far, dark side of Vesta, waiting for the bad guys to make a break for it while hoping they didn't.

Being bored while wasting valuable time she could ill afford was the best part of it.

As bad as being bored was, and Katie hated being inactive - she liked to act not react - it was better than the alternative.

Sadly, she had to hope nothing happened. She had to hope that the bad guys were either intimidated by the *Resolute*'s blockade or that if they weren't, they decided to make their get away during Iris and Zhang's watch.

Because if they weren't complete idiots that getaway was likely to mostly succeed.

They'd been ordered to give anyone attempting to escape Vesta a warning that they'd use lethal force if the would-be escapees didn't heave to and await boarding.

Given Space Force regulations and the unwillingness of the senior officers on the *Resolute* to depart from them it was an empty threat.

Railgun rounds were fast and had tremendous kinetic energy. Railguns were devastating weapons against anything they could hit. Unfortunately, deliberately hitting anything, that wasn't static or nearby, wasn't that easy. Easier if it was moving directly away from or towards one, but distances in space are huge. One couldn't rely on a target being where one expected it'd be when you fired on it. It would have certainly moved. If one's projectile was very fast, or the target was very close, then the target may not have moved very far at all. If it wasn't, fire control was an exercise in prediction. Given that crystal balls were still a technology in development, a largely futile exercise.

The theorists said that railgun combat would mean a reversion to medieval times. Military force based on them would be effective against surprised soft targets and enemy military forces willing to accept battle. There'd be none of the forcing the enemy to decisive battle of the Napoleonic and the early modern times of the 19th to 21st centuries.

Missiles might be the answer to that conundrum, but they had their own drawbacks. Not that it mattered under the current circumstances. Missile warheads tended to be indiscriminate in their destruction. Certainly against moving targets. The *Resolute* didn't want to kill any hostages the bad guys might have taken. It didn't even want to kill the bad guys it wanted to capture them for questioning.

So, no missiles.

Katie sighed.

Not only no missiles, but she couldn't even use her railgun and its most effective projectile to their full effect. Those were reserved for one mission and one mission only, the protection of planetary populations from imminent mass destruction.

Anything short of that and Katie, and every other Space Force officer, was bound by stringent rules of engagement.

Her best railgun rounds, capable of a limited degree of maneuver, were also designed to be her most destructive. Couldn't use those.

She couldn't aim her gun directly towards any ship between her and Vesta. Even a round that hit its target was likely to sail straight through it and do significant damage somewhere on Vesta. Vesta was a big rock, some 500 kilometers wide. Chances were she'd not hit anything or anyone important, but the Space Force's rules of engagement did not let her take that chance.

Also, she was not allowed to fire a round at a ship coming directly at her or moving directly away from her. She couldn't take her easiest shots. A round hitting a target with those aspects would travel its full length, likely killing everyone on board.

Finally, and rather redundantly in Katie's mind, she wasn't allowed to fire a round in such a fashion that it'd be hard to impossible to retrieve. The Space Force was sensitive to the issue of railgun rounds zipping around in interplanetary space for years to come and maybe eventually hitting some innocent civilian.

Basically they could fire on a close-by ship that wasn't in the direction of Vesta that they could hit from the side with a good chance of just surgically taking out engineering or the engines and that was all.

And miracle of miracles, if they were only faced with a single fleeing ship they could likely do just that. If they were lucky, they might manage to succeed against a second ship.

If the bad guys had more ships, and the sense to use them, some of them were bound to get away.

Everyone knew the poor jerks on the spot were more likely to get blamed for that unfortunate outcome than Space Force standing orders. So, yeah, Katie was cheesed and hoping somebody else besides her and Bobby got to be those poor jerks.

Katie knew she needed to get her head back in the game and maybe develop a little more emotional maturity and calm. So she forced her thoughts away from contemplating the cosmic injustice of it all and back to passively observing the space around her. The more she was aware of how things were now, especially on the dark surface of Vesta, the quicker she'd notice any changes.

That change came three quarters of the way into their watch. Made sense. The bad guys probably figured they'd be tired but not alert in anticipation of the end of the watch.

Multiple bright lights, engine plumes, broke out against the dark surface of Vesta. Katie elbowed Bobby beside her awake. "Unauthorized departures in progress from Vesta's dark side," she announced both for Bobby's benefit and that of the *Resolute* who she'd opened a channel to with a flick of her other hand.

"Weapons free," Bobby ordered. "Give them the warning."

Space Force doctrine held that cautions from female members were more likely to be heeded than those by male ones. Might or might not be true, but it meant the job fell to Katie. "Unauthorized ships in Vesta space. This is the Space Force. Heave to now or we'll use lethal force. This is your last warning."

Katie didn't really expect a reply. She was surprised.

"Katie Kincaid! Kincaid is that you?" came a voice she thought she recognized.

"Don't bother. It's you. You're like a fly to shit when it comes to trouble, girl. Haven't forgotten you. Never going to forget you. It's Guy Boucher. Just calling to let you know I've just bumped you up on my bucket list. Going to get you for what you did to Billy and me. Try sleeping on that. As for heaving to we both know you're bluffing."

Bobby next to her looked her way, questions in his eyes.

"Smuggler from Ceres. No time now," Katie said. She'd picked a ship to track automatically. Bobby needed to maneuver the boat to give them a shot as soon as that ship came out of Vesta's shadow. The fact that it didn't seem to be the ship Guy's signal was coming from was moot. They had to do this right, which meant quickly, if they were to get any of the bad guys.

"Matching course with Bad Guy One," Bobby said.

Katie flicked on the active tactical radar. A quick adjustment and their target was painted perfectly. To Katie's shock, it looked like a Bird class scout, not some stripped-down merchant or miner. "Designating aiming point. Will fire as soon as you bring us to bear."

Bobby was a good pilot. It might have been a fraction of a second before the red target cursor jittered over their aiming point. Katie pushed the firing button. The whole boat shuddered as the gun fired at maximum force.

"Bring us around to Bad Guy Two," Katie said. Bobby was supposed to be in command, but Katie had no time for niceties. Enough of these bastards were going to get away as it was.

"Coming around to Bad Guy Two," Bobby replied. Damned if he didn't sound amused. Cool as a cucumber in any case. A good thing.

The aspect wasn't as good this time. It took long seconds for the tactical radar to paint their second target, and the aiming point Katie found was less than perfect. They were likely to make a mess of the whole aft end of their target. This time at least it did look like a stripped-down merchant. Just control and living with a long empty cargo spindle before the engines were reached. Hopefully there was no one down there tending to them. Katie really didn't want to become a killer any sooner than necessary.

She didn't waste any time on that depressing thought. "Steady as she goes," she said quietly. There. The targeting cursor briefly touched the aiming point. She pressed the firing button. "Firing," she said as she did so. "Third target?"

"No chance," Bobby replied, not sounding so amused now. "They're past us and gone. We could fire off a bunch of rounds and maybe hit one and who knows what else."

"Your call."

"That it is," Bobby said with a crooked grin and a tilt of the head towards their control consoles. A reminder that this was all being recorded. "Check our results with our first two targets."

Katie did so. "Radar shows extensive damage to the engines of both targets," she said. "Neither is under acceleration. Target two has a slight tumble. Visuals show some slight gaseous content in a debris field surrounding it. No ongoing out-gassing. Target one is more intact according to radar, but visuals show a degree of ongoing out-gassing. Hope they got to their suits. Should have had time."

Bobby looked distracted. Likely on a separate channel to the *Resolute*. That was shortly confirmed. "*Resolute* says they'll send Boat Alpha with the marines to evacuate Bad Guy Two. We're to rendezvous with Bad Guy One, but not to board or let anyone transfer until the marines are available."

"Yes, sir."

It was all pretty anti-climactic from there on in.

Four of the six escaping ships had gotten away, though. One of them had been Guy Boucher's.

Katie didn't feel good about that.

\* \* \*

Katie was angry and frustrated. Katie was tired of being angry and frustrated. It achieved nothing useful. It was exhausting. It was off-putting to the people she needed to live with and get along with. It was also likely to lead to poor decisions. But all the same she was tired, angry, and frustrated.

"Calm down," Bobby, who was in the pilot's seat next to her, said. He smiled. "That's an order."

Katie couldn't help smiling back. Bobby was disgustingly laid back, but he was a genuinely nice guy too. She was becoming quite fond of him. "Yes, sir. Sorry, but I hated seeing those guys get away."

"Especially that Boucher guy," Bobby asked with comically raised eyebrows.

"Guy Boucher was logistics chief back on Ceres," Katie answered, more worried than angry now. "Head of the smuggling ring there. His son was a bully. Big, mean, and dumb. Guy wasn't so big, and he certainly wasn't dumb, but as smooth as he could be, I think he was plenty mean."

"Doesn't scare you, does he?" Bobby asked in a perfect schoolyard double dare tone.

"Guy Boucher concerns me," Katie answered, "because I'm not stupid. The man is dangerous and it seems he's got a grudge against me. That's not why I'm upset though."

Bobby was lining up for their final approach to the *Resolute*. Katie certainly didn't begrudge him a few moments to do that job right. Shortly, they were right on track. "No?"

Bobby asked.

"Nope. It's not even that so many of the bad guys got away."

"You shouldn't feel bad about that. We did well to get even one of them back there. We got two and pretty cleanly too. You kicked everything off perfectly and didn't make any mistakes later. You did good, Katie."

"Yeah, I guess so," Katie said. "You know people will pick at the decisions we made in split seconds with weeks and months to think about it."

"We did our jobs the best we could under the circumstances," Bobby answered. "That's what matters. There'll always be Monday morning quarterbacks."

One of the undeniable benefits of an Academy education for Katie was that she'd gained some familiarity with Americanisms. The Americans might deny it, but they still had disproportionate influence both at the Academy and in the Space Force. At least many of the other Earth born seemed to think so. They were all dirt huggers to Katie. But at least she understood what Bobby was saying. There'd always be those who'd criticize what you'd done in the heat of the moment at leisure afterwards.

"Okay," Katie replied. "But what really bugs me is that, having put constraints on us that made our job almost impossible, the Space Force will blame us for it not having worked out better."

Bobby sighed. "Both true and not useful. We live but to serve and sigh."

"Ha! And that's useful?"

"Yes, it's best not to worry about what you can't change. Accept it cheerfully. Look, you'll feel better about it once you've had some decent sleep."

"What do you want to bet they send me to Vesta with the marines pronto to clean things up?"

Bobby flinched. Answered that question. "Well, they'll probably want to give the marines a bit of a rest," he said with a crooked smile.

"There is that," Katie admitted. She was glad he was here to humor her. "I know you're right. Even if it's objectively not justified, it's best to be cheerful and accept the things I can't change in good humor."

"That's my girl."

"Thanks, Bobby."

\* \* \*

Ravi was tired. He was also pissed off, annoyed, and unhappy with the Space Force and the world in general. Oddly, he was also feeling more optimistic about the future than he had for years. Ravi wasn't that old. As far as he could remember, he'd been a dutiful kid rather than a happy one.

Maybe Ravi was feeling more optimistic than he'd ever had in his entire life.

Being genuinely responsible for something that had mattered in its own right and not just been another test had been a revelation.

Ravi had been a rule follower and a test taker his whole life. He'd been serious and competitive. It'd been what he'd been comfortable with. Ravi had set high standards and more often than not he'd met them.

It was convenient in a zero-sum world that other people often didn't. It had also been a source of ongoing frustration to him when he'd had to depend on the often inadequate efforts of such people.

Now he was thinking he'd had it all wrong.

Ravi had just spent the last few days running the Weapons Department himself in the midst of a serious, routine upsetting, crisis. The captain and the XO had told Lieutenant Novak, who normally held that responsibility, in no uncertain terms, that she was to leave it all to Ravi. Novak was to stand bridge watches and make sure she was well rested and alert for them. Period. That's all.

And so Ravi had got thrown in the deep end and discovered he liked the water.

Ravi was in the tiny Weapons Admin office right now. He was doing "paperwork" though there was precious little actual paper involved, thank heavens. Most of the last few days he'd spent down in the spindle with his senior techs, just waiting for the weapons systems to be called on and fail. Fail and need immediate intervention.

Fact was, that the Space Force rarely fired its weapons. Sad from a technical point of view, if good from a wider one. The incidents in which it'd done so for real could be numbered on the fingers of one hand.

Given that fact and the known problems with their

long-range missiles, Ravi had thought it a good idea to be prepared for the worst.

In the event, the *Resolute*'s weapons hadn't been called upon. That dubious honor had fallen to Boat Beta and SLT Maddox and ENS Kincaid.

Ravi didn't begrudge them that.

They'd done as well as could be expected given the circumstances. They'd stopped two out of six ships attempting to escape without killing anyone and without any collateral damage. Pretty impressive in Ravi's mind. Somehow, though, he felt sure it wouldn't stop the brass and the public from going over the whole thing with a fine-toothed comb and second-guessing everything the pair had done.

From Ravi's point of view it was also a relief that the smaller, less complicated railgun on the boat had operated as intended without any issues. He wasn't at all sure the same would have been true for the larger weapon the *Resolute* carried.

Ravi and his men had done everything possible to see the thing was in working order. Any failure wouldn't have been his fault, only his responsibility.

And it was that sense of real responsibility for something that mattered that had been the source of Ravi's epiphany.

Not just responsibility for the *Resolute*'s weapons working, but for the happiness and well-being of the men and women under his command.

It was true in some sense that he hadn't really done that much, and nothing that in substance Novak hadn't delegated to him at other times, but he'd been solely responsible this time.

Maybe having Miller at his side giving advice and pointing out things had helped him along to understanding that his decisions, and the way he presented them, had a real effect on the lives of genuine people. He was probably getting both too reliant on and too chummy with Miller. Ravi would have to watch the optics of that, but the man had been an invaluable help.

Ravi had long been frustrated that his sincere efforts didn't seem to be recognized. Now he realized he'd been something of a cargo-cult officer. Ravi had had the motions and forms of the job down without really understanding what he was doing.

Ravi still had a lot to learn, but at least now he realized that. It was a huge can of worms, to be sure. Part of the problem being that the Space Force was largely a cargo-cult Space Navy. The oldfashioned states of Earth did need an organization to keep the high ground of space from being used to undermine their autonomy. That was a real mission, but not one that was openly admitted.

The Space Force's ostensible mission was to be the core of a defense force once interstellar contact was fully made. It was one nobody really understood. The Space Force's centuries of tradition were largely inspired by a combination of science fiction and history.

No wonder it'd been so difficult trying to make practical sense of it.

Ironically, it left Ravi feeling some considerable sympathy for Kincaid. Kincaid had come into the Space Force as a practical spacer, albeit one who was barely out of childhood. She had acted like one. Like someone concerned with achieving real results. In fact, Ravi was convinced he owed her an apology over the incident with Able Spacer Jones. Ravi had been so concerned with not disappointing the captain and with preserving his own authority that he hadn't even realized he was endangering the man's safety.

It was a sort of mistake he was going to be careful to avoid in the future.

Unfortunately, at this point in time as much as he thought he ought to apologize to Kincaid, and as much as he'd like to talk to her about the nature of the Space Force and how to cope with it, neither was going to happen.

Ravi wasn't that much older than the girl, and he didn't outrank her by that much either. If they'd been peers in separate chains of command, there would have been no problem. Problem was that he was going to get her as a trainee. Kincaid was going to be in his chain of command.

Theoretically, he could call her in for a private purely off-the-record talk, give that apology, and discuss his new insight into the nature of being a Space Force officer. In practice, that idea was a non-starter.

Worse, in practice, neither he nor the other senior officers were in any place to step out of their assigned roles and cut her any slack. This mess at Vesta was going to come under profound scrutiny by SFHQ. That scrutiny would extend to the *Resolute*'s entire tour. Any deviations from Space Force orthodoxy were likely to meet with severe correction.

So as bad as he might feel about it privately, he wasn't going to be able to reduce the outrageous workload she'd been assigned. Ravi was going to have to demand adherence to the highest formal standard. There was going to be no being reasonable, realistic, or practical, and allowing her a little slack.

And he wouldn't be able to explain why either. There was an altogether too great a chance she'd put it all down to personal animosity and resent him because of it.

He wouldn't blame her.

He'd have been feeling sorry for himself about that.

Only there was no doubt at all that Kincaid was going to be getting the shorter end of the stick.

\* \* \*

Amy was feeling tired, but basically pleased with both herself and her people.

She'd just come from the main galley and was checking in with the stewards that took care of the wardroom. It'd been a chaotic last couple of days, but she'd managed to make sure that nobody lacked for anything they needed. Above all, nobody had missed regular, hot meals that were both nutritious and tasty. Served in comfortable and convivial settings at that. It made for good morale. Good morale made for an effective ship's company.

Amy was proud of what her people had managed.

Usually they had an established routine and a much smaller number of watch keepers to provide for. They'd had no warning when shore leave was canceled and the ship had gone to battle stations. But they'd risen to the occasion without complaint.

She'd already checked with the supply techs and the victualer, and all was well with them. Same with Med Bay and the main galley and the folks manning them. Now she was back at the wardroom. She was going to grab a cup of bitter caffeine and a hot meal herself and get some sack time.

First the stewards. She was in luck. She caught both of them, "Mama" Cruz and "Rob" Maric, in the little kiosk adjacent to the wardroom that was grandly named "The

Wardroom Auxiliary Galley". "Hi, guys. All's well?" Amy asked.

"Been busy. They've all been burning the midnight oil. Nothing we couldn't handle," Head Stewart LS Cruz answered. "I was just telling Rob here he should get some down time. Figure the worst of it's over, right?"

"Yep, looks like we've caught the bad guys or they've escaped," Amy replied. "Looks like they're all gone either way, and the governor is back in charge on Vesta."

"That's good, ma'am."

"Great, I'll just grab a coffee and bite and be on my way then."

Amy found the wardroom empty except for Katie Kincaid, who was staring at a coffee and meal of her own. Amy plumped herself down across from her friend. "Sounds like you did good," she said.

Katie nodded slowly. "Could have gone worse I imagine."

"A lot worse. Blockade's done, right?"

"Yep. Had to go to Vesta with the marines and read everyone the riot act."

"Problems?"

"Nope. Everyone was glad to have someone to tell them what to do. Still felt pretty tense for a while. Didn't know what to expect."

"So I can see you're tired, but you seem unhappy too."

"Nothing much could have done about it, but most of the bad guys got away. Not happy about that."

"Eat your food. Go get some sleep."

"Yes, mother."

"Looks to me like you could use a little mothering."

Katie looked up at Amy blearily. "Supposed to be able to handle this. Not sure I can."

"It'll look better after you've had some rest." Amy wasn't at all sure how true that was, but she had to try.

"Yes, ma'am."

"There's the spirit. Eat." Amy resolved to pay particular attention to her cabin mate's well-being for the next while. Somebody had to.

## 11: Katie, Just Suck It Up

The XO had come down to watch Katie and the marines train.

The mess on Vesta was now officially somebody else's problem. The *Resolute* was on its way to the Jovian system. Governor Porter was more or less back in control of Vesta. The *Renown*, one of the *Resolute*'s sister ships, was on its way from Earth to the asteroid accompanied by several corvettes and a full squadron of scout ships. It was carrying a full set of extra Space Force officers to replace those currently serving on Vesta.

Katie was pretty sure that no Space Force member currently serving on Vesta was going to escape with their careers undamaged. The careers of the officers in particular were done. Most of them had likely done nothing wrong. So it certainly wasn't fair. Only if Katie was right, it was never going to be possible to fully untangle what had happened on Vesta. And that was assuming that the powers that be didn't try to deep six the whole event out of embarrassment. So there was no hope any officer who'd been posted to Vesta for the last few years would ever be free of a taint of suspicion. There'd always be questions about their integrity. They wouldn't be given positions of importance or trust.

Completely unfair to most of them.

Right now, however, Katie was more concerned about how unfair the whole thing was proving to her.

The training schedule she'd been assigned prior to the *Resolute*'s arrival had already been too much. Realistically, she could see that now. Katie's additional duties as a pilot and with the marines were more than the straw that was breaking the camel's back. They were a whole extra load. The proverbial camel was being crushed.

Katie was desperately hoping the XO was down here to tell her that her responsibilities were being cut back to something bearable.

As soon as Sergeant Suvorov signaled their latest exercise was done and they could all take a break, Katie made her way over to the XO's vantage point.

"Sir?" she asked, throwing him a quick salute. Not technically necessary, but an entirely acceptable military courtesy. See, Katie could be political and butter her superiors up if need be.

"Ensign Kincaid," the XO replied, returning her salute. He gave her a bleak smile. The XO didn't seem angry with her. He did seem very tired. It occurred to Katie she wasn't the only one who'd been tossed into the deep end by recent events.

"Anything I can do for you, sir?"

"Well, for one you can pass on my appreciation for their performance to Sergeant Suvorov and his marines."

"Gladly, sir."

"I'd do so myself, but I want to cement your position as their leader."

Katie was surprised by that. Katie was certain the XO had only intended her as a legal placeholder. She was pleased she'd managed to be more. Even more pleased the XO recognized that. Katie was also concerned by the implication he was planning to leave her in the marine command role. What effect was this going to have on the training plan she'd been assigned? "Thank you, sir," she said.

The XO's smile widened and thinned. Katie recognized the expression as grim amusement. "You did well. I'm impressed and so was the captain. I'm afraid your reward for doing well at a series of difficult tasks is going to be getting more of them."

What could Katie say? "Yes, sir."

Whether the XO heard her reservations in her voice or already understood the predicament he'd placed her in, Katie didn't know. In either case, he answered the question Katie hadn't asked. "And, no, Ensign, I'm afraid I'm not going to be able to relax your training schedule or even relieve you of any of your other tasks."

"Sir?" She might as well hear his reasons for this disturbing decision before trying to make her case.

The XO sighed and shifted his hold on the nearby bulkhead. Whatever his thinking, he didn't appear happy about what he was telling her. "I wasn't kidding you when I said I was soft for an XO. Too soft. Also believe it or not, I'm on your side politically. I'm well known as belonging to the faction that believes in your grandmother's vision for the Space Force."

As a mere ensign, Katie hadn't concerned herself with the internal politics of the Space Force. Katie's grandmother hadn't forced them upon her either. Katie had known that sooner or later that would have to change, but for the next few years she'd figured she could just concentrate on being the best young officer she could. "Haven't really thought much about politics, sir," she said. "Figure they're a bit over my pay grade."

The XO's smile became much thinner and significantly sadder. It almost disappeared. His eyes bored into her. The XO seemed to be mentally weighing her in the balance. He finally relented, running a hand through his hair. "In an ideal world, none of us would need to worry about politics."

"But we don't live in an ideal world, sir?"

"That's correct, Ensign. And ours is looking a great deal less than ideal." The XO stared past Katie at the marines who were just beyond earshot and carefully pretending to ignore the two officers. Whatever he had to say, he didn't want to share.

"My grandmother has been clear about need-to-know and discretion, sir."

"That's good. I'm guessing she hasn't been overly pressing about her vision for the Space Force or the politics of getting it accepted, that right?"

Katie thought about her conversations with her grandmother during what she'd viewed as vacations. "I guess so. She hasn't really tried to press her particular vision on me. I already thought the main concern of the Space Force ought to be how we'll handle the rest of the galaxy once we get into full contact with them. My grandmother didn't have to convince me of that. As for the politics, like I said, sir, it's above my pay grade. I might have seemed arrogant, I guess I really was, but I'm not presumptuous enough to think an ensign ought to be second-guessing Space Force policy. I've got a lot to learn first, sir. I know that."

The XO smiled. "Good to hear. You need to at least seem humble at times. Only I'm afraid events have wrong-footed both of us."

That felt generally right to Katie. When she tried to think what the XO meant specifically her imagination failed her. Katie licked her lips. This was awkward. Suddenly she understood why he was holding this conversation where nobody could overhear them, and nobody, especially the rest of the officers, could see their interaction. This conversation was not entirely appropriate. The XO was going out on a bit of a limb to explain to her. "Exactly how, sir?" she asked, hoping she was right and wasn't being too bold.

"Given your origins and who your grandmother is, you're either doubly cursed or blessed depending on how you want to look at it. What you aren't and can't be, is completely apolitical. Your very existence as a Space Force officer is a political football. Whether you like it or not, both people off of Earth and the faction of Space Force officers who bought into your grandmother's vision are going to see you as the standard bearer for their hopes. At best, the Earth firsters, and the *'the Space Force should be a police force devoid of visions of grandeur'* people are going to see you as a pawn in the hands of their political opponents. You might not be interested in politics, but politics is interested in you."

Katie frowned. Katie was sure that the whole point of the training schedule the XO had foisted upon her had been to teach her some humility. How did this square with her being politically important? "I think I understand what you're saying, but I don't understand what I can do about it. As a junior officer, I don't see what I can do other than try to do my job to the best of my ability."

The XO smiled. Katie supposed it was better than open hostility, but she was really beginning to hate those smiles. They always seemed to signal some irony that was only amusing if you weren't sitting at ground zero of the contradiction. "Normally on one of these cruises we'd have had a lot of freedom to do things our own way. The brass would have been happy to forget about us for the year we'd be gone showing the flag in the outer system."

"But not after what just happened at Vesta. That's an issue, sir?"

"It certainly is, Ensign. I'd hoped that the training program I'd assigned you would teach you a little humility and deference to authority without the need of putting a reprimand on your record."

"That hasn't worked?" Katie asked. Then she felt a rush of indignation. "You know it was a matter of safety, sir?"

"I'm aware, Ensign," the XO replied grimly. "I'm also aware, as you should be, that in a trade-off between a small risk to a lowly spacer and the preservation of good order and discipline the powers that be in the Space Force will come down on the side of good order and discipline. They prefer not to make that preference explicitly clear to the public, but that is the case. You should never forget it."

Katie's indignation started to morph into outright anger. If what the XO said was true, had her choice in careers, her whole life plan, been a terrible mistake? That was a truly depressing thought. Depression wasn't useful, though. Anger was not appropriate. Katie choked down her feelings. "I appreciate the effort, sir."

"That's nice, because my fudge didn't work out. Not after Vesta, it hasn't. Everything that happens on this trip, every decision we make is now going to be subject to critical scrutiny."

Katie could see that. Anything out of the ordinary, anything that needed to be explained was going to be questioned. The XO was saying that whatever his personal feelings, he didn't have much room to maneuver anymore. He was, in effect, apologizing to the greatest degree he could. Not a good sign that he felt the need. "Ouch. Sir?"

"Good. Complaining would only make it worse. I'm glad to see you can learn, Kincaid. You've got a choice to make. You make the choice I expect you will and stay the course and you're facing a truly steep learning curve. Alternatively, you can formally request that I release you from having to complete the training program I gave you if you wish. If you do so, I will."

"Thank you, sir."

"Not so quick. You want command, right?"

"Yes, sir."

"You bail on the training plan and maybe, just maybe, that won't kill your chances at command. After all, the circumstances are extraordinary and you did do well on Vesta. Only not everyone will see it that way, and promoting you to real responsibility was going to be controversial anyhow. Show any hint of weakness and you'll be giving your enemies ammunition against you. Both they and your own would-be supporters will tend to see you as a weak reed. You'd probably get plum technical assignments that sound impressive, but you'd probably not get real command responsibility. Do you follow me?"

Katie did. Katie didn't like what he was saying, but she understood it. She wanted to complain that it wasn't fair. It would be less than helpful to do so. "Yes, sir. I do, sir."

"On the other hand, it may have been hard, but so far you've managed to hit all your training benchmarks. You've also done good work as a pilot and with the marines. Some people will debate that, but most will understand it that way. If you can keep up the good work and nothing goes sideways when we reach Jupiter, then you can expect to be seen as a rising young star on the command track."

"I'd like that, sir. What are the chances of problems in the Jovian system?"

The XO grimaced. "We're not sure, but I'd say high. Most of our escapee smugglers seem to have gone that way. Callisto Base is a Space Force installation and I'm fairly confident we won't have problems there. Ganymede, on the other hand, we've never paid much attention to. It's mostly a science station, there's ice mining and some other commercial activity, but if the scientists weren't paying to keep the base active it likely wouldn't be worthwhile. I have a bad feeling that once we take a closer look, we're going to find all sorts of things we won't like."

"I see, sir. You might need the marines and the boats again. Also you might have to go to battle stations again and you won't want untried junior officers on watch."

"Exactly, Ensign. I'm glad you understand. I hope you also

understand that I need your decision some weeks before we get to Jupiter. I want time for everyone to settle into their assigned roles. I know you're tired. You should sleep on this. Having done that, I'd like your decision as soon as possible. Two weeks max."

"Yes, sir. I'll sleep on it and get back to you as soon as possible. Can I ask for advice from others?"

The XO made yet another unhappy face. "Very discreetly, if at all. I want this all to be as discreet as possible. You are not to share the details of this conversation with anyone."

"Yes, sir."

"Any more questions?"

"No, sir."

"Good. Later, Ensign." With that, the XO spun and took off down the spindle towards the gravity ring lifts.

Katie took a deep breath and tried to absorb what she'd just heard. It made her head spin. Katie had already felt tired, and now she felt like she had the weight of the world on her shoulders.

"Ma'am, we can finish the exercises without you."

Katie looked up to see Sergeant Suvorov before her. Great, she had her head so far up her butt that she was losing situational awareness. "Do you think that's a good idea, Sergeant?"

"Yes, ma'am. I don't know what you and the XO were talking about, but it looks like he left you a lot to think about. And, forgive me for saying so, ma'am, but you already needed a break. It's difficult, but after all the up time you've had, you've got to slow down and recharge your batteries."

"Very well, Sergeant," Katie replied. Katie smiled. "On due consideration, I believe I'll retire to my cabin and other duties. Please, carry on with the training exercise. If I understood the XO, we may need to secure a moon base once we arrive at Jupiter. Please don't repeat that."

The sergeant looked at her with concern. Right, she should have known there was no need to caution him about discretion. "Yes, ma'am." He saluted and moved quickly back to his waiting charges. They'd been rather ostentatiously ignoring the byplay between their bosses.

Katie wasn't sure if she was more amused or alarmed at the whole charade. She really did need to get some rest. Katie started picking her way back to her cabin.

Katie had no good choices as far as she could tell.

Damned if she did, damned if she didn't, it seemed to her.

Maybe it'd look different after a solid nap.

Somehow she doubted it.

*** 

The *Resolute* was cruising. Gone ballistic on the long trajectory out to Jupiter and her moons. Her crew was cruising too. Relaxing and recovering from the stress of the events back at Vesta.

Katie had got a good ten hours of solid, continuous sleep. It felt odd.

It was a sign of just how tired she'd been that she'd slept through the set of maneuvers involved in the *Resolute*'s burn for Jupiter. She'd always prided herself on being alert to any major change to a ship's state. Not this time. She'd been completely oblivious.

Katie had woken to find herself ravenous, and the *Resolute* stood down to a relaxed state. The XO had decided the ship's crew needed a rest after being stood up for the events at Vesta. He'd stopped short of ordering every crew member not actually on watch to stand down, go to their rack, and sleep. What he wanted was pretty clear for all that.

Katie had made her way through something like a ghost ship to a wardroom that was practically empty. Even the stewards were missing. They'd left out a large buffet and a collection of pre-prepared meals that could be heated up. The only other person in the wardroom had been Amy, who was heads down at a table in the corner, apparently going over a collection of figures on her personal computing device.

Katie had just nodded at her on her way to pile up a plate at the buffet. Amy had just absentmindedly nodded back.

Katie inhaled half the food on her plate before pausing to contemplate it all. Checked her device and found the XO's orders. Noted that it'd be a day and a half before she could hope to get started on whittling down the pile of tasks she faced. Some more study on weapons and operations might be possible, but she felt she was already into diminishing returns on that front. Might be better just to get the rest the XO had recommended.

"Feeling better?" Amy asked. She must have finished

whatever she was doing.

Katie gestured at Amy to sit down. "Physically. A bit discombobulated. Been on the go so long that it feels weird to not be rushed."

Amy sitting down leaned forward and peered into Katie's face. "Hmm, you do look better. Starting to wear some dark circles into that baby fat under your eyes, though. Wonder if you're ever going to be the chipper young thing you were when we first met again."

Katie snorted. "Never thought of myself as a chipper young thing ever."

"Maybe you should start."

Katie blinked. It was unusual for Amy to be so blunt. Even in jest, Amy wasn't one to be pointed. "Being optimistic is good. Even when it's not completely realistic. I know that. That's not exactly the same as being chipper. Being chipper can be annoying. At least it always seemed to annoy my mother."

"You always agreed with everything your mother thought?"

Katie half gagged, half giggled. No, she'd certainly not always agreed with her mother. Not that they'd indulged in open conflict. You can't have that on a small ship with a tiny crew where it's impossible to avoid each other for months on end. "No, we didn't always agree."

"Didn't think so," Amy said. "Seriously, Katie, in circumstances you can't completely control, it's easy to get depressed. You don't want to get all uptight like Shankar either, do you?"

"No, but I don't think I'm that bad."

"It's a slippery slope. Anyhow, you are feeling better, right?"

"Yeah, but I've got a whole lot of work to do to qualify in operations and weapons, and I have to train with the marines, and I have to hold down a pilot's slot. I think I need to clone myself. Missed my chance to get some bridge watches in during actual maneuvers while at Vesta too."

Amy looked pensive. "Vesta was a surprise all around. You have any idea what we can expect at Callisto and Ganymede?"

Yes, Katie did, and she'd also been warned not to discuss it. Katie smirked. "I don't know anything I can discuss," she said. "Furthermore, I can neither confirm nor deny your speculation that we may expect surprises in the Jovian system."

Amy smirked back. "Well, thanks for your non-information you didn't share with me. I'll be careful not to be obvious about any preparations I make."

"Thanks."

"I'm guessing you're worried you won't get the bridge time you need to stay on the command track."

"You'd guess right."

"It's not going to be easy, Katie, but you never wanted easy anyway, did you?"

"No, but not so hard I couldn't handle it either. I know my career isn't the most important thing at stake here, but it is important to me and I'm worried about it. I like to plan so I can be in control of things. Don't know what to expect. I have no plan. I'm not in control, and I'm not happy right now."

"You've done okay so far. Trust yourself. Keep plodding. Accept you'll never know everything you'd like to, or have a perfect plan. Don't worry, be happy. You'll cope better that way."

"That does seem to work for you."

"I've been thinking, too. It has, but I've been coasting. I've stayed too far inside my comfort zone and not pushed myself enough. Just bobbed along like a cork on top of the waves of events. The opposite of you."

"Yeah, I get these ideas and want to make the whole world go according to plan."

"Never going to happen, but doesn't mean you can't keep yourself ready to give it the odd nudge now and again."

Katie nodded. Amy hadn't really told her anything she didn't already know, but somehow she'd made it easier for Katie to face the future. She didn't feel so much like giving up anymore. Curling up in a corner and dying didn't seem as appealing as it had scant hours before. "Makes sense. Lots of sleep, some food, and a little helpful advice, and it doesn't seem quite so hopeless."

"Good. You're going to have to try to get as much signed off as possible before Jupiter. Pace yourself, but no slacking. Not because of some delusion that it's hopeless or for any other reason. Understood?"

Katie grinned wanly. "Yes, ma'am."

"Good."

\*\*\*

Iris was briefing Kincaid in the Ready Room. Katie was pushing her limits regarding her allowed time in low or zero gee Given her other workloads, especially the training time she needed to spend with the marines, Iris was trying to go as light on Katie as she could with regarding her duties as a boat pilot.

The Ready Room was Boat Ops' main space that resided in the gravity ring. It wasn't currently being used by anyone that needed to rest, and it had pretty good facilities for giving briefings and even provided a mild form of virtual reality for simulating boat operations. Not as good as the simulation mode of the boats themselves, let alone actual flight, but good enough to count as partial credit towards maintaining one's pilot qualification.

Iris was pleased to see her youngest pilot wasn't looking quite as thinly stretched as she had during their time at Vesta. Not that she didn't look a lot more worn than the young woman that had first boarded the *Resolute* a few months ago.

Much more worn than the young teenager Iris remembered from Ceres. There'd been a bounce there that was simply missing now.

There were faint dark lines spreading down from the corner of the young woman's eyes instead. Not a good trade. It made Iris sad.

"It's too bad about Lieutenant Wong," Katie was saying as she studied the proposed training schedule Iris had given her. They'd left Wong behind at Vesta. Wong had been beaten so badly that he'd be recovering for months yet. Recovering in some place with proper medical facilities and professionals if he was to have any hope of doing so fully.

"Even more unfortunate we couldn't draft anyone from Vesta to make up for the fact we're now short of pilots, especially if we end up facing another period of high tempo operations in the Jovian system." Iris knew she should be feeling more sympathy for Oswald Wong, but she had her own problems.

Kincaid flinched. "We're stretched pretty thin, aren't we?"

"We are. They simply didn't anticipate the demands we'd face when they designed these frigates. We didn't really have enough boats or pilots for something like Vesta even before we lost Oswald."

Kincaid looked up at Iris wide eyed. "You know I did talk some with my grandmother about the Space Force. Particularly about purely technical issues of design that didn't seem all that political. They were thinking of only having a single smaller shuttle and improved docking facilities on the Renown class at first. The civilian designers and politicians thought two full sized boats were a boondoggle as it was."

"But your grandmother and most every other Space Force officer with any real experience insisted on a couple of real boats. Thank heavens. Space Force does manage to get things right sometimes."

Katie grimaced. Iris knew the girl hated negativity. Sometimes you just had to face facts, though. Katie must have realized her feelings were showing on her face. The look vanished as quickly as it had come. "You know, even without all the politics, it's not an easy task we have. I think after this they'll be looking at adding a couple more boat bays to the next design. It's been a major learning experience. Maybe they'll even revive the idea of aircraft carriers in space."

Iris shook her head. "They'd have to drop the prohibition against using small craft in deep space. Hard to see that."

Katie bit her lip and thought about that. "Don't know. Sometimes even having gone to the Academy, I wish I was more plugged into how the senior officer corps thinks."

"Would have thought your grandmother would have helped with that."

"I don't know how typical she is."

"There is that. She is rather unique. So, to get back to the here and now. What do you think of your schedule? I did my best to not cut too much into your zero gee time, but there is only so much I can do. Even if it didn't look like I'm going to need you fully up to snuff when we reach Jupiter, there are hard criteria for a pilot to remain qualified on boats. We can't fudge those."

Katie nodded. "I appreciate that. Thanks. It's going to be tough. If we don't get any more nasty surprises, I think I can handle it. Probably. The XO isn't so sure. He says he'll let me have a reduced training schedule if I want, but it'd severely impact my chances of progressing on the command track. He doesn't want that spread around by the way. I want to go command, but I don't want to mess up because I bit off more than I can chew. What do you think?"

Iris was heartbroken to see the desperate look of someone who felt trapped in Katie's eyes. The girl's invincible optimism had always been one of her more attractive traits. Didn't mean Iris was going to soft pedal the truth. "You've been lucky so far. I know it's been hard work, but you've been lucky, too. The smart thing would be to cut your losses and specialize in Boats or something like me. They're simply not going to make command an easy option for you."

"Be better for you too, wouldn't it?"

"It'd be better for Boat Ops. Personally, I'd really like to see it work out for you. But your burning of the candle at both ends is a potential problem. If you're focused on weapons, ops, and bridge ops and tired out from juggling too much, you're not going to be as sharp as both me and the marines need you to be. That's a real issue."

"I've managed so far."

"Yes, and like I said, you've been lucky. Maybe you can stumble through to the end of this on sheer perseverance if we don't get more surprises. But ..."

"We're expecting surprises."

"Right. And they could be very problematic. Look, Katie, I'm not going to twist your arm here, but if you don't do something about your workload, you're trusting to dumb luck to make it through."

"Not fate or destiny or anything?"

"You can call it what you like, I call it dumb luck."

"Ouch."

"Your call. Be warned, if you don't look like you're managing to handle it, if your reaction times slip, or you miss your assigned times exercising, then I'll go to the XO myself about it. We need you here on boats. We need you able to do the job."

"Yes, ma'am. I understand."

"Good. Sorry, but we have a job to do."

\* \* \*

Katie and Lieutenant (Senior Grade) Haralson had the ship's briefing room to themselves. Haralson was both the *Resolute*'s ops officer and her designated training officer. Katie was finding he was a really great guy. Smart as all hell, but not full of himself. Always polite and possessed of a gentle but subtly penetrating humor. Infectiously enthusiastic too.

Enthusiastic about both physics and history, which was amazing. Made sense in the context of spaceship combat operations, though. Katie was beside herself with glee. It was exactly the sort of thing she'd dreamed of being immersed in as a young girl wanting to join the Space Force and make a difference. With a guilty twinge, she couldn't help thinking how jealous Amy would be of the quality time she was getting with the ever so attractive Lieutenant Thor Haralson.

Said individual sighed with regret. "This is all so fascinating, but also not what we're here for."

Katie didn't exactly crash back to Earth. Earth was some hundreds of millions of kilometers away. She crashed back to reality. Reality being that the tin can she was living in was due to arrive in the vicinity of Jupiter in a few weeks and that before that happened she had a lot to do. Most of the training involved in qualifying for weapons, ops, and several bridge stations in fact. The ship wasn't likely to have much time to accommodate her training needs. She had to be prepared to seize what opportunities came up. Also, much sooner than that, she was going to have to render a decision to the XO.

A decision about whether she'd accept a reduced, more manageable training schedule, but one that might cost her chance at ship command, or whether she'd gamble both on her own ability to handle an inhuman workload and the ship's ability to accommodate her.

Katie tried to smile despite not feeling so happy anymore. "Yeah, I know. It was nice not to be worried about ticking off some training goal or answering some formulaic question for a change. I like studying, but I'm feeling like some sort of goose that's being force fed. I'm starting to gag on all the answers I'm supposed to memorize."

Haralson nodded. He didn't speak right away. He seemed to be picking his words very carefully. "The course of study you and the XO have agreed on is less than ideal. It's not necessarily the one I would have settled on as Training Officer if it'd been entirely up to me."

Between her own hubris and the XO's missteps, Katie was in an awkward place. Katie knew the XO wanted to keep just how badly off of the record, but she also wanted to play it straight with Haralson. "The XO has informally indicated to me that he'll give me a reduced training workload if I ask for it within a week from now."

"Nice to be kept in the loop." Haralson might be a nice guy. Didn't mean he didn't have feelings. "Did he make it clear how fishy it'd look?"

Katie felt bad. She took a deep breath. "Yes. I guess Vesta not only gave us all more to do, it means a lot of extra scrutiny by high command too. He thought they'd probably have enough doubts because of the whole mess and my failure to cope with the workload I accepted, that it'd probably mean no chance of ever getting ship command."

Haralson nodded his head ruefully. "All too true. Did he also mention that your chances of ship command aren't very good, anyway? Nothing to do with you at all. We don't like to discourage ambitious young officers, but there just aren't that many command slots to go around."

"About three dozen scouts, and just over two dozen larger ships."

"That's right. Most young officers are glad to get scout command for a year or two. That's enough to establish a solid career for those that don't get out and go into politics of some sort."

"That always bothered me about the Academy. The cadets weren't that bad, but from what they said, the people running the Space Force are more into Earth politics than being an effective military force."

Haralson made an act of puffing his cheeks out. Katie saw that he was trying to lighten the impact of what he had to say. "You know the history. When has military force not been about politics? Constitutionally, serving military members are supposed to stay out of domestic politics, but it's always political. Most of that's above my pay grade, let alone yours, so we're not going to discuss it. However, you have to understand that getting ship command is political."

"It's not about being the best commander possible?"

"It's about both. And you're doubly handicapped."

Katie had hoped to get some career advice from Haralson, but this wasn't sounding good. "Okay?"

"Use what you know about history. Don't think just about ship's captains back in Napoleonic times, think about fighter pilots a century and half or so later."

Katie thought she saw where Haralson was going with this. "Or submarine captains once they were nuclear armed too? You've got a very few men. They were all men back then, weren't they? Anyways just a very few people and the fates of whole nations, even the world rested on them. *'Never in the history of human conflict was so much owed by so many to so few.'*"

"You've got the idea." Haralson looked thoughtful. "Churchill might have been exaggerating for effect in one respect. I think that might be something that happens over and over, that a few people in a critical place and time determine the fates of a much larger number of people. That's off topic, though. Key thing is that ship command in the Space Force falls into the category. It's not something conferred lightly. Also, we've learned the hard way from history and our own experience that we don't dare cycle people through the command slots too quickly. Not with the larger ships anyway."

"How so?"

"It takes time for commanders to get to know their people and their jobs and show what they can do. Takes time for their crews to settle in and meld into effective teams too. Move people around too much and they don't get to learn their jobs or how to work with each other properly."

"Okay, that seems like common sense."

"Maybe, but it's also very inconvenient. Means at any given time there are only a few dozen people who've ever had ship command in the Space Force. Of the entire human race there are, at any given time, little more than a couple of hundred individuals who've commanded a military space ship."

"And yet the fate of the whole human race could depend on them."

"And you can be damned sure they're chosen very carefully indeed."

"Not just for competence?"

"That's a prerequisite. It's necessary, but not sufficient. Above all, a captain in the Space Force has to be trustworthy. Both in temperament and politically. A captain might have to make critical decisions without much time or information. They have to be people who won't crack or go off the rails under extreme pressure. Also, they have to be people who are reliable in the first place. A single captain has the power to wipe out cities and the population of whole regions on Earth. Not something anyone is eager to remind the public on Earth about, but not something the board assigning ship command ever forgets either."

"Wow. I guess I knew all that, but I never looked at it quite so starkly."

"So you can see how Space Force command might not want to give ship command to anyone whose judgment or politics were suspect."

Katie did. It gave her a hollow feeling in her gut. "So the slightest doubt, and they're going to go with better safe than sorry."

"They're not going to take any chances. Quite reasonably."

Katie couldn't help feeling the law of unintended consequences was coming into force. "Also means anybody who's a little bit different or inclined to thinking outside of the box isn't going to have too much of a chance."

"It's a conundrum. Anyhow, enough philosophy, the point is ship command was always going to be a stretch. You shouldn't feel too bad about that. If you don't overstretch yourself, you can still have a very good solid career in the Space Force. You've proven yourself adept at engineering. Lieutenant Sarkis thought you did well in Supply, and that's important if not glamorous work. I suspect from what I've seen of a very energetic and competent young woman that you can do most jobs on a ship. Do them better than most. I think you'd probably make a good Ops Officer and be outstanding influencing policy from staff positions. The fact that you're a bit of an anomaly in personality and background shouldn't handicap you much in such roles."

"Just if I want ship command."

"Exactly. I suggest, Ensign Kincaid, that you take the XO up on his offer. Sounds like he's gone out on a limb to be fair to you. Take the bird in hand and don't go beating the bushes for a bird that might not even be there."

"That's a twisted metaphor, sir."

"You get my point, think about it."

"Yes, sir."

## 12: Katie, You've a Lot to Learn

Amy was in the cabin she shared with Katie Kincaid. For a change, she was getting to see Katie awake. It'd been crazy back at Vesta, and they'd almost never been in the cabin and awake at the same time. Now, a week out of Vesta on the way to Jupiter, things were getting back to something resembling normal.

Well, normal for everyone but Katie. Katie's normal didn't seem to be anything like anyone else's normal.

Amy had a thick sheaf of hardcopy with a set of questions Katie had printed off.

Katie was studying. Amy was trying to help.

Amy thumbed through the thick sheaf of paper and picked a question. "What is a Renown class frigate's longest ranged weapons system and under what conditions would it be used?"

"The long-range missiles of a frigate have the greatest effective range. They can reach out thousands of kilometers and then adjust for the fact their targets aren't where predicted any longer. Railgun rounds can do damage at vast distances, but cannot obtain effective fire control solutions for anything that's not static except at short range. The long-range missiles have large, very destructive warheads and are to be used to destroy, even annihilate, targets that pose a threat to civilian populations. In a hypothetical combat with other armed vessels, they'd be used to soften up opposing targets and to confuse their firing solutions."

"That's right," Amy said.

"Certainly found out about the limitations of railguns back at Vesta," Katie said. "A little less hypothetical than some of the questions on those sheets."

Amy ruffled the sheets in question. Questions? How many questions were on them exactly? She tried to guess how many A dozen questions per sheet and over a hundred sheets easily. Five minutes a question and they'd be here an hour for each piece of paper. Amy hadn't thought it through before, and suddenly it occurred to her that neither had Katie. She must be as tired as she looked. This was simple arithmetic. "You realize we could be here a week and not get finished all these?"

Katie looked blank and then blushed. "Maybe I didn't think this through," she admitted, "but I do need to know the answers to all those questions. It helps in remembering them to have someone else ask me them."

"Didn't you mention something about having to make a decision about how much of this you can handle within the next week?"

"Don't think I said anything specific. It's a bit sensitive. I messed up trying to do so much."

"Yeah, and that was before Vesta."

Katie looked sick. "Yep."

"You did well. You've done well at everything you've had time for. Only you've heaped far too much on your plate for any one human being to handle."

"I don't think there's anything in my training schedule I can't do."

"No one thing. Katie, seriously, I think you can do anything you want. What you can't do is everything. You have to set priorities. You've got to go to Haralson or the XO or whoever has the power to change what you're assigned." Amy had a good idea it was the XO, but that neither Katie nor he wanted their little game of chicken to go on the public record. "You've got to ask them for a more reasonable workload. This isn't reasonable."

Katie sighed. "Maybe not, but I said I could do it so I have to try."

"Katie, do you try to be reasonable with other people?"

"Of course, I do."

"Good. You should be reasonable with yourself too. You're tough, you're smart, kind of, and you're willing to work hard. You're also only human, and there's only so many hours in a day. Be reasonable."

"I promise I'll think about it."

"Please do."

"Next question?"

Amy sighed. "What is the purpose of watch keepers on the bridge making regular reports even when nothing has changed?" she asked.

As usual, Katie's answer was by the book.

Maybe she really could handle it.

Amy had her doubts.

\* \* \*

Iris had a headache. Multiple problems were contributing to it.

It was over a week after Vesta and Iris was finally getting the "Boats and Bays" post action inspection done. Iris had figured giving her people some rest and getting a training regime set up was more important. She didn't imagine her flight engineers minded the extra time to get everything in order either.

The inspection was mandatory. It was also picky in ways that made no sense. It was unnecessarily time-consuming. Iris figured some staff puke who'd put in the bare minimum of time actually working on boats must have composed it. Whoever it'd been had thrown in everything but the kitchen sink. Iris was sure if there'd been a sink in the vicinity she'd be looking at instructions to inspect it for being watertight, not having chips or dents, having the correct capacity, being clean, and clear of a long list of stains and crud. Her imagined staff puke would have been determined to leave nothing off of the list and not at all concerned about the practicality of actually using it.

Didn't matter. Iris hated paperwork and administrative overhead. All she'd ever really wanted was to be a pilot. She'd never hungered for command. Iris had no desire to organize people or give them orders. Only it was her job now. It was her job to make sure Boat Ops was ready for whatever they were going to face at Jupiter. Iris was determined to do that job to the best of her ability.

SLT Bobby Maddox made a noise in his throat.

It reminded Iris that a time-consuming formal inspection was the least of her problems. She glared at Bobby.

"Don't blame me," Bobby said. "Whatever's bugging you, it's not my fault. You want to get this over with, right?"

Iris guessed they must have been floating in the big airlock giving entry to the starboard boat bay for some minutes now. Bobby was right to give her a bit of a nudge. It wasn't his fault she was feeling overwhelmed. It wasn't his fault that he and not Zhang was here as commander of Boat Beta. Didn't stop either of those things from being irritating, but it wasn't Bobby's fault. "I'm not. I'm just annoyed at the entire situation. Also, this is a good opportunity for us to talk things over. I want us to be as ready as possible for whatever we're asked to do when we reach Jupiter as possible. A little advice might be helpful."

Bobby nodded. Zero gee could make body language a bit awkward, so he did so carefully. "Dumped us in the deep end, didn't they? You in particular."

"True, but it's our job to cope with it. That's why they pay us the big bucks."

Bobby smirked at the hoary old joke. "Maybe we can take this slow and careful and talk about it between list items. I'm guessing me being here and not Lieutenant Zhang is one issue. Let's get that out of the way."

Iris nodded and pulled herself into the Boat Bay. She stationed herself to the side of the Emergency Medical Station just outside of the airlock. Bobby took the opposite side. "First off, you and Kincaid did a great job back at Vesta. You make a good team," she said to him.

Bobby smirked again. Somehow, maybe because he didn't seem to take himself too seriously, it wasn't annoying. Good that something wasn't. "Only I'm a mere sub-lieutenant and Myleen is a lieutenant. It doesn't look good for her that you passed her over for boat command. Doesn't look good for you either unless you have some good reason for it."

"Myleen is too much like me. Myleen wants to fly, not order folks around. And she's not a grumpy old woman who's figured out over the years that sometimes you just have to be pragmatic and bang people into place."

Bobby grinned. "Ouch."

"Yep. If need be."

For a change, Bobby looked serious. "Doesn't help that

Kincaid's the exact opposite. She's always got a plan, and she's always eager to tell everybody what it is."

"Put those two together and Kincaid is likely to take charge without either of them noticing it's happening. That could be a problem."

"So you give Myleen command of Alpha with me as her co-pilot and take Kincaid on as your co-pilot on Beta?"

"Probably work, but I don't think it'd be optimal. I think I'm going to rotate us all through the various positions as a training exercise for the simulations and when we reach Jupiter, it's going to just happen that we're in the same teams as at Vesta."

"So it all looks proper on paper, but we get the teams we know work?"

"Exactly."

Bobby nodded. Iris knew he knew it was a little dodgy. "Ought to work. We're not going to get the zero gee simulator time on the boats we want are we?"

Iris sighed. "Let's go through the list of medical supplies."

"Don't forget to check the cabinet is properly secured, in proper shape, and the lid opens and closes easily as it should."

Iris threw a mock glare his way. "It is a very thorough list, isn't it?"

"It is."

Iris had a little time to think as they went through the formalities. The medical cabinet done, they moved on to the fire station on the other side of the airlock. Iris reached the conclusion there was no good way to say what she needed to. "Kincaid's the problem."

Bobby fidgeted with the fittings that held some fire extinguishers in place. "Katie's not bad people. It's not her fault."

"No, but she's green as a pilot and we only have her as a very part-time one. It's bad enough the marine training is cutting her zero gee quota, but the rest of it is worse."

Bobby inspected the manual overrides to the automatic fire suppression system pensively. "Yeah, not only is she studying for Ops, weapons, and several bridge position qualification exams, but they're going to require actual time first shadowing watch keepers and then actually doing at least a few watches herself."

Iris pushed a bright red button labeled "Warning Test". A loud hooting horn, bright flashing lights, and an urgent repeating message bellowing over all of it resulted. It stopped when she released the button.

"Wow. Can't see anyone ignoring that," Bobby exclaimed.

"Get caught in here when the suppression system goes off and you're a goner," Iris replied. "They'll sacrifice crew members to save the ship if they have to."

"So, Kincaid?"

"It's a problem. If we had her full time, we could all train together intensively. That'd be best. Only we don't for reasons we can't change and neither can she."

Bobby frowned. They both knew that wasn't entirely true. Katie could free up some training time, most likely at some cost to her career prospects. It made no sense, but it was the way it was. "Have you thought of going to the XO and asking him to relieve her of her other training responsibilities?"

"I have. Only the marine thing is pretty much baked in and I'm not willing to torpedo Kincaid's career so that she can get some more, maybe only marginally useful, simulator time even if it'd make me feel better."

"That's decent of you."

"Don't worry, Bobby, if it turns out that I have a choice between what the mission requires or the ship needs, and being fair to Kincaid, too bad for Kincaid."

They didn't talk much for the rest of the inspection.

They did their duty properly, if gloomily.

\* \* \*

A week and a half out of Vesta and Ravi was down in the missile bays with his new trainee. At least Ensign Katie Kincaid didn't have any trouble getting around in zero gee. She was better at it than Ravi himself, to tell the truth. Ravi always tried to be truthful. A problem in a couple of ways.

To be able to train Kincaid properly, he was going to need her respect. "It's excellent that you're so adept in zero gee," he said. "Unfortunate that your zero gee budget is so tight. We could use another set of commissioned eyes down here more often."

"Yes, sir."

"You don't wonder why?"

"Aah, yes, sir, but I didn't want to seem impertinent."

Ravi kept his face blank. It was unfortunate. He turned to face her. "Please, don't worry. We started off on the wrong foot. I regret that. I'm sure you do too."

Kincaid still looked wary. She paused before responding, though. Maybe there was a crack of hope there. "Yes, sir. That's true," she replied a bit too fervently.

"Anyhow, I intend to do my job as professionally as possible and I trust you'll do the same. No hard feelings."

"Of course, sir." Kincaid seemed to relax some. "Sir? Aren't the missiles and all the other weapons designed to be largely maintenance free and storable for decades if need be?"

Ravi made a point of not sighing. There was no good place to start the talk he was going to have to give to the young ensign. No sugar was going to help this medicine go down easy. "Theoretically," he said. Might as well start by answering her question. "You're familiar with the Space Force Secrecy Act and how it applies to you?"

"Yes, sir. Just out of the Academy, sir. They covered it in detail. Also, my grandmother had something to say about the practical issues involved."

Her grandmother the Admiral, somehow Ravi had forgotten about that delightful little wrinkle. He forced a smile and tried to sound as if this was all normal and above board. "Okay, that's good. What follows falls under that law. You're not to discuss or even hint at it without first discussing it with me, the captain, or the XO. You can check with them if you like. I suspect they'd prefer not to have that conversation, but that is your right." He did sigh at this point. It was warranted. "In fact, if you have any doubts about it, it's your duty to do so."

Kincaid looked very serious as well she might. "Yes, sir. That's clear. I understand."

Ravi nodded. "Excellent. With regard to our long-range missiles the theory is not bad. We have stringent standards for them. Some parts are literally supposed to be made out of gold so that we don't have to worry about corrosion issues. The Space Force pays through the nose to have missiles that are supposed to be storable without the need of careful maintenance. Not that we don't do that maintenance, anyway. The people who set us up knew their history. They understood how a military not actually at war can deteriorate and get hollowed out. They were determined that wouldn't happen to us. The current brass thinks the same way. You follow me so far?"

"Yes, sir. Supposed to be gold?"

Well, give Ensign Kincaid one thing, she might be an arrogant pain in the patoot of a know it all, but she was quick on the uptake. "Exactly. Apparently that was too much of a temptation for someone in the supply chain for our current load out. Our missiles test out as meeting all their specs, only if you strip them down and look at what they're made of, it isn't gold. Lieutenant Novak and PO Miller are consummate professionals and insisted that we check them after we left Earth. Otherwise we'd have never noticed."

"Yes, sir. They're so expensive we hardly ever fire them. So do they work anyways?"

Well, that was an awkward question. It was possible that even the few missiles that had been test fired had been deficient. There was no telling how far back this scam went or how widespread it was. Was the entire Space Force armed with Below-spec long-range weapons? Ravi shrugged. "We've got no idea. We could test fire a few, they could work, and we'd still have no idea if the next one we fired, maybe under operational circumstances, would work as designed. It's unlikely they're anywhere near as durable and robust as they're designed to be. How far short they fall we simply don't know."

"Ouch." Kincaid screwed her face up in unhappy thought as she realized how bad it was. It was obvious she had a lot she'd like to say. A lot of questions she'd like to ask. "Sir, I get that this is way above our pay grades."

"Good. I'll answer any questions you have the best I can, but you're not wrong." As awkward as Kincaid's first question had been, it wasn't the most awkward one she could have asked. She hadn't asked who'd decided to keep the whole problem secret, or what the political ramifications might be. It could be the rot went a long way up and that someone might try to deep-six the whole issue. Deep-six everybody who knew about it. It was dangerous to be privy to secrets like this.

"Do all the watch officers know about this?"

Another awkward question. Other questions might have been more awkward. Also ones he couldn't answer. So Kincaid wasn't entirely clueless. The question she'd asked was one he could answer. One she potentially might need to know the answer to. "Lieutenant Novak does. So do I, the captain, the XO, and our senior techs, Miller, Korona, and Pong. And now you do too. That's it. We're the only ones on the ship who do."

"I see, sir."

Kincaid gained some more points in Ravi's book by not pointing out that the only reason she'd been read in was that she might figure it out on her own otherwise. That she'd not bothered making the point that watch officers could theoretically find themselves commanding the ship in combat without realizing a major weapon system wasn't up to snuff was worth even more points. Ravi didn't like it any more than Kincaid likely did, but neither of them could do much about it. Ravi appreciated not having to explain that. "Glad to hear it, Ensign. I'm not sure I do."

Kincaid nodded thoughtfully. For better or worse, she didn't seem to see herself as Ravi's equal. She also didn't seem to see herself as a junior trainee who should hang on every word her more experienced superior deigned to share with her. Kincaid looked at Ravi coolly. "Nothing much we can do about it, is there?"

"No."

"And to get back to more immediate challenges, you're not going to give me any breaks, are you?"

"Not a chance. I regret how unfair it is. Only after seeing how it can mess things up, I'm in no mood to be cutting corners."

Kincaid nodded grimly. "My training schedule is brutal. There's no room in it for even little surprises."

"You should have never agreed to it. You should go to the XO and ask to have it canceled. Not reduced. You've been assigned two full-time jobs already because of operational necessity. You don't have time for training, let alone extra training."

"If I can't stand bridge watches by the end of this tour, I'll likely never get ship command. Fair or unfair, whatever the operational circumstances, it's just not the way things are done."

"Personally, I sympathize. Believe me."

"But?"

"There's a lot more than one junior officer getting the career she wants at stake here."

"So, that's it. It's just too bad?"

"At the very least, you should go to the XO and ask to be relieved of all duties that aren't essential or related directly to qualifying as the Officer of the Watch. This might be hard to believe, but I'd miss having you available in Weapons. But it'd be the best thing for you."

"Everything about this tour is going to be carefully scrutinized by SFHQ. I think he'll be reluctant to do that."

"It won't look good for him and he's got a lot more on his plate than we do, but it's what would be best for you."

Kincaid sighed. "Anything more before we get back to weapon systems? This is costing zero gee time."

Ravi smiled. Not happily, but the girl was starting to grow on him. "Ensign Kincaid," he said gently. "Please, remember I'm in charge here. I think this has been time well spent. Honestly, don't hesitate to ask me anything. I'll help you learn anything you want. I'll give the best advice I can if you want it. My time is your time. I'd like to see you succeed."

"But you're not going to take it easy on me. You're going to make me dot every 'i' and cross every 't' before you qualify me on anything."

"Precisely."

"Going to be tough."

"True."

\* \* \*

Yet another learning experience. One with one lesson that Katie found herself being taught over and over again. There were far more roles to fill on a Space Force warship than there'd been on her family's civilian survey ship.

Right now Katie was doing a damage control watch. She was trying to get the necessary quota of them to qualify as a full-blooded Damage Control Officer. Katie wanted to do that before giving the XO her final decision in a couple of days. The more she had ticked off on her list of training tasks, the better. Katie still wasn't sure what she'd tell him.

She certainly wanted to maximize her chances of getting ship command one day. Which meant going for the gusto.

Katie had certainly underestimated how much she didn't know about running a Space Force frigate.

For one thing, although accidents did happen to civilian ships and civilian crews had to know what to do in the case of an emergency, they didn't deliberately put themselves in danger's way. They also didn't seek to keep operating in the event of damage and to make repairs on the fly in order to do so.

Nobody in humanity's experience had ever fought a space battle. They didn't know what it'd take. Going from the experience of oceanic naval battles, damage control could be critical.

Historically, it'd been important to keep warships fighting as long as possible. Even after they'd fallen out of the fight, it'd been important to get them back into it as fast as possible.

Katie still remembered reading the story of the WWII aircraft carrier *Yorktown*. It'd sailed for the Battle of Midway with dockyard repair crews still on board. It'd seemed exciting to her as a young girl. Now she was beginning to understand the human cost and desperation that it had represented.

Still, the Americans had won that battle. It had all counted for something.

One small thing it meant was that Katie wasn't bored by damage control watches. Nothing much ever happened on damage control watches. It was all very routine. The hands assigned to the damage control watches did their jobs professionally. Only Katie could tell it was out of a sense of personal pride rather than any sense of urgency. Even at Vesta, the *Resolute* had never been threatened. It was hard to imagine.

Katie wouldn't mind at all when she'd finished this last watch as the Damage Control Officer. It'd mean she'd be ahead of the training schedule the XO had assigned her. Haralson was the designated Training Officer, but the training plan had definitely been the XO's idea. Katie was now well aware he'd never intended her to actually attempt it, let alone succeed at it.

Katie was proud of herself for having managed it. Katie also knew she was skating on thin ice, though. Rather too late, she regretted not having caved to the XO's unstated wishes and begging off of it. One little snag in getting qualification time at something. Anything she didn't get quicker than most people. A bad cold or just the wrong time of month, anything really that slowed down the breakneck pace she was setting and it could cost her her desired career.

Katie had been too proud, stubborn, and, let's admit it, too stupid to do the smart thing. Hopefully she'd know better in the future.

In the meantime, she needed to convince herself and the XO that she could handle the whole insane program.

Katie had to show she could handle positions as both an Ops Officer designing battle plans and a Weapons Officer making sure the tools to execute those plans were ready. On top of that she had several different bridge positions to qualify for; helm, communications, sensors, and fire control. Not as fully trained to be sure, but she had to demonstrate a knowledge of the basics and spend some time in the positions to get a feel for them. Katie had to be able to take those positions in a pinch. As a prospective Officer of the Watch, she was supposed to know what they involved.

And that was in addition to her duties as both a pilot and the nominal leader of the marines. If the XO decided she was too stretched to do those jobs properly, he might cancel her training program himself. Cancel her chances of ship command along with it, but the mission came first.

Katie had to get all the comparatively easy stuff out of the way first. If there was trouble when they reached Jupiter or even if the captain and XO expected it, then her training needs were going to come a distant second to making sure the *Resolute* was ready for it. Katie had to get as much done before then as possible.

Katie had to work hard, but not so hard she burned out.

She had to hope her luck held.

## 13: Kincaid on the Spot

At Sergeant Suvorov's signal, Katie kicked off and cannonballed through the upper right corner of Boat Beta's main hatch. The boat bay it was in was large, but not that large. Katie hit a bulkhead hard after only a few meters. Feet first this time, so no more new bruises.

The people that had designed the ship's boats had not anticipated them being used in possibly opposed assaults. The marines, and Sergeant Suvorov in particular, had more active imaginations. And so Katie and the marines were practicing getting out of Boat Beta as quickly and in as unpredictable a manner as possible. The better not to get shot.

Katie got a quick fix on her surroundings. There was something new in them. The XO was waiting in a corner. Katie flashed the sergeant a stand down signal and went to see what her superior officer wanted.

She had a pretty good idea. They were just short of two weeks out of Vesta. The time the XO had given her was about up. Now she had to decide whether she could continue to handle the ambitious set of tasks he'd given her. Tasks that included a rather insane training schedule that nevertheless she needed to complete if she was to have the career she wanted.

Right now there didn't seem to be any sure way to qualify for the ship command she wanted. It'd be a strike against her if she bailed on her current training program. It'd be even worse if she burned out attempting to stick to it, and the XO had to relieve her of some of her workload. Worse of all would be if she screwed up some vital function because of being tired, or because she simply didn't have the time to do it all.

What it boiled down to was that Katie could avoid disaster by bailing, but her chances at getting any serious future command position would be greatly diminished. Alternatively she could attempt to remain on the command track without being handicapped but only at the cost of risking outright disaster. Showing a lack of judgment regarding her capabilities or failing at an important task could easily crater her whole career or at the very least, disqualify her from any command position. Katie might get low-pressure positions that required technical proficiency, but never command. Not if her judgment or ability to perform under pressure were considered suspect.

So, Katie thought as she made her way over to the XO, no pressure.

Snapping off a salute in zero gee was something of an art. Katie had mastered it. The XO returned her salute and smiled thinly. "So, looks like it's going well. You and the marines look smooth. Lieutenant Gregorian is happy with you. You're ahead on your training schedule too. Consider me pleased."

Katie nodded. "Thank you, sir. Been working hard to get ahead of things."

The XO gave a small nod at that. "Smart. We're stretched thin. Sad fact is, Ensign, is that the Space Force didn't expect to ever have to deal with anything like the mess we've stumbled into."

Katie didn't have to be told that this was a private conversation. Space Force officers were expected to avoid anything that could be construed as critical of the service in general. In particular, they weren't supposed to gripe about the missions they'd been assigned or the adequacy of the resources they'd been given. Only sometimes you needed to face up to reality. In such cases discretion was expected. "Yes, sir."

"For whatever reason, it remains that the *Resolute* doesn't have the officers it needs to be fully combat capable. We expected a show-the-flag cruise. We're not set up for either marine Away Ops or ship to ship combat, let alone both. We would have been spread thin even before losing Roth and Wong."

"I see, sir."

"I do hope so, because the upshot is something that's completely unfair to you even before our unfortunate missteps with each other. You've done very well at a variety of tasks. Like I said, I'm pleased."

"Thank you, sir."

"And your reward for that is that I'm using you as my switch hitter for all the roles I don't have a more experienced officer available for. Having you double timing as a pilot and marine lead both is already a stretch."

Katie wondered what the XO was leading up to. They both already knew this. "Yes, sir, but sir, I think I'm managing to handle both roles. Lieutenant Gregorian and Sergeant Suvorov both seem happy enough with me."

"They are. They've been pleasantly surprised, I think. Still doesn't change the fact that they'd each like to have you to themselves."

"Yes, sir."

"Lieutenant Shankar has briefed you on our weapons situation?"

Yet another twist. The XO was using her to plug holes in his organization chart. It was a desperate shift. He was doing it out of necessity. That same necessity would put paid to her training if push came to shove. "Yes, sir. Could be a problem."

The XO shook his head. Not in negation. The man was understandably unhappy. Not with Katie, it seemed. "It is. And the fact we haven't told several of our officers of the watch about it is more of a problem. But an opportunity for you, Ensign."

Somehow Katie sensed that opportunity had its drawbacks. "Glad to hear that, sir."

The XO gave her a genuinely amused smile. The XO knew very well that she knew that this wasn't unadulterated good news. "Yes, yet another responsibility to place on your young shoulders. Lieutenant Novak knows the score. So does Lieutenant Shankar, so I'm giving him a bridge watch too. You're going to get to be his understudy. A solid step on the path you want to take, but another demand on your time."

Katie thought for a moment. This was good, even if it could be awkward. There was a missing piece. "You have a plan to make sure it's one or the other of them on the bridge if something happens?"

"I do. It's a good one too. I'm rather pleased with it. Lieutenant Haralson wasn't so happy."

"Because he doesn't fully understand why you assigned Novak, Shankar, and me, especially with all the other things I'm doing, the roles you did."

"Exactly. Lieutenant Haralson hasn't said so, but he probably thinks I'm being a vindictive jerk and placing the mission at slight but definite risk in indulging myself."

It was a nasty irony. Katie could understand the XO feeling rather bitter about it. "Well, sir, for what it's worth, we both know you're putting the mission first."

"I am. I'm glad you understand that. The mission comes before the good of any of us as individuals. In your case, I think my plan means we'll be able to avoid using you as either a pilot or as marine lead. Can't guarantee that. If you're not sure you can step up at need, you need to tell me now."

"Yes, sir. Can you outline the plan before I decide?"

The XO looked past her at the far side of the Boat Bay. Katie followed his gaze. He didn't seem to be looking at anything in particular. The XO was lost in thought. Contemplating something. The XO sighed. "I planned to. And I will. It is highly irregular, you know. Normally a junior officer would be assigned a specific task and not given more information than necessary. There have been debates about that, but that's the standard practice. In this case, with so many variables in the event something goes wrong, with your having multiple possible roles, and with many more senior officers not fully in the know, it seems prudent to read you in fully."

"But you're not happy about it, sir?"

"No, but let's move on, Ensign. Our plan is to get to the Jovian system somewhat earlier than any smugglers will be expecting. We can't change the fact they know we'll be arriving there, but we can advance the timing some. Get some tactical, if not strategic surprise. That's the main reason we left Vesta so fast with things still in flux there. We'll also be burning some extra fuel and be having to top up at Callisto too. Having burned a little harder we'll get there a little sooner."

"That's a good idea, sir. They won't see us coming?"

"We think they're likely down on Ganymede at or near the base there. As you know, it faces Jupiter. We're going to time our arrival so that the bulk of Ganymede is between the base and Callisto. We'll swing by Callisto on the way in. Make sure all is well there and pick up extra marines and some scout ships."

"So we won't need the boats, maybe."

"Exactly."

"Don't they have a marine officer on Callisto?"

The XO sighed. "Yes, but I don't know him. Moreover, neither he nor his marines have had a chance to train for what's coming. We're only going to be able to give them a few days warning if we don't want to compromise comms security."

"Ouch."

"So, if we do have to use both them and our own marines, I'll still want you with Sergeant Suvorov. We'll have to work out the exact command structure on the fly."

Katie was flabbergasted. As her grandmother liked to say, '*it was no way to run a railroad.*' "Sir?"

"I'm well aware it's not ideal, Ensign. If all goes according to plan, we won't have to use the marines."

"I see, sir."

"Really? I doubt it, but thanks for the vote of confidence." The XO shifted his body slightly. Even in zero gee, remaining motionless in one position for too long was uncomfortable. "Our plan is to come in from the far side of Ganymede fast and slot ourselves into a highly elliptical orbit with its high slow point above Ganymede base. We should come over the horizon and control the space over the base without the bad guys getting enough warning to escape."

"You're hoping they'll surrender. That they'll realize they can't escape with the *Resolute* and Callisto's scouts holding the high ground. You don't think they might choose to dig in and fight? Use the civilians on the base as hostages?"

"You're right, I'm hoping they'll see reason and surrender I'm also hoping that if they try to run for it like at Vesta we'll be better set up to stop them. I don't think they'll try to hold the base against us. It'd be ugly if we had to fight for it, but the outcome wouldn't be in doubt. Also, right now they're guilty of smuggling and ignoring Space Force orders. The penalties aren't light, but they're not that heavy either. Not as heavy as getting Space Force members or civilians killed anyhow. Theoretically, there's even the death penalty for that."

"Locked away for good at least sir. So this can work, if everything goes right and the bad guys see reason."

"I believe so."

"But if it doesn't?"

"Then we'll have to improvise and prioritize between bad and worse options."

"They could try to wait us out. It could be a long blockade."

"Yes, and a certain young ensign's training plan would go in the trash bin."

"Or we might have to assault."

"Would also kill that ensign's training plan. Could get the ensign herself killed. Risk of the job, Ensign."

"Your plan requires precise timing and everybody knowing what needs to be done."

"It does. If I think your workload is wearing you down and making you less than fully copacetic, I will unilaterally reduce it myself."

"And my training for bridge watches has the lowest priority."

"Exactly. The best possible plan which requires you continuing to be some sort of super girl mightn't be workable. It could be the better plan is the good one where I relieve you of everything but your marine and pilot roles. They're both tough enough in their own right and you can't really train enough for either."

"I imagine if I'm on the bridge and mess up at a critical point, it could be pretty bad too."

"There are no jobs available here that aren't important and where failure won't have consequences. There's no easy path forward for you, Ensign. Which one do you choose? The merely hard, fraught one, or the truly insane, demanding one? The one that requires nothing go wrong."

Katie grinned grimly. The XO wasn't such a bad guy for all that he was putting her in an impossible situation. "Gee, sir, you know how to make a girl's day. You know the old tag; *Fortune favors the bold'.*"

"And *'the best laid plans of men and mice',* Ensign," the XO replied. "Okay, that's resolved. Remember if it looks like you're flagging I'll step in."

"Yes, sir."

"If the needs of Ensign Kincaid's training comes up against the ship's mission, the mission comes first."

"Yes, sir."

"Dismissed, Ensign."

They saluted each other, and the XO spun around and started back forward to the gravity ring.

Katie watched him go. She hoped she'd made the right decision.

\* \* \*

Katie felt different. She had finished up the exit drills with the marines in a bit of a trance. Fortunately, Sergeant Suvorov simply put them through the paces of what they already knew and didn't throw any wrinkles into the mix as he occasionally did.

Katie made her way back to her quarters in the gravity ring alone. The marines had more zero gee quota left than she did. They kept training without her. That bothered Katie on one level, but it also gave her a little welcome time to think.

Katie was all in. It was a sea change. It was a do or die situation. Katie had only played a little poker, and that no well. Katie's experience at sea was a day's excursion as a tourist whale watching. Do or die, unfortunately, she had a bit more familiarity with.

All the same, they were useful concepts in trying to capture what she was feeling. Something, something important, had changed.

Katie hadn't realized it before, but she'd been anxious. Not nervous finger-biting levels of anxious, but a tiny sliver of anxious. Constantly. What she was trying to do was risky. More risky than made sense by a normal reckoning. She'd known it. When Katie thought about it, she realized she'd been constantly second-guessing herself. Constantly evaluating what she was doing for its sanity. Wondering if it made sense to be doing it and not something else. Like sleeping or making better friends and relaxing with them. Or simply taking more time to do each of her tasks more slowly and learning them in greater depth.

That was gone now. It was like someone who'd been sitting

in the corner only listening to everyone talk had left the room. There was a presence missing.

There was no point being anxious now. Katie's course was set.

Picking that course could turn out to have been a mistake. Katie's career might end up a shipwreck. She might end up on the rocks.

It was even possible she'd chosen the wrong destination.

Didn't matter. There was no turning back now. She was committed.

It was a relief.

\* \* \*

A couple of days and they'd be entering the Jovian System. A couple of centuries before, people would have said "reaching Jupiter". Only the intervening years of true interplanetary travel had brought home just how much the gas giants and their accompanying flocks of moons were like mini-solar systems in their own right. Hence the current usage.

Katie knew her focus was blurring. She needed to get her head back in the game for the final stretch of taking her first step on the command track. She'd stumbled out of the gate. She'd been running hard to make that up, and now the finish line was in sight.

The last month and a half of their trip out to Jupiter had been like a dream of sorts for her. The time had disappeared with a surreal quickness. She'd been very busy. For a change, so had everybody else.

Everybody knew that what they were as like as not facing in the Jovian System was going to make Vesta look like a walk in the park. They'd been working hard to prepare.

If nothing else, it meant the coffee in the wardroom was always fresh. It never got time to sit. Katie was pouring herself a cup right now. She'd just finished another training session with the marines and had a bridge watch in the sensors position in a couple of hours. After having her coffee she'd likely fill the time with some virtual reality simulator time flying a boat in a blockade simulation.

It was daunting to think that all the training was likely to be over in a mere couple of days and that then it was all going to turn real.

Katie looked around the wardroom and spotted Lieutenant

Jeffries, the Engineer, sitting by himself. He was idly reading something on his tablet, but didn't seem too absorbed in it. He looked up, caught her eye, and gestured her over.

Walking over, Katie, couldn't help but think that her time in engineering, just a few months ago now, felt like something from a prior life.

"Been a while," the Engineer said as she sat down.

"Sorry, been real busy."

"Seems everybody has been going full out for the last month. Want to be ready for whatever we find when we reach the Jovian System."

"Even engineering?"

"Sure, the specialists might take the lead regards damage control, but it's us engineers that do most of the work. Heck, I've even had the spindle watch back in propulsion practicing how to steer the ship with the engines."

"Not likely to need that."

"No, two full sets of cross connected control conduits running on both the port and starboard sides. Not much chance anything short of losing the front half of the ship would take them all out, but still not theoretically impossible. This business of remotely controlling equipment on the ass end of the spindle from the gravity ring or the spindle's front end at a pinch has always made me a bit nervous."

"What, sir, no faith in all our wonderful theory about what'll happen in combat?"

"Even in engineering what you hear about in the classroom or see in the docs never quite seems to match what you find when you get hands-on for real."

"Amen, sir."

"Anyhow, I've been following your adventures. Have to admit I wouldn't have minded if you'd given it up and elected t go engineering track after all, but you seem to be coping. This damn the torpedoes and full steam ahead routine is nothing new for you, is it?"

"No sir, and I don't feel proud of it, but it's nice not to be the odd body out for a change."

"Got most of that crazy training plan signed off on?"

"End's in sight. I'm trying not to get cocky, but I've passed all the written exams. I've done them for Ops, Weapons, and all the bridge positions, up to and including the Officer of the

Watch one."

"Just need time on the job then?"

"Yep, only need several watches shadowing Ravi Shankar during some maneuvers and then I think he, and Haralson, and the XO, as well as the captain should be willing to sign off on letting me be in charge of a bridge watch of my own. It's something I've been working towards for years. Hard to believe I'm almost there."

"You've worked hard. You deserve it. Worried about something going wrong at the last moment?"

"Yeah, for sure. When I'm not busy, I've begun getting the flutters. You know the XO's plan?"

"Don't we all. Quick check-in at the Callisto Space Force Station to make sure all's well and get some reinforcements, then right into a sneak attack around the bulk of Ganymede on the base there."

"Well, not necessarily an attack," Katie said. "We don't know for sure the fleeing smugglers went there, and even if they did we're hoping they'll surrender, right?"

The engineer grimaced. "The XO made it sound logical for them to do that. Not my wheelhouse, but sure hope they share his logic. Callisto is not Goddard Station if we get banged up."

"Even if they don't surrender, a blockade, or at worst a surface assault are the next most likely scenarios. The ship-to-ship space combat scenario is the least likely one."

"Says the girl who's one of the few pilots to ever fire a weapon at another ship. Anyhow, won't those scenarios mess up your training plan? Are they going to want a trainee on the bridge during actual combat? And aren't you likely to be helping lead any ground assault?"

It was Katie's turn to grimace. The Engineer's concern was far too justified for her taste. She took a sip of her coffee before speaking. "Yes, I'm afraid so. I suspect the captain will want his senior and best trained officers on the bridge for any combat." She wished she could mention the issue with the long-range missiles. It seemed dishonest not to. Only the captain's wishes in the matter were quite clear. "And, yeah, if they need to use the marines I'm probably going to get drafted to go along with them. There are civilians on Ganymede and only one actual marine officer stationed at Callisto. And that's it for the whole Jovian System. So, yeah, I'm hoping the

XO's plan works out."

The engineer looked sympathetic. "Otherwise, a career setback could be the least of your problems."

"Yep. Anyhow, we'll know soon enough. Doesn't help to worry."

"You're right there."

They didn't talk a lot after that, and not about anything too important.

Katie couldn't slack off quite yet.

Yeah, only a little longer and it'd all be decided.

One way or the other.

\* \* \*

Callisto Station filled the large forward-mounted screens of the *Resolute's* Battle Bridge. The bridge deep in her spindle designed for controlling the ship under combat conditions. Zero gee conditions where surviving combat was more important than the crew's long-term health.

They were in the process of docking. It was a trial run for the combat they might be facing a couple of days from now.

Katie was filling the role of Junior Officer of the Watch. Basically, she was Lieutenant Ravi Shankar's deputy and apprentice as he acted as the Officer of the Watch. Technically, Ravi was fully responsible as the current OOW and the docking maneuver currently in progress was his sole responsibility.

In fact, the captain was present and there was no doubt he'd take charge if he felt the need. It'd be a bad thing indeed if that happened. The careers of all of them - the captain, Ravi, and Katie herself - would end up in the crapper. The Space Force didn't have that many biggish ships. It was rather protective of them.

Overly protective in Katie's mind. She'd docked her family's ship dozens of times. In her experience, you got better with practice. She figured the Space Force would have been better off taking more risks and giving its people more practice. None of her superiors had felt the need to ask for her advice, though. She'd had enough sense not to offer it. Never say Katie Kincaid couldn't learn. Given enough figurative whacks alongside the head, of course.

"Ensign Kincaid, confirm closing velocity," Lieutenant Shankar ordered.

Katie glanced at what both her heads-up display and the

instruments in front of her were saying. It was remotely possible one might be wrong or you might misread it. "Closing velocity is two kilometers an hour and directionally correct," she calmly but clearly enunciated.

It was very slow compared to the kilometers per second delta Vs they normally dealt with, but given the mass of the *Resolute* and Callisto Station even a very slow collision would do immense damage.

That would be very bad. Not only for all of their careers, but for the prospects of their mission succeeding.

Callisto Station was one of the few places in the Solar System that could dock a full sized Space Force ship. Putting those docks out of commission would have been a very bad thing at the best of times.

It was not the best of times.

The XO's plan called for a quick pickup and consult dock here at Callisto Station. Callisto Base's commander, with responsibility for the entire Jovian system, was up from the surface to meet with them. He was accompanied by all the marines he'd felt able to spare.

The plan was to confirm all was well with the military base and its command structure. If all seemed right, they'd take the marines on board and immediately depart for Ganymede while they were still invisible to the base there. Hopefully before the possible bad guys they expected there could learn they were coming.

If they flubbed the docking, that plan would be trashed.

And although it was a far from perfect plan, it was likely by far the best possible one available. They didn't want to give the smugglers time to get away or maybe worse, dig in.

So Katie found herself holding her breath and wishing she could take charge.

The seconds stretched as the Station and its docking cradle grew closer and larger.

Finally. "Helm, prepare to cancel velocity on my mark," Ravi ordered. Then a brief pause. "Mark!"

And as they hovered in place, the docking grapples reached out and grabbed them with a loud dull multi-part clunking sound. It shivered through the *Resolute*'s hull. Who said there was no sound in space?

"Ship is secure," the Helm announced.

Katie let out a breath she hadn't realized she'd been holding. From the quiet, almost inaudible sounds around her, she hadn't been the only one.

"Well done, Lieutenant Shankar," the captain said. "Well done, all of you."

Katie felt a certain totally personal glee. Being present as Junior Officer of the Watch during a docking maneuver had been one of the boxes she'd needed to get ticked off for her Officer's Bridge Watch qualification. She was so close. She'd done her time familiarizing herself with all the other bridge positions except for the quartermaster's. It wasn't unheard of, but most officers never bothered to get qualified as a quartermaster. It wasn't necessary, and the stringent requirements included more experience than most of them would ever have. What she had done, just within the last couple of days, was to have been present as Junior Officer of the Watch during both a gravity ring despin and a major navigation burn.

With those boxes ticked off, all she needed was more hours as JOOW on the bridge. That and the captain's sign-off that he believed her competent to act as his deputy in commanding the ship.

The captain spoke again. Katie realized she'd been woolgathering while on duty. "Lieutenant Shankar, as soon as possible I want the gangplank deployed. Take on what air, water, and supplies as you can, but they're not our top priority. Nobody but myself, the XO, and Lieutenant Haralson is to go ashore. Nobody is to come on board until I give permission That clear?"

"Yes, sir. Right on it," Ravi replied.

Katie busied herself making sure the rest of the docking procedure was going as it should. They weren't going to be here long. The XO's plan called for them to get back on their way as quickly as possible. Still, there were consumables it wouldn't hurt to top up as much as possible.

Katie really hoped the XO's plan worked. It was a huge bluff, based on a number of assumptions and guesses in the absence of solid information. It looked like Callisto, as a purely military base, could be trusted. The only civilians were the immediate family of serving members. There might be the odd spy, but it had seemed unlikely the bad guys had managed to subvert its administration. Their gamble that they wouldn't encounter the same problem as they'd had at Vesta seemed to have paid off.

Hopefully their gamble that they'd find the smugglers and their ships at Ganymede and that they'd surrender if they managed to surprise them and catch them on the surface would also pay off.

Katie hoped so.

Katie's future career prospects weren't anybody's top priority, not even Katie's, but she'd sure hate to see them go down the drain all the same.

A long blockade would likely have that effect. Either the XO or the captain were going to be present for the critical time periods in the XO's plan. If it worked, they didn't appear to intend to read the rest of their senior officers in on their long-range missile problems.

If it didn't, they wouldn't have much choice. They'd brief Lieutenants Haralson and Campbell on the problem and likely all the weapons and fire control ratings too. They'd put their senior officers and ratings on watch. They wouldn't trust Ravi or Katie on watch unsupervised. If the XO's plan failed, the smugglers would have the initiative and the *Resolute* and her crew would have to be prepared to react at any time.

Somehow Katie doubted the bad guys would pick a time convenient for the Space Force.

May you live in interesting times.

Ravi came up beside Katie. "Look sharp. You're overthinking things. Just do your job. Forget everything else for the next couple of days. I want you resting when you're not on watch."

"Yes, sir."

"Couple of days. Forty-eight hours or fewer, and we'll know if it's worked out or not. Remember, you're not alone. This'll make or break all of us."

Katie nodded.

## 14: Kincaid Shows Initiative

They would know soon.

It would be only a few more seconds. The *Resolute* wa coming around Ganymede fast and low. So fast that even Ganymede's wisp of an atmosphere was having an effect. The *Resolute* shivered with a keening sound.

"It's only a noise," the XO said. "I had Lieutenant Haralson do the numbers."

That mere noise put Katie's teeth on edge. She was Junior Officer of the Watch again. Ravi, Lieutenant Shankar, was OOW.

The captain and the XO were both present with them on the *Resolute*'s Battle Bridge.

And in a few seconds they'd cross the horizon and have a clear line of sight on Ganymede Base.

They'd know then if the smugglers were really there. A short while later they'd know if they were going to surrender.

The XO had prepared plans for every scenario he could think of. They had prepared broadcasts in the can for every eventuality. All they had to do was to see what the situation on the ground was and follow the prepared plan.

And Ganymede Base, and more importantly its landing field, slipped into sight.

Sensors reported. "Sir, they're here. Extra ships in the open. Four of them. Scout, miner, and stripped merchant." A pause and they continued in less clipped tones. "Sir, one other ship. I don't recognize the type. It's big and rather odd."

"Very good, Sensors," Ravi answered. "Comms, broadcast surrender demand 'B'."

Katie snuck a look at the captain and XO. The captain looked calmly pleased. The XO could barely contain his glee.

The broadcast played over the bridge's speakers. "Unauthorized ships at Ganymede, this is the Space Force Ship *Resolute*. You are under arrest. Surrender now. Shut your systems down cold now and evacuate your atmospheres. Assemble your crews, unarmed, and in neat lines in the base's hanger. You have three minutes to acknowledge and begin to comply. Fail to do so and we will use lethal force. *Resolute* out."

It wasn't a long time for the smugglers to reply, but the physics of the situation required they know what to do next with only minutes to spare.

"Sir!" Petty Officer Delong at the Sensor position didn't sound panicked. She did sound surprised. Worried even. "It looks like they're closing hatches. Firing engines. *Merde!* There are still people on the tarmac."

Katie sucked in her breath. In better times, any of the senior officers on the bridge would have reprimanded the PO for her profanity. Not now. They were too busy watching all their plans go into the dumpster. What were the odds the bad guys wouldn't have got warning in time to be gone completely, but still enough to be ready to lift when the *Resolute* appeared? Almost non-existent, she'd have thought. The XO certainly had. They must have had sensors or lookouts put out.

It was something for the post-mortem. This wasn't over yet.

"Weapons, short-range missiles, full salvo, two missiles each on the civilian ships, three each on the scout and the big guy," Ravi snapped out. "Fire!"

Katie's heart swelled with pride. Ravi had reacted quickly and appropriately. She hadn't been sure he'd had it in him. She glanced over at the captain and the XO. Too many cooks spoil the broth. They were giving Ravi his head. This was no time for an impromptu change of command. The captain looked focused but calm. Katie decided never to play poker with him.

The XO looked for all the world like he had bad gas.

It was the XO's plan that had just gone up in flames. Both he and the captain had to be aware that Ravi's missiles might kill or maim innocent civilians. They couldn't be certain who was present on Ganymede Base's landing field. They'd be answering to both SFHQ and their civilian masters for Ravi's missile salvo.

Delong on sensors must have routed the long-range cameras to their main screens. They got what seemed to be close ups of their missiles screaming in to explode on the landing field. They caught the scout as it was lifting and flipped it over. It wasn't going anywhere. Someone cheered. Then the other ships pulled free of the debris field the missile salvo had created. A gloom descended.

"Helm, begin escape burn now," Ravi ordered. "Bring us to bear on the miner, the merchant, and the big guy in that order. Execute."

The gees of the maneuver were crushing. Katie prayed everyone on the ship was strapped in like they were supposed to be. If anyone had decided a short biobreak was in order, they were going to get hurt.

The *Resolute* started killing its forward momentum and clawing for the sky. They had planned on that much. Only they'd planned to beat the supposedly surprised bad guys to the punch. They were supposed to be ahead of the smugglers and ready to intercept any escape attempt. Only they weren't. They were behind and playing catch up. It was a stern chase. A proverbially long and fraught exercise. Would have been against one target, let alone three.

Katie saw Ravi glance at the captain. She couldn't tell what if anything passed between them.

"Weapons, long-range missiles," Ravi bit out. "Full salvo, one each on the miner and merchant, two for the big one."

"Yes, sir," Weapons responded.

Long-range missiles are large. Katie felt the shudders of their launch even over the general shaking of the ship. Ganymede's gravity might be a bare one-seventh of Earth's, but it was still more than the missiles were designed for. It could have been only minutes, but it seemed to take forever for them to reach their targets.

And something happened, or rather didn't happen.

"Sir," Weapons reported. "Our missiles all seem to have failed in their final approach sprint. None of them altered course. None of them have detonated." He sounded almost more puzzled than disappointed. He wasn't one of the senior missile techs who'd known they weren't up to spec. That they might not work when needed.

Ravi had known. That was why he'd put them in position to use the railgun. "Helm, Weapons, does the railgun have bearing on the miner?" The miner was tail end Charlie. Ideally they'd have worked from the furthest ship to the closest, but that wasn't what the geometry was giving them.

"Coming to bear now, sir," the Helm responded.

"Weapons, fire when you bear," Ravi ordered.

"Yes, sir," Weapons responded. "Firing on target acquisition." Tens of seconds later he was good to his word. The entire *Resolute* hitched. Railguns dump a lot of kinetic energy into their rounds.

Seconds later, Sensors reported. "Sir! Clean kill on the miner. Holed her right in the engine compartment. She's shedding life boats." Katie could see that. The wreck would continue to rise a while longer but then fall back to Ganymede and crash, making a new crater hopefully not too close to the base. Nobody wanted to be on board for that.

"Helm, time to bearing on the merchant?" Ravi requested.

"They're not making it easy, sir," the Helm replied. "Estimate about 100 seconds."

"Weapons, prepare to fire as soon as we bear on target."

"Yes, sir," Weapons replied. "Fire on target acquisition." He sounded fractionally calmer this time.

They were all holding their breath, waiting for it when the ship rang like a gigantic bell that'd been hit with a hammer. The screens flashed bright white and the interior lights all flickered. Indicator lights here and there on different consoles blinked out. Others turned red.

"Sensors, what was that?" Ravi demanded.

"Sir," a junior fire control rating spoke up. "I think we were hit with a beam weapon from the big ship."

"Thank you," Ravi answered. He picked a channel on his console. "Damage Control, status?"

"Holed amidships," came the answer. "Looks like it's clean through, port to starboard, a meter or two wide easily, immediately forward of the boat bays."

Well, that was interesting. Until several seconds ago, beam weapons had been something theoretical you read about in Science Fiction. Not anymore.

Ravi continued to impress Katie. He didn't dwell on it. "Weapons, do we still have the railgun?"

"Yes, sir."

"Helm, time to bearing on the merchant?"

"Sir, I don't have control."

Katie briefly wondered if the unknown, likely alien, ship had known how to knock out both sets of control conduits or if they'd just got lucky. Again, something to worry about later. She looked around, did the calculations, and realized she had no time to explain to Ravi, the captain, or anyone else what needed to be done. Damn, this could be her career.

Katie opened a channel on her console. She spoke loudly so everyone could hear. "Engineering, Bridge. Perform emergency engine steering maneuver now." She checked the numbers. "Immediately. Twenty-nine degrees to port in the current plane. Execute."

The whole ship shuddered with a prolonged rumbling.

Ravi glanced at her. "Weapons, fire when you bear," he said acting as if nothing unusual had happened.

The rumbling ended, and the *Resolute* seemed to hitch all at the same time.

Seconds passed.

"Sir, we have hit the merchant," Sensors announced. "I have explosive de-gassing and a large debris field. No lifeboats."

Katie figured they'd likely killed everyone on board that ship. She had very mixed feelings about that which she'd work out later.

"What about the big ship, Sensors?" Ravi asked.

"Picking up acceleration, sir. Maybe she was hanging back to help the others?"

"Helm, Weapons, report."

Helm spoke first. "Sir, still no control from here. Distance is opening quickly. Honestly, engine steering isn't very precise. We were lucky. I don't think we have any hope of catching them or getting a fire control solution on them."

"Sir, I second that," Weapons reported.

"Lieutenant," the captain spoke.

"Yes, sir," Ravi replied.

"I suggest we're done here for now. You did well." The captain looked Katie's way. "As did you, Ensign Kincaid. I approve of your initiative."

"Thank you, sir." Katie noticed the XO staring at her. He nodded.

There was still a lot to do. The rest of the watch was busy, but it turned out they'd weathered the worst of it.

Not turned out ideal, but much better than it could have.

\* \* \*

Katie was exhausted. Body and mind she had nothing left to give.

Back in her and Amy's cabin now, she slumped on the edge of her bunk, aching with fatigue, but with her mind still racing.

Katie had been busy. It'd been hours since their climatic battle with the fleeing smugglers and what would probably prove to be an alien ship.

The end of the battle hadn't been a signal for the *Resolute*'s crew to stand down and rest. They'd still had the battle's aftermath to deal with. A ship to get patched up and working and survivors to rescue. Ganymede Base to deal with. A blockade of that base to co-ordinate with reinforcements from Callisto until they were sure they'd winkled the last of the bad guys and their collaborators out.

And Katie had been right in the middle of it.

Katie and Ravi had been relieved of their watch early with the captain's praise ringing in their ears. Ravi had disappeared to check out his beloved weapons systems. Katie had been drafted to help restore access to the boat bays and engineering. Her reward for having cross trained in both engineering and damage control.

As soon as they'd gotten access to the boats back and even before the control conduits had been repaired, she'd been drafted again.

This time by Iris Gregorian. They needed to take the boats out and rescue survivors from the ships they'd wrecked. They'd taken those survivors down to Ganymede along with a contingent of marines and returned with repair materials and extra workmen.

With the arrival of that help, the captain had stood most of the ship's crew down. One of the damage control techs, the engineer, and a couple of senior NCOs had stayed on the job to supervise the Ganymedian help.

Katie had been one of those ordered to get some rest.

"Too tired to even sleep," came Amy's voice. Guess she'd been here all along, Katie had to think. Rather dully.

"It was wild. I can't process it and I can't stop thinking about it."

"The rumors I heard were insane. Alien battle cruisers and you taking the ship over from Shankar and the captain both to fight them. Crazy what people will say."

Katie made a sound that was almost a giggle. "Yeah, very exaggerated. To the point of not being true. There was a strange ship. I did issue one order to engineering without checking with anyone first, because there was no time. Ravi and the captain were both okay with it."

"Really?"

"Really. You can't trust rumors."

"Okay, but tense at times, I bet."

"You'd win that bet."

"Too wiped to clean up and get a hot meal?"

"Yeah."

"Well, at least we've got lights and gravity back. You lie down, close your eyes, and empty your mind. I'll rouse you and make you eat a proper breakfast come time. We've broken out the last of the maple syrup. Pancakes, bacon, sausage, beans, eggs, and ham. Re-hydrated some melon and strawberries too. I'm going to make you eat a proper breakfast. No pecking and running. Now sleep."

Katie smiled a little. "Yes, ma'am."

Katie lay back as told.

She fell off into a dreamless slumber.

* * *

Ravi was discombobulated. Proud of how he'd done. Happy with himself and the world in general. Feeling confused and adrift for all that.

It wasn't until after he'd finished the post-action inspections of both the railgun and missile systems with Miller that he'd had any time to think about it. Up until then, he'd been too busy with alligators to worry about the swamp. Hadn't worried much about it then either. He'd grabbed a quick snack from a buffet that the stewards had put out in the wardroom and gone right to sleep.

A few words from the captain in passing had made it clear that for the next few days he was going to be neck deep in doing a postmortem on how their weapons had performed. Ravi had figured he'd better rest while he could. Turned out he'd needed it. He'd slept like a rock for eight hours plus. Now he found he was ravenous and was packing away a huge breakfast. Seemed that Supply had relinquished their last supplies of the good stuff. Even the coffee was fresh.

"Hear you did us proud."

It was Lieutenant Novak, nominally his boss, but they'd both been too busy to see much of each other recently. "Just did what I had to," Ravi replied. "Kincaid stepped up at a critical moment. Glad she showed initiative that time. Biggest ship still got away. We didn't lose anybody. Smugglers did. People got hurt on Ganymede."

Novak sat down across from him. "You done good, Ravi. Bask in it for a bit. Your reward will be greater trials to come. Don't doubt it."

"Reports to SFHQ?"

Novak smiled. "Yep, and the bean counters back on Earth will want to be reassured you fired off our missiles in a cost-effective manner."

"Ouch. It does kind of put it all in perspective, doesn't it?"

"It does that."

\* \* \*

Amy watched Katie eat.

It was good to see. When people lost the will to eat, or became too focused or strung out to bother, then there was something wrong with the world.

Amy was basically content.

She hadn't played the most critical role in the events of the last few days, but she'd done her part. None of the techs had lacked for spare parts or tools. The whole crew had had ongoing access to regular hot meals. Good, tasty, nutritious meals. Nobody may have thought much of it. They'd all had other concerns. But if they'd missed meals, or those meals hadn't been good ones, Amy was willing to bet they'd have noticed that. It wouldn't have helped morale at a stressful time.

So, yeah, Amy figured she'd done her job and helped make her little piece of the universe a better place.

All the same, there was no doubt that her roommate, young Ensign Katie Kincaid, had done even more.

Katie had gone out on a limb at a critical time, and it'd made a difference. Amy wasn't sure there'd be an honest appraisal of the action just completed in her lifetime. With aliens, probably the Star Rats, involved, and major missile systems failing, and their having been sent out inadequately prepared, she'd figure a lot of the implications of what had happened would be swept under the rug.

All the same, Katie had done well on the bridge from what Amy had heard.

Amy had no doubt at all she'd also done the job of two other officers turning to for both damage control and boats duty.

Amy figured that was likely worth a letter of commendation from the captain. The captain was basically a fair guy in Amy's experience, and Katie did have an admiral as a grandmother, so again Amy would be willing to bet on it.

Katie looked up. "You're awful quiet. Pensive."

"Just thinking about it all. You did well, Katie. A little exciting for my taste, but I wish I could have done more myself."

Katie waved her fork at the breakfast she'd mostly demolished. "This was at least partly you. This is something."

"Yes, but being modest like I am, I still think maybe if I'd been a bit more ambitious maybe I could have done more."

Katie paused and sighed. "It's worked out more or less, I guess, but believe me you can be overambitious. I think you've been the reasonable one."

"But the world's changing. Honestly, the world's always changing, isn't it? What's reasonable now according to conventional opinion isn't necessarily what's going to work in the future."

Katie diced some ham up into small squares. It was damned good ham, Amy knew. She'd paid extra for it. Katie speared a piece and examined it. "Nobody knows what the future holds for sure. My grandmother is big into the theory of prediction. Seriously, I'm good at math, but I've never had the time for evolutionary population dynamics and the theory of best adaption to niches that change in accordance with a punctuated disequilibrium model."

"That a complicated way of saying it's complicated?"

Katie grinned. "Yeah. Guess I have to admit going all out at things is my strength. I'm a kind of anything worth doing is worth overdoing sort of girl. But maybe the best thing is moderation. Test the envelope some, but don't go overboard or be doing it all the time."

"Sounds right. Maybe you need to be more careful and I need to be less comfortable."

"Could be."

"I think I'm going to think about it."

## 15: Kincaid Takes a Step

The weeks at Ganymede had been busy ones. Iris hadn't got much time to rest and think. She was tired.

For a change it was a happy sort of tired. The aftermath of a job well done more than the portent of grim, ceaseless days to come of plodding along towards a horizon that never seemed to get closer. Iris hadn't realized how unhappy she'd been.

Not until she'd started feeling better.

Iris had never been one to indulge her moods. She was even less inclined to show them to others. But now the Boat Bays were deserted for the first time in months. There weren't even any marines training. They were getting some well-deserved rest. So Iris had time to mull things over undisturbed.

Turned out all the smugglers and any associates or collaborators they'd had on Ganymede had attempted to flee. From what Iris had heard, there'd been no bad guys at all left on Ganymede. One comms tech on Callisto had come forward to confess to being blackmailed into being a smuggler informant, and that'd been that. The marines hadn't had any fighting to do.

Only it had taken some time to establish the facts and the marines had been on guard or patrol that whole time. So, yeah, they were due some rest.

Iris was also glad they weren't cluttering up her Boat Bays for a change. Technically, she was down here doing a routine inspection prior to departure from Ganymede and the Jovian system. True, as far as it went. She was hurrying the task, though. She wanted some time to depressurize and think events over. A little time to survey the swamp now that the alligators weren't so pressing.

She'd done good work. The *Resolute*'s boats had been a key part of its being able to do its mission. Unlike Callisto Station, Ganymede Base didn't have proper docking facilities for a frigate. All the transfers back and forth between the ship and the base had gone on one of Iris' boats. They'd been kept busy.

Iris was sure the captain and XO had noticed. Iris' career had been resurrected. Iris had been telling herself she didn't care about her career being stalled. She'd had herself convinced all she cared about was having a job she liked and was good at. She'd been kidding herself.

Now that she had a career again, she realized that.

It made her doubly happy that Kincaid's career hadn't gone in the crapper. Iris hadn't felt good about pushing the kid, now a young woman and an officer, so hard, but she hadn't fully appreciated how devastating failure would have been for her either. Iris had tried to broach the topic with Katie and perhaps implicitly apologize.

Tired and busy herself, but in a happy high mood, Kincaid had hardly noticed. Apparently a lot of her optimism had, like Iris' resignation, been something of an act. Now that things had worked out Katie was beside herself with relief.

Exactly how things had worked out, Iris wasn't sure. From the degree of relief everyone was feeling, it'd been touch and go. From what Katie had said piecemeal during their man short trips, very little had gone according to plan and they'd had a lot of dumb luck.

The ship losing power even briefly and then losing way made that clear. Apparently some of their weapons had malfunctioned too. The entire crew knew this. They'd also been warned not to discuss it even with each other, let alone any outsiders. There were multiple sensitive issues involved, they'd been told.

But if Katie thought it'd been a close-run thing, then Iris figured it'd been a close-run thing indeed.

Oddly enough, that didn't bother her. It meant that what Iris did, what the Space Force did generally, mattered.

Iris' life and her career had a meaning now that they hadn't had before. She'd been simply enduring before.

Now she wasn't.

\* \* \*

Ravi was meeting with his boss, Lieutenant Novak, in the Weapons Admin Office. Very close quarters. The Space Force recognized sometimes privacy and security required a dedicated office, but they hadn't wasted much space on it.

"Be on our way soon. It's been crazy," she was saying.

Ravi nodded. "Been busy, but after that dust up when we arrived here, nothing else seems worth getting too worried about."

Novak smiled. It was a nice smile, and Ravi regretted not seeing it more often. Ravi reminded himself that she was his boss. "Well, don't be too obvious about it," she said.

"Yes, ma'am."

The smile became a grin. "Good news, Ravi."

"Ma'am?"

"The captain just showed me a letter of commendation for you and Kincaid. You done good, Ravi. People know it, too."

Ravi was almost embarrassed. He had done well. It was true. Ravi wasn't used to being praised so effusively all the same. "Kincaid showed initiative at the exact right time." He paused and chuckled. "It's ironic. There really is no telling what life is going to throw at you."

"Nope. Glad to see you've learned that. Happy you're good with it."

"It's weird how I feel. I mean, I've always liked things predictable. I like clear rules to follow."

"Noticed that."

"That hasn't changed, but somehow it's refreshing to know life can throw you curveballs. Before I felt I was playing a lost chess game out to the bitter end, out of a forlorn hope my opponent would make an unlikely mistake."

"I'm guessing your family had unrealistic expectations. They should be happy when you get that letter."

"They will be, and that's a relief."

"You don't sound like you care that much."

"And that's the weirdest and best thing about it. I don't. It's good. It's great. Only the best thing about it is that I'm happy with myself. Never realized it, but I've been putting other peoples' opinions and goals ahead of my own my whole life. I think I resented that, and it made me unhappy."

Novak nodded at that. "I can see that. You did seem a little wound up. Didn't know why."

"Trip back to Earth is going to seem odd. We're not going to have that much to do, right?"

"Just routine checks and a very relaxed watch schedule," Novak confirmed. "On the other hand, we're going into refit as soon as we get back."

"That going to be slack, too?"

"Maybe normally you'd be getting time ashore catching up on training, or taking some extended leave."

"Not this time?"

"No. This is not going to be a normal refit. You're going to be busy at the yards and not able to tell anyone why. They're going to want to tear the whole ship apart, figuring out how our weapons did and what the effects of that alien beam weapon were."

"Going to be busy again."

"Very, and that's not all. Everybody and their grandmother is going to want to debrief us about the incident."

"Ouch. That might not be so much fun."

"Impress the brass and boffins and your career could take off. Also, we've got a chance to make a real difference."

"Think I mightn't mind shaking things up a bit."

"Amen."

* * *

"Go get them, Tiger," Amy told Katie. Cheerfully and brightly, and Amy did cheerful and bright pretty damned well if she did say so herself. Katie was about to do her first independent Bridge watch as OOW.

Katie was nervous. You had to know her well to see it. Katie was trying a bit too hard to seem like the picture of a perfect Space Force officer. "I can do this. I know that. It's just that I've been looking forward to it for so long. Hard to believe the day's come."

Amy slapped her roommate on the back. "Don't overthink it. Just be the Katie we all know and love. On your way. Forward March!"

Katie gave Amy a grin as she exited the cabin. "Thanks."

After she'd left, Amy let out a deep breath and sighed. She lay back in her bunk. She hadn't been as busy as Katie or, to be honest, most of the *Resolute*'s other officers, but she'd been busy enough.

They were cutting their deployment short to return to Earth space and a refit. Also, they'd spent their time in the Jovian system off of Ganymede instead of docked at Callisto Station. It'd complicated their resupply. And, of course, the disruptions to the ship's routines had knock-on effects for Supply when it came to the provision of meals, etc.

It'd kept Amy occupied.

Amy had done a good job. She ought to feel good about that.

And she did, after a fashion.

Only, although she had no desire to emulate Katie's headlong overachievement, she did have the feeling she wasn't living up to her potential.

Damn Katie Kincaid, Amy thought fondly.

Well, they'd all have some extra time on the trip back to Earth.

Maybe Amy could finagle herself a little cross training.

Might be interesting.

\* \* \*

The day had come.

Finally, Katie was going to command a bridge watch. A key step to eventual independent starship command. Katie was beside herself with happiness. She just hoped she didn't mess up in her excitement.

Also, excited happiness wasn't exactly the right demeanor for a responsible, confident Space Force officer. So, she stopped for a moment at the entrance to the bridge to compose herself. She checked her wrist display. It was precisely 19:43:32. The Evening watch began at twenty hundred hours, but regulations required being fifteen minutes early.

Katie stepped onto the bridge and glanced around. Both the Last Dog and Evening watches were present. Petty Officer Catherine Caldwell was taking over the helm. All the other watch keeping stations had already been turned over to members of her Evening watch. Katie didn't doubt they'd made a point of all being a little early so that her first turnover went smoothly. It warmed her heart. It was great to be part of a supportive team.

Enough lollygagging, she had goals here. To keep the *Resolute* safely on course to start with, but to be sure her first independent watch went smoothly and without fuss too, and lastly to enjoy reaching this milestone she'd spent the last five years striving towards.

Lieutenant (Senior Grade) Thor Haralson had had the Last Dog watch and was turned slightly towards her, waiting. She wasn't sure, but he might be smiling slightly. There was a definite twinkle in his eyes. She stepped up to him, braced, and stood at ease.

"I am ready to relieve you, sir," she said.

"I am ready to be relieved," he replied.

Katie turned to the quartermaster. "Have the ship's log record the watch turn over."

"Yes, ma'am."

Lieutenant Haralson gave her a second to return her attention to him and spoke formally. "Ship's navigation status is as follows. Our solar relative heading and course are both one hundred and seventy degrees and in the ecliptic plane at a velocity of six km/sec. We have just cleared the Jovian planetary system on a course out from Ganymede Base. There are no close-by bodies and we should not encounter any during the watch. The captain has ordered our initial burn for Earth return to take place at twenty hundred hours and twenty minutes."

Katie replied, "Understood," and repeated back the lieutenant's report.

"Good," Lieutenant Haralson said when she was done. "Radiation watch status: no solar flares are predicted and we are clear of the Jovian radiation belts."

"Understood. No radiation hazards expected."

"Ship's readiness is currently at level X-ray. The crew has been warned to expect a major maneuver. The bridge, the engineering, and damage control officer watches have all been assumed by the Evening watch."

"Understood. Ship state X-ray, crew has been warned of major maneuvers, and the watch turnover is complete."

"Except for the Officer of the Watch," Haralson said with a smile.

"Yes, sir," Katie answered. On one level she appreciated the tiny bit of levity, but for the most part she wanted this to go by the book. She had little doubt the captain would review the record of what was happening. He might even be quietly watching right now.

"Other than the burn at twenty-twenty, there are no other special orders or incidents that you need to be aware of."

"Yes, sir, the burn for Earth at twenty hundred hours and twenty minutes is the only special order for the watch."

"That's correct."

"I relieve you, sir," Katie said. Her heart thumped. This was a unique moment in her career. For the first time she would have command, if only temporary, of a Space Force ship.

"I stand relieved. Attention on the bridge. Ensign Kincaid has command," Lieutenant Haralson stated loudly.

"Ship's log, watch turnover completed," Katie said loudly and crisply herself.

"All yours, Ensign," Lieutenant Haralson said in a low kindly voice before turning to stroll off the bridge.

The rest of the Last Dog watch followed suit, most of them pausing briefly to give her a nod or smile of encouragement.

Pride and glee warred in Katie's heart. Best not celebrate too early, though. The watch wasn't done yet, and she had a major maneuver coming up in less than a half hour. Checking the ship's displays for herself, she could see there were precisely twenty-seven minutes and twenty-eight seconds remaining. Not that she was counting. Ha.

She'd done maneuvers like this many times on the *Dawn Threader* and even docked her family's big survey ship several times. Still, this was different. Not only was the rest of her career potentially riding on her not making mistakes, she had to do the whole thing in proper Space Force fashion. The *Resolute* was a bigger ship with a much bigger crew. It wouldn't do to be nervous, but she shouldn't be overconfident either.

The next seventeen minutes crawled along with infinite slowness. The bridge crew went about its duties with quiet efficiency. Something of her mood must have conveyed itself to them. There was little of the usual casual chatter and low-key banter.

Finally, it was time to start. "Quartermaster, please give the ten-minute major maneuver warning," Katie ordered.

"Aye, aye, ma'am."

The announcement rang out over the ship's internal intercoms. This was really happening.

Five more minutes and another warning.

Another at one minute. Katie couldn't help feeling it was overkill, but it was also standard Space Force procedure and at least nobody could claim they weren't warned.

At exactly twenty hundred hours and twenty minutes, Katie spoke. "Helm, bring the ship around to three five five degrees solar relative."

"Aye, aye, ma'am, bringing the ship around to three five five degrees solar relative."

Katie watched the star field slowly move port on the bridge's large screens. The heading shift took several minutes. She made a point of not checking exactly how long or giving any other signs of nervousness. They slowed, then stopped. The sun blazed just to the port of dead ahead and Jupiter hung in the sky, almost out of sight to the starboard.

Petty Officer Campbell on the helm spoke. "Ma'am, heading is now three five five solar relative."

"Quartermaster, announce burn imminent," Katie ordered. She waited a solid minute before speaking again. "Helm, on my mark initiate a zero point five gee burn for two zero zero seconds."

"Acknowledge. On your mark a half gee burn for two zero zero seconds."

"Three, two, one, ignition!" Katie said.

The engines rumbled and Katie felt herself being pushed back into her command chair. Three and a third minutes later, the force subsided.

"Navigation check our course," Katie ordered.

A few moments later, the response came. "Course nominal, ma'am."

"Well done, Helm," Katie said. "Bring our heading back to five zero degrees solar relative."

"Thank you, ma'am. Bringing course back to five zero degrees solar relative."

This time the star field swung starboard, but not as far.

Once the ship's course had steadied, Katie gave her final orders. "Quartermaster, announce maneuvers are done. Stand the ship down to readiness state Yankee."

"Aye, aye, ma'am." Once more the announcement echoed.

It was done. Katie felt everyone on the bridge relax a little. Nothing easily pinpointed, but her watch seemed a little less stiff.

The rest of the watch was totally uneventful.

All was well with Katie and her world.

The *Resolute* and her career plans were both on course.

Katie was one step closer to being a starship commander.

# Appendix A: 24th Century Military Ranks

## Space Force Naval Officer Ranks:

Fleet Admiral
Admiral
Vice Admiral
Rear Admiral
Commodore

Commander
Lieutenant-Commander

Lieutenant (senior grade)
Lieutenant (junior grade)

Sub-Lieutenant
Ensign
Cadet

The traditional rank of Captain is absent to avoid the traditional conflict with the title of a Commanding Officer (CO) of a ship.

Abbreviations are FADM, ADM, VADM, RADM, CDRE, CMDR, LCMD, LTSG, LTJG, SLT, ENS, and CDT.

## Space Force Naval Officer Ranks (annotated)

Fleet Admiral   *(rare; in wartime only)*
Admiral   *(the Space Force at the time Katie joined had, but did not use this rank)*
Vice Admiral   *(the Space Force at the time Katie joined had, but did not use this rank)*
Rear Admiral   (flag) *(Highest rank in active use in the Space Force at the time of Katie's entry, CO of Space Force. Some retiring senior officers were given the rank as a courtesy prior to retirement.)*
Commodore   (not flag) *(commands squadrons and flotillas)*

Commander   *(COs of districts, outposts, small groups of ships, and large capital ships)*
Lieutenant-Commander *(COs of corvettes and frigates, Executive Officers (XOs) of larger ships)*

Lieutenant (senior)   *(COs of small ships, XOs of corvettes & frigates, watch officers, dept heads)*
Lieutenant (junior)   *(watch officers, deputy dept heads)*

Sub-Lieutenant (fully qualified commissioned rank) (*inexperienced LTJG in essence, promoted after year or two of good service*)

Ensign (*provisional commission prior to being fully qualified pending completion of all training*)

Cadet (*not commissioned, basically officer candidates, commissioned to ensign on completion of basic and initial specialization training - command or engineering generally, there are technical and medical specializations but usually they're direct entry from civilian university or mustangs and have capped or special career paths*)

## Notes on Roles of Ranks

Cadets, Ensigns, and Sub-Lieutenants are all essentially officers in training.

A Sub-Lieutenant is fully qualified but inexperienced and will normally be promoted to LTJG after a year or two of satisfactory service.

The bulk of the officer corps has ranks between LTJG and CMDR inclusive. Most posts are filled by senior lieutenants. Most junior lieutenants are promoted to senior lieutenant after several years of satisfactory service. Lieutenants, senior and junior do most of the watch keeping. Lieutenant-Commanders and Commanders are considered senior officers and act as the COs of larger ships, groups of smaller ships, and shore units.

Commodores command squadrons and flotillas. At the time of Katie's enlisting there were very few of them. Essentially it was a rank Commanders received shortly before or upon retiring or which prospects for the command of the Space Force (a RADM slot) were given usually upon receiving a very senior unit or staff position.

The head of the Space Force Academy was and remains a Commodore's slot.

## Training requirements:

Note that in Katie's time all cadets took command courses, but also engineering ones if choosing that path or if they were at all ambitious. Katie's superiors tried to guide her down the Engineering path.

Cadets take Basic officer training*, and at least one* of Command or Engineering. (Taking just Engineering was career restricting and generally the Academy preferred not to so restrict the careers of officer candidates at first. On the flip side engineers were always needed. Most decently ambitious cadets who could hack it would take both sets of courses.)

Ensigns receive courses in Watch keeping*, Navigation*, Communications*, Sensors, and at least one* of Piloting or Engineering.

At the time of Katie's entry almost all Ensigns would have taken Basic Officer Training as cadets as direct officer entries were rare to non-existent. This changed later as the Force expanded quite drastically. Generally Basic officer training would have either all cadets (Academy) or all ensigns (direct entry) in a class but there could be exceptions.

Lieutenants (junior grade) receive courses in Weapons*, Ship handling*, Ship command*, and optionally Logistics and Intermediate engineering

Lieutenants (senior grade) receive Advanced officer training* and optionally Staff training, Tactics, Operations, and Advanced Engineering.

Senior officers take very select limited enrollment in courses given by the Space Force Staff College.

Intermediate and Advanced Staff Courses, Fleet Operations, Fleet Tactics, Military History, Political and Economic Issues, Intelligence and Special Operations, and Engineering Administration and Logistics are some topics given at various times.

These courses are non-standard. Individuals are being groomed as candidates for specific higher command positions at this level.

At least that was the case for most of Katie's career later on the vast expansion of the Space Force led to an expansion in senior and flag ranks and a greater standardization of training for them.

(*) training necessary for promotion

## Marine Officer Ranks:

General
Lieutenant-General
Major-General
Brigadier-General*

Colonel
Lieutenant-Colonel

Major
Captain
Lieutenant

Ensign
Cadet

Note the Marine rank structure is flatter than that for fleet officers. They don't have as many training ranks essentially.

Abbreviations are:
GEN, LGEN, MGEN, BGEN, COL, LCOL, MJR, CPT, LT, ENS, CDT

(*)At the time Katie joined Brigadier-General was the highest Marine rank. It was held by the CO of the Marine Corps. The "Corps" being essentially brigade sized. Tradition again.

Equivalencies with Naval ranks:

GEN = ADM
LGEN = VADM
MGEN = RADM
BGEN = CDRE

COL = CMDR
LCOL = LCMD

MJR = LTSG
CPT = LTJG

LT = SLT
ENS = ENS

CDT = CDT


Marine officers have different training courses. Promotion from captain to major is not automatic and generally although a marine Captain is technically equivalent to a naval Lieutenant junior grade they pull a lot more weight.

Marine Captains are rarely posted aboard ships but when they are, are brevetted to Major. There is only one Captain on a ship and it is a position of command not a rank.

## Notes on Rank Structure in Planetary Armies

Most planet bound armies have a rank structure similar to that of the marines. They're numerically larger so have more filled out higher ranks.

So typically something like

Field-Marshall (FM) *(rare)*
General of the Army (GA)
General (GEN)
Lieutenant-General (LGEN)
Major-General (MGEN)
Brigadier-General (BGEN)

Colonel (COL)
Lieutenant-Colonel (LCOL)

Major (MJR)
Captain (CPT)
Lieutenant (LT)

Ensign (ENS)

Cadet (CDT)

## Space Force Enlisted Ranks

| | |
|---|---|
| Master Chief Petty Officer (MCPO) | E-7 |
| Chief Petty Officer (CPO) | E-6 |
| Senior Petty Officer (SPO) | E-5 |
| Petty Officer (PO) | E-4 |
| Leading Spacer (LS) | E-3 |
| Able Spacer (AS) | E-2 |
| Trainee Spacer (TS) | E-1 |
| Recruit Spacer (RS) | E-0 |

Coxswain (Cox'n) is the senior enlisted man in a ship's complement, Boatswain (Bosun) the senior non-engineering hand, Chief Engine Room Artificer (CERA) the senior enlisted man in engineering. The men in this case can be of the female gender, because tradition.

## Marine Enlisted Ranks

| | |
|---|---|
| Master Warrant Officer (MWO) | E-7 |
| Warrant Officer (WO) | E-6 |
| Staff Sergeant (SSGT) | E-5 |

Sergeant (SGT)               E-4

Corporal (CPL)               E-3
Private (PVT)                E-2

Trainee (TRN)                E-1
Recruit (RCT)                E-0

Master Sergeant, Command Warrant Officer, and Command Master Warrant Officer are all titles (positions) indicating the senior enlisted man in a unit. The 'man' may be female. Tradition.

That said older men in general and most women dislike long deployments on smaller ships and age and gender imbalances persist in the fleet.

The marines make few allowances for smaller people with low upper body strength which disadvantages small men and many women.

On the other hand the smallest ships have very constricted quarters in the form of sleeping tubes which larger individuals simply cannot fit into.

Smaller people also use less life support and consume less food. Some believe they tend to have better co-ordination and hold up better under variable gees.

# Appendix B: Renown Class Frigate Fact Sheet

The Renown Class Patrol Frigate was designed in the 2320s to provide more sustained patrol capability then earlier scouts and corvettes had proven capable of providing.

It was also inspired by the idea of the "Prepare for Contact" strategic school that the Space Force's primary mission ought to be to train a cadre of officers and men capable of manning a prospective interstellar navy able to hold its own against hostile alien forces.

As such its hull size was picked to allow deployments of up to a year and it was given a full spectrum weapons suite including both short and long range missiles as well as a 60mm railgun as its main armament. Short range rapid response guns and a complement of torpedoes rounded out the on board weapons suite.

Two Hellas class ship's boats each mounting a 12mm railgun and a configurable combat module usually consisting of an ECM and sensor package with a small number of small missiles usually dual purpose Anti-Missile Missiles (AAM) and Anti-Ship Missiles (ASM) provide the class with additional combat capability.

## Class includes:

Renown 003
Repulse 004
Resilience 005
Revenge 006
Resolute 007
Redoubtable 008

## Manning:

Ship's Total Crew (76 to 95) (9 to 14 officers) (67 to 81 enlisted men)

Seventy-six crew is adequately manned, ninety-five is fully manned. Additional berths are available for two officers and fifteen enlisted supplementary personnel usually trainees of one sort or another. Enlisted personnel in particular start off narrowly specialized and receive cross training as well as more in depth training as their careers progress.

# Layout:

The shape of Renown class Patrol frigates is basically a 94 meter long, mostly 12 meter diameter main spindle with the shape of a cylinder with an octagonal cross section. There are bulges for for the gravity ring mounting and boat bays of 4 and 10 meters respectively. The gravity ring mounting bulge is symmetric. The boat bays protrude more to the port and starboard then they do "up" and "down". The main spindle penetrates a large rotating gravity ring mounted forward of its middle. (Between the 22m and 34m marks starting at the ship's nose and counting back to the 104m mark at the end of its engine nozzles)

Also appended are a sensor array and "flying bridge" on its forward end, and on its stern end, the propulsion systems and main engines.

The appendages give the ship an overall length of 104 meters.

A set of detachable external propellant tanks are arranged around the very rear of the main spindle around the Engineering spaces and ahead of the engines.

## Spindle section lengths are:

| Section | Length | Cumulative |
|---|---|---|
| Sensor array | 3 m | 3 m |
| Flying bridge | 3 m | 6 m |
| Armored passage | 3 m | 9 m |
| Battle Bridge | 4 m | 13 m |
| Forward Guns | 5 m | 18 m |
| Forward Missiles | 4 m | 22 m |
| Combat Information Center & Gravity Ring Mounting | 12 m | 34 m |
| Storage | 12 m | 46 m |
| Boat Bays (port & stbd) | 24 m | 70 m |
| Aft Missiles | 4 m | 74 m |
| Torpedo Bay & Launchers | 7 m | 81 m |
| Aft Guns | 5 m | 86 m |
| Armor, shielding, hatch | 2 m | 88 m |
| Main Engineering Control (Engine Room) | 4 m | 92 m |
| Auxiliary Machinery Space | 4 m | 96 m |
| Inboard Propulsion Space | 4 m | 100 m |
| Engines | 4 m | 104 m |

## Gravity Ring:

The provision of gravity is essential for the long term health of crew on sustained deployments. To this end the class mounts a large gravity ring on its spindle within which the crew spends most of its time. Generally the spindle is only manned by skeleton watches. The exceptions are for maintenance and during battle stations. At full battle readiness the gravity ring is despun and locked down.

All the crew's normal living activities and regular cruising watches are performed from within the gravity ring. Their exposure to zero gravity is logged and limited by regulations. Exercise programs are mandatory.

The gravity ring has a 25 meter radius or 50 meter diameter. The ring has a cross section of 10m wide and 6m high.

From the inside the gravity ring has the form of a long corridor that runs for some 160m and has "spokes" with lifts, damage control stations, and escape pods at 40 m intervals. To each side of the corridor are the ship's living quarters, eating and recreation areas, and a variety of work spaces. The corridor splits and zig-zags in the vicinity of cabins and other living quarters in order to provide some privacy and quiet to resting crew when they're off duty.

Using the cruising bridge as our starting point and working clockwise around the ring when looking aft at its forward wall the interior space of the gravity ring is divided as follows:

Cruising bridge
Captain's cabin
Other officers cabins
Wardroom
Admin offices
Galley
Damage control and escape pod stations, lifts (first quarter spoke)
NCO's mess
NCO living quarters
Hand's mess
Hand's living quarters
Canteen
Laundry
Medical Bay and Infirmary
Damage control and escape pod stations, lifts (second quarter spoke)
Remote Engineering Control Room (opposite bridge on ring)
Hull, comms, and electrical workshops
Tool crib and parts storage.

Marine barracks
Armory
Gym
Damage control and escape pod stations, lifts (third quarter spoke)
Remote Weapons Control
Weapons workshops
Ready storage for victuals.
Remote Situation and Briefing Room
Ready room
Damage control, escape Pods, and lifts including one dedicated to flight crew. (fourth quarter spoke)
*And back around to the Cruising bridge.*

# Appendix C: Hellas Class Boat Fact Sheet

The Hellas class Ship's Boats are the mid-twenty-fourth century Space Force's work horse small utility craft.

Two of these are carried by each frigate, four by cruisers, one by corvettes. They're also used as general purpose utility boats by Space Force stations and bases.

They are capable of stern end bottom down propulsive landings and take off from both Luna and Mars, though most passengers prefer the dedicated shuttles available if they have a choice.

## Manning:

Each boat has a pilot, and a co-pilot that doubles as a combination comms, sensors, and weapons officer. Each boat also carries a Flight Engineer, usually a senior NCO technician, responsible for all maintenance and ensuring both the propulsion systems and life support systems function correctly during operations.

## Layout:

| | | |
|---|---|---|
| Bridge | 3 m | 3 m |
| Cargo Bay | 6 m | 9 m |
| Engineering | 3 m | 12 m |
| Engines | 3 m | 15 m |

Total length 15 m

The boats do not normally carry external tanks, they have a single co-axial 12mm railgun and belly and ventral mounted combat packages, normally composed of limited tactical sensors, ECM devices, Anti-missile missiles (AMM) and anti-ship missiles (ASM). They have two rapid entry and exit hatches port and starboard amidships. There is a starboard side airlock in the cargo hold just aft of the bridge. Opposite it is a drinks and small meals dispenser. There is a port side airlock in the cargo bay just forward of engineering. The boat's heads are opposite it.

The Cargo Bay despite its name is multi-function and configurable. It can carry crew and VIPs in relative comfort or marines and their gear in somewhat less comfort, as well as cargo in a variety of containers and forms. Seats and tie downs are removable and configurable.

Typical capacities would be twenty passengers in luxury mode, thirty-two marines with heavy gear in assault mode, forty crew in regular passenger mode, and maybe eighty refugees in emergency evacuation mode.

Engineering contains the life support, power supply, and auxiliary propulsion machinery. Also all the controls to them which are normally monitored by the flight engineer.

# Appendix D: Typical Ship's Organization

## Standard Crew for a Renown Class Patrol Frigate:

*All numbers approximate but those below are the usual minimum to be expected for safe sustained operations.*
*Also note that the Bridge watches and Away Operation personnel are part of the Operations Department. The Supply department subsumes all the support personnel.*

### Command:

Captain
Executive Officer
Department Heads (Operations, Weapons, Engineering, Supply)
Deputy Department Heads

So ten officers in command positions when fully manned. Plus boat pilots, also supplementary officers or trainees may be carried.

### Bridge Watch:

Officer of the Watch
Quartermaster
Helmsman
Sensors
Weapons
Communications

Three watches so: 5 X 3 = 15 personnel total in addition to watch officers who are drawn from Operations and Weapons officers.

### Away Operations:

#### Marine detachment:
An additional 7 personnel, sergeant, two corporals (fire team leads), four privates

#### Boats:
Two Boats (Alpha Starboard, Beta Port)
Pilot, Co-pilot, & Flight Engineer X 2

Pilots and Co-pilots are officers but do not normally stand Bridge watches, the Flight Engineers are senior enlisted.
Another 6 personnel.

In total the Operations Department has approximately 30 personnel, including six officers.

## Weapons:

Chief Weapons Tech
Tactical sensor watch keepers X 3
Fire control techs X 6
Missile maintenance techs X 3
Guns maintenance techs X 2

Minimum 15 personnel in Weapons.

## Engineering:

Chief Engine Room Artificer
Propulsion watch keepers X 6
Maintenance Electrical/ Internal Comms/Aux Machinery X 6
Maintenance Hull X 2
Damage Control Techs X 3

Total 18 Engineering personnel approximately

## Support Staff:

Chief Supply Tech

Victualer
Cooks X 6
Stewards X 2

Supply Techs (parts) X 2
Supply Tech (consumables)

Senior Med Tech
Junior Med Tech

Minimum 15 personnel in Supply and other support.

## Ship's Total Crew (76 to 95) (9 to 14 officers) (67 to 81 enlisted personnel)

# Appendix E: Resolute's Ship's Company

## Officers:

| | |
|---|---|
| **Captain:** | LCMD James Hood |
| **Executive Officer:** | LTSG Kyle Winters |
| | |
| **Operations Officer:** | LTSG Thor Haralson |
| **Deputy Operations Officer:** | LTJG Cara Campbell |
| | |
| **Pilot/Chief Boats Officer:** | LTSG Oswald Wong |
| **Pilot/Deputy Boats Officer:** | LTJG Iris Gregorian |
| **Co-pilot Boat 1 (Alpha):** | LTJG Myleen Zhang |
| **Co-pilot Boat 2 (Beta):** | SLT Robert Maddox |
| | |
| **Weapons Officer:** | LTSG Anne Elizabeth Novak |
| **Deputy Weapons Officer:** | LTJG Ravi Shankar |
| | |
| **Engineering Officer:** | LTSG Allan Jeffries |
| **Deputy Engineering Officer:** | LTJG (but empty, LTJG Anita Roth had a skiing accident) |
| | |
| **Supply Officer:** | LTSG Michael Vann |
| **Deputy Supply Officer:** | SLT Amy Sarkis |

## Supernumerary and Officers in Training:

ENS Katie Kincaid

## Enlisted with supervisory or directly reporting positions:

| | |
|---|---|
| **Cox'un:** | MCPO Norman "Norm" Kothen |
| | |
| **Operations:** | |
| | |
| **Bosun:** | MCPO Michael Roberts |

| | |
|---|---|
| **Quartermasters:** | CPO Elroy "Roy" Walters<br>SPO Rowena Pritchett<br>SPO Danel "Dan" Dicherry |
| **Lead Sensor Tech:** | PO Simone Delong |
| **Lead Helmsman:** | PO Catherine "Cathy" Caldwell |
| **Lead Communications Tech:** | PO David Parnell |
| **Lead Deckhand:** | PO Mathieu "Matt" Laplace |
| **Flight Engineer Boat 1:**<br>**Flight Engineer Boat 2:** | PO Alice Morgan<br>PO Timothy Ferguson |
| **Senior Marine:**<br>**Fire Team One Lead:**<br>**Fire Team Two Lead:** | Sgt Peter Suvorov<br>Cpl Javier Diaz<br>Cpl Jean-Pierre Lebrun |
| **Medic:** | PO Jonathan "Doc" Bethune |

## Weapons:

| | |
|---|---|
| **Senior Weapons Tech:** | SPO "Dusty" Miller |
| **Missile Techs:** | PO Joska "Josh" Korona<br>PO David "Smelly" Pong |
| **Gun Techs:** | PO Gil "Gilly" Chen<br>PO Karisa Rodi |
| **Tactical Sensor Operators:** | PO Chakradhar "Chaka" Chatterjee<br>LS Kitty O'Dowd<br>LS Megan "Megs" Rabani |
| **Fire Control Operators:** | LS Isolde "Issie" Powe<br>LS Decha Benjawan |

## Engineering:

**Chief Engine Room Artificer:** MCPO James McIsaac

**Senior Propulsion Tech:** CPO Glynn Pembroke

**Senior Propulsion Watchkeepers:**
SPO "Mo" Khoury
SPO Pavel "Pie-face" Borzakovsky
PO Torri Bowens

**Senior Electrician:** CPO Gregory "Greg" Baddell

**Senior Electrical Watchkeepers:**
SPO Kemal "Sam" Samim
PO Heidi Fahr
SPO Mats "Mattie" Thorne

**Senior Hull Tech:** CPO Tal "Tally" Peretz

**Senior Damage Control Tech:**
SPO Waluyo "Wallie" Pane

## Supply:

**Chief Supply Tech:** CPO Susan Cooke

**Head Cook:** SPO Thomas "Cookie" Callahan

**Head Stewart:** LS Tuhina "Mama" Cruz

# Enlisted not in supervisory positions:

## Operations Dept:

**Sensor Techs:** AS Tam Doan
AS Valdemir "Vald" Ghezzo

**Helmsmen:** LS Karli Saltik
AS Alexei Toporov

**Communication Techs:** AS Ingrid Ohlson
AS Bernardo Napoles

**Deckhands:** AS Kazimir Jakubek
AS Chiamaka Okuro

**Medic:** LS Candice "Baby Doc" Agina

**Marines:** Pvt Tony Anders
Pvt Hans Mueller
Pvt Lew Kalchik
Pvt Pedro Barca

## Weapons Dept:

**Fire Control Techs:** AS David Jones
LS Rosa Lund
AS Rakin Nassar
AS Katry "Kat" Mach

## Engineering Dept:

**Engine Techs:** LS Jessie Brimer
AS Akona Fall
AS Stefan "Stef" Risberg
LS Parin Tara

| | |
|---|---|
| **Hull Techs:** | AS Luke "Lucky" Milligan |
| | AS Pia Balderas |
| **Electricians:** | AS Rashid Halabi |
| | LS Wilmot "Willie" Amsel |
| | AS Jamila "Jammy" Sane |
| | AS Kara Ghilarducci |
| **Damage Control Techs:** | AS Lisa Elo |
| | AS Bernard Hartman |

## Supply Dept:

| | |
|---|---|
| **Stewart:** | AS Robert "Rob" Maric |
| **Cooks:** | AS Laban Jamal |
| | AS Gert Kinsky |
| | LS Okoth Sow |
| | AS Jela Algafari |
| | AS Chandrak Malik |
| **Victualer:** | LS Mia Oohara |
| **Supply Techs:** | AS Francis Jertel |
| | AS Abdal Issa |
| | AS Winnie Couch |

# Appendix F: Simplified In-System Navigation

Orbital mechanics are very complicated, but the Space Force by making a number of assumptions has created a simple robust system that minimizes errors during operations.

Basically the Space Force is interested in position, course, and heading.

Course is the direction a ship is moving in. The heading is the direction it is pointed.

Everything is relative to a main local body. This reference body can be the system primary, a planet, or even a moon close up.

Co-ordinates are spherical with two angles relative to either the system ecliptic or the plane through the center of the reference body and its primary that its orbit lies in. This is the reference plane. One angle lies in the reference plane and the other in the plane perpendicular to it.


## For Position:

The first position parameter is the angle in the reference plane.

It is against a reference line (meridian) defined as a line through the reference body's center to the center of its primary. The positions being those at noon on the 21st of March 1957. For the solar reference the line between Earth and the Sun is used. Similar arbitrary meridians are assigned to all systems. If no planet or sister star has been formally designated the largest is used.

Sometimes this first angle can be relative to a nearby major body orbiting the reference one. For example "10 degrees ahead of Jupiter solar relative". In which case this usage will be made clear.

The second position parameter is angle perpendicular to the reference plane. It can be up to 90 or -90 degrees out of the plane. Zero degrees is straight inside it.

The third parameter is the distance to the reference body. Usually in kilometers. Usually between thousands and hundreds of millions of them.

**For Heading and Course:**

The first heading and course parameter is the in reference plane angle.

It is defined against the direction line to the primary:

| | | |
|---|---|---|
| Zero | (0) | degrees is straight toward primary. |
| Ninety | (90) | degrees is heading of body in perfectly circular orbit. |
| One-Eighty | (180) | degrees is straight away from primary |
| Two-Seventy | (270) | degrees is back bearing along perfectly circular orbit |

The second heading and course parameter is also an angle. It has values between zero and 360 degrees in the plane perpendicular to the reference one. Up 10 degrees is 10 degrees, down 10 degrees is 350 degrees.

Lastly for courses there is a velocity parameter. It is in km/sec and relative to the chosen reference body.

During docking maneuvers velocity is in km/hr. Docking is always relative to the object being docked with.

# Appendix G: Clocks and Watches

## Watches:

*Note this is the traditional system of periods used by Anglo-Saxon nations. The Americans managed to get it adopted when the Space Force was formed by letting it be presented as the British RN variant rather than the USN one. Politics can be weird, international politics weirder. Hence UTC as the civilian abbreviation for standard time, what is called ZULU in all modern militaries including the Space Force.*

Technically a ship at the discretion of her Captain can institute whatever watch system it wishes to. In practice some variation of the following watch system is used. One in three watches is a tough, hard to sustain for long periods of time tempo, four in one is more usual and considered sustainable for long periods, and five in one is quite relaxed and for slackers.

| | |
|---|---|
| 0000-0400 | Middle watch |
| 0400-0800 | Morning watch |
| 0800-1200 | Forenoon watch |
| 1200-1600 | Afternoon watch |
| 1600-1800 | First Dog watch |
| 1800-2000 | Second Dog watch |
| 2000-0000 | Evening watch |

More often than not crew will also be expected to "turn-to" during the "day" from 0800 to 1600. However, traditionally crew that have the Middle watch are excused the Forenoon, and crew that have had the Morning watch are excused the Afternoon. All again at the discretion of the Captain and XO.

The Evening watch may be called the First watch, and the Second Dog the Last Dog. Official Space Force documents punt the issue by presenting a large number of possible watch schemes and leaving it up to the ship's Captain. The Captain will usually delegate to the XO who will normally simply follow tradition with a few tweaks sometimes.

No perfect watch system has yet been designed and it's rare that everybody is completely happy with whichever one is chosen.

## Time:

In space a standard "Zulu" time scheme is followed which mirrors British Standard, Greenwich, or UTC time as it is variously labeled.

A 24 hour clock is used. So 1:00 pm is 1300, 5:00 pm is 1700, 8:00 pm is 2000 etc..

Years, days, and time are exactly the same as on Earth's surface in London.

Military outposts, bases, and ships will tend to keep a 24 hours 3 in 1 or 4 in 1 schedule with no particular emphasis on one watch.

Other places with less need for constant readiness and large civilian (particularly ones with a high proportion of children) populations will have a day or main watch in which members with non 24/7 roles concentrate themselves. Factories or jobs having to share resources may deviate at need. Traffic control, docks, and life support operate around the clock.

If you enjoyed this novel, please leave a review.

To be notified of future releases visit my website at
http://www.napoleonsims.com/publishing

Manufactured by Amazon.ca
Acheson, AB